Secrets...
& Mistakes

...Plus!

ARE YOU A WORRIER?
TRY OUR FAB QUIZ AT
THE BACK OF THE BOOK

SOME SECRETS ARE JUST TOO GOOD TO KEEP TO YOURSELF!

Sugar Secrets...

1 ... & Revenge
2 ... & Rivals
3 ... & Lies
4 ... & Freedom
5 ... & Lust
6 ... & Mistakes
7 ... & Choices
8 ... & Ambition
9 ... & Dramas

Sugar SECRETS...

...& Mistakes

Mel Sparke

Collins

An imprint of HarperCollins*Publishers*

Published in Great Britain by Collins in 1999
Collins is an imprint of HarperCollins*Publishers* Ltd
77–85 Fulham Palace Road, Hammersmith, London W6 8JB

The HarperCollins website address is
www.**fire**and**water**.com

9 8 7 6 5 4 3 2 1

Creative consultant: Karen McCombie

ISBN 0 00 675444 9

Printed and bound in Great Britain by
Caledonian International Book Manufacturing Ltd, Glasgow

CHAPTER 1

HAPPY BIRTHDAY

"What is it?"

"I don't know," Sonja Harvey answered, delicately probing the object that her friend Kerry Bellamy was staring at.

Kerry shuddered. "I don't like the look of it, whatever it is..."

The boys all leant over for a good nosy.

"Oh, for goodness sake, stop poking at it," drawled Cat, rolling her eyes at Anna, who was surveying the scene with a smirk. "It's dead, whatever it is, so just eat it!"

Making her way back from the loos, Maya Joshi slipped between the tables of the nearly empty Indian restaurant and wondered why her friends were all huddled together over the candlelit table.

"What's up?" she asked, gazing down at the array of food that had arrived in her absence.

Kerry was staring uncertainly at her plate, still wrinkling her freckled nose at what she saw there.

"Unidentified object in Kerry's curry," grinned Ollie, his soft brown hair flopping into his eyes as usual.

Maya peered at Kerry's plate then gave a cursory look at everyone else's.

"Kerry, you've got my prawn bhuna and I've got your vegetable korma," she pronounced. "Here, swap. Though now I've seen it, I wish I'd gone for the vegetable korma too."

"What, that thing's a *prawn*?" gasped Matt, pointing at the sauce-covered object as the plate was lifted past his nose. "But it's *huge*!"

"It's a king prawn, you prat," Maya teased him. "Don't you get them in Pot Noodle?"

"I don't eat Pot Noodle *all* the time," he protested, pretending to be hurt. With his father constantly away on business or ensconced at the golf clubhouse, Matt Ryan led an almost home-alone lifestyle in their vast house, which involved paying minimal attention to a balanced diet. "I cook too!"

"Matt, you do *not* cook," said Catrina, giving him a who-are-you-trying-to-kid? stare as she tore off a chunk of nan bread. "What you do is take a ready-meal out of the freezer and stuff it in the microwave. And you don't even do that often, since you still haven't worked out how to use it."

"Oh, yeah!" Sonja chipped in excitedly. "Remember the time we went round and Matt was trying to make toast in the microwave?"

"Uh-huh," nodded Cat. "And he was so lazy that he still ate it, even when he saw it hadn't worked."

"That's right – instead of beans on toast, it was beans on hot, floppy bread!" shrieked Sonja.

"OK, OK!" Matt interrupted the giggles that had erupted around the table. "So I won't be going on *Masterchef* any time soon..."

"And you won't be eating what you ordered tonight either," said Maya coolly.

"What?" asked Matt, flipping his gaze over the food in front of him.

"You ordered chicken biryani, right? Well, what you've got there is chicken tikka masala, which is what *Joe* ordered." Maya pointed at his plate. "And Joe's already eaten half of your biryani."

Joe paused, a forkful of food lifted to his mouth. "Oh, Jeez, sorry, Matt!" he mumbled. "I forgot what I ordered!"

"You lot – what are you like?" Maya gazed round the table. "I leave you alone for a few minutes..."

"...and we're lost without you!" Ollie finished the sentence for her, clutching his hands dramatically to his chest and gazing heavenward.

"Very funny, Ollie." Maya raised her eyebrows at him. "But not as funny as the fact that you've just smeared curry on your suit."

Ollie looked down at his clasped hands and the fork clutched between them, still laden with the food meant for his mouth – not his best clothes.

"Oh, Ollie, here," flustered Kerry, dabbing a serviette in a glass of water and rubbing at the offending stain.

Sonja winced when she saw Ollie's face – his thin-lapelled mod suit, an original from the '60s, was his pride and joy and only worn on special occasions.

"Listen, everyone," said Sonja, suddenly rattling her freshly manicured nails against the glass in front of her to get their attention – and to take Ollie's mind off what had happened. "Aren't we forgetting something?"

She looked knowingly around at the others and, for a second, they looked blankly back.

"Ahhh," muttered Ollie, the light suddenly dawning. He gave Sonja a nod. "C'mon, everybody: *Happy Birthday to you, Happy Birthday to yooooooo, Happy Birthday, dear Ke–rry, Happy—*"

Kerry clapped her hands over her face with embarrassment as her friends launched into a loud and reasonably tuneless version of the song – not that she had much cause to be embarrassed; being a quiet Tuesday night, the only people they were disturbing were a middle-aged couple in the window seat and the staff of the Kamil Tandoori restaurant.

"How does it feel to be seventeen then?" asked Matt, who at eighteen was nearly the oldest (Anna beat him by a couple of months) but certainly not the wisest of the friends.

"Um, fine," shrugged Kerry, hoping the hot flush in her cheeks wasn't too visible. "Much the same as yesterday, I guess."

"But what about all that stuff you're legally entitled to do now?" enthused Sonja. "You can, er... well, learn to drive! That's about it, I think..."

"Maybe Matt will teach you," Catrina suggested wickedly, knowing that her ex was as likely to let anyone loose at the wheel of his precious Golf as shy-boy Joe Gladwin was to stand up and do a striptease on the table.

"Well, I—" spluttered Matt, before he saw the Cheshire cat grin on Catrina's face and knew he was being wound up.

"I want to propose a toast," Ollie interjected. All heads swivelled his way. "To... Irene!"

"Irene?" squeaked Sonja, picturing – as they all did – the sprightly ex-dinner lady who helped out at the End-of-the-Line café. "What's she got to do with anything?"

"It's thanks to Irene helping out at the café tonight that we're all here," Ollie reasoned.

"That's true," nodded Anna. "If she hadn't offered to give Nick a hand, either Ollie, Joe or me would have had to work this evening."

Well, it would have been me, being honest, she admitted to herself. It was really sweet of Kerry to have invited her along tonight – her first proper night out by herself with the crowd. But, if it had come to the crunch, she would have worked, of course. Ollie, as Kerry's boyfriend, and Joe, as one of her best mates, could hardly miss out on the celebrations.

"Exactly," said Ollie, raising his glass. "So here's to Irene!"

"To Irene!" the others all bellowed.

"And, of course, a toast to Kerry," Ollie added in a softer voice, "for being seventeen, for being beautiful – and for being mine."

A chorus of cheers and "aww"s rumbled round the table and even Cat, for once, kept her cynical comments to herself.

As Ollie leant over and kissed his moist-eyed girlfriend, Sonja gazed round at the rest of her friends and thought how brilliant it was to be together like this.

Who needs the hassle of boyfriends when you have good, solid mates like these? she thought, smiling a private, contented little smile. The fact that she had lately been burned by not one but two lads went a long way to colour her opinion (though she knew she'd got her comeuppance – she'd been two-timing them both). And she was also viewing the friendship of the crowd through slightly rose-tinted specs: although everything was fine now, over the past few months her cousin Catrina had certainly tested everyone's patience and goodwill, to say the least.

And look at the way they've all got into the spirit of Kerry's night out! Sonja enthused to herself, putting to the back of her mind the fact that only the day before Cat had moaned that going to a club would be much more fun than a meal in a restaurant (but then Cat *always* wanted an excuse to go out to a club).

She gazed round at them all: there was Ollie Stanton in his (curry-stained) suit, instead of his omnipresent combats; Maya Joshi looking effortlessly sleek and gorgeous in a slash-neck, three-quarter sleeved black top and baggy, black linen drawstring trousers; and Catrina Osgood in a low-cut, crochet cardie that showed ample amounts of bra (the waiter had struggled to keep his eyes on her face when he took her order) and a ruby red, A-line satin mini that matched the red streak she'd put through her dyed blonde hair for the night.

Matt Ryan looked handsome – but then it wasn't hard for him – in a new designer T-shirt, the name of which Sonja didn't recognise. But Matt would love that; being so ahead fashion-wise that only he and a handful of style mag editors knew what the next hip trend was. Joe Gladwin was wearing a new, loose-fitting white shirt and, with a summer's worth of exposure, his brown hair had taken on the faintest of highlights.

Wow – our Joey's almost turned into a bit of a looker! thought Sonja suddenly, gazing proudly at her friend's lightly suntanned features. *Who'd have thought!*

It was the same with Kerry, Sonja realised. Kerry Bellamy had always been pretty – even though she could never see it herself – but after a summer of going out with Ollie, her confidence seemed to have grown in leaps and bounds. Tonight, wearing a long, rust-coloured hippy dress, and with her browny-red curls shiny and bouncing, she looked almost exactly like a shot Sonja had seen in *OK* of Minnie Driver arriving at some awards do or other.

I must tell her that later, Sonja thought, knowing that Kerry still found it hard to handle compliments, and would stumble and splutter a "No that's not true!" if Sonja said it now in front of everyone.

"Kerry, this is for you..." said Anna, interrupting Sonja's musings.

Sonja felt guilty for a second: Anna had turned up tonight in the old jeans and stripy T-shirt they'd all seen her wear around the café – she obviously hadn't been told that everyone was getting dressed up. And Sonja knew that she was supposed to have let everyone know... Oops!

Anna smiled shyly and pushed a small, ribbon-wrapped parcel across the table towards the birthday girl.

"Oh, Anna! You didn't have to! I mean—"

What Kerry meant was that Anna Michaels was still a relatively new addition to the crowd – she hadn't *had* to buy a present; she didn't know Kerry that well.

Feeling all eyes on her and the gift in her hands, Kerry's fingers trembled a little as she fumbled to unravel the ribbon.

"Oh, it's so pretty!" she gasped, holding up a necklace that was made of tiny, uneven chunks of semi-precious stones, strung together on black string.

"It's called a chakra," said Anna, looking pleased at Kerry's reaction to her gift. "All the stones are meant to make you feel more centred. Like, you know, if you've got lots of thoughts racing around your head, it's meant to make things a lot clearer."

Kerry looked flustered all of a sudden and shot an unreadable, sideways glance at Ollie. Oblivious to Kerry's consternation, Cat reached over and touched the small, polished stones as they dangled from her friend's hand.

"Maybe I could do with one of these," she mused.

Sonja and Matt both burst out laughing.

"What, you getting into New Age stuff, Cat?" snorted Sonja. "What's next – yoga? Not in that skirt, girl!"

It was impossibly hard to do, but Cat bit her tongue. Her cousin and the others had no idea about the whirlwind of thoughts running around her head, or had any clue about what she'd been up to today.

God, she thought, crossing her fingers under the table, *I hope I'm not about to make a really big mistake...*

CHAPTER 2

CAT KEEPS QUIET

"If you want to wait a while, I'll phone for a taxi," Matt offered. "I'll pay."

"No thanks, Mr Moneybags. You don't have to waste Daddy's allowance on me," trilled Cat, always quick to get a dig in at Matt and his cushioned lifestyle. "I'll just keep Joey company. And I fancy a walk."

She's up to something, thought Sonja, gazing at her cousin through narrowed eyes as she kissed Kerry goodnight and waved at the others.

Years of growing up with Cat and watching her get in and out of scrapes was qualification enough for Sonja to suss out when trouble was brewing. And apart from that, when was Cat – who never wore anything on her feet less than three inches high – ever in the mood to walk anywhere?

But this is Kerry's night, Sonja reasoned, *so I'm not going to spoil it by saying anything. Cat can't keep anything to herself for long, so we'll find out soon enough what she's up to...*

"Well, tonight's been great, Kerry – I've never actually had an Indian meal in an Indian restaurant before. I've only ever eaten it out of a foil tray when it's been delivered," admitted Matt, gazing round at the ornately papered walls and intricately decorated wall hangings of the restaurant.

"Really?" said Ollie in surprise, sitting up straight and pulling the small, wet towel off his face. While the girls had delicately wiped their fingers with the lemon-fragranced hot towels given to them by the waiter, Ollie had walloped his across his face with a groan of pleasure.

"You didn't say that when we came in." As often happened, Sonja was surprised that while Matt was one of the oldest and most 'privileged' (big house, posh boarding school, buckets of cash) of them all, he could be pretty naive too.

"Why give Cat *more* ammunition to have a go at me!" Matt shrugged good-naturedly.

"But you two love sniping at each other!" laughed Sonja.

"Oh, I don't think Matt loves it, do you, Matt? You've just got used to answering her back, haven't you?" Maya said intuitively.

"*She* always starts it. All I do is try and give back as good as I get."

"What is it – a bit of self-protection, then?" asked Anna, whose favourite hobby was working out what was going on inside people's heads. But she hadn't had anyone to practise her amateur psychology on since she'd moved to Winstead, until she'd started to hang out with Ollie and his friends.

"Whoa! It's like sitting in between Ricki Lake and Oprah here!" Matt laughed, holding up his hands.

"Yes, but you haven't got as hard a shell as you pretend, have you, Matt?" smiled Maya.

"Me? I'm tough as anything!" he jokingly boasted, holding his arms out and flexing his muscles theatrically.

Maya reached over and tickled his armpit, and Matt crumpled up laughing.

"Hey, you know who you sounded like there!" said Ollie, reaching down into Kerry's bag.

"Furby!" the girls all squealed as Ollie placed the black and white furry toy – Matt's present to Kerry – on the table. He tickled its tummy and the creature burst into a mechanical rattle of giggles.

Looking over at Matt's grinning face, Sonja felt guilty at joining in with her cousin's teasing of him earlier in the evening. She was so used to

Catrina and Matt's constant bickering that it hadn't really occurred to her that it might sometimes get a bit wearing for him.

So he's cocky and overconfident a lot of the time, but he's so sweet and kind too, she said to herself, thinking specifically of the goofy but perfect gift he'd chosen for Kerry. "I just saw it and thought it looked like Barney!" he'd explained when she unwrapped it. It was true – the fluffy toy did look like Kerry's lovable, daft dog.

In fact, Matt's a bit like Kyle and Owen rolled into one... Sonja mused. Before her latest attempt at romance had fallen flat on its face, she'd been torn between Kyle's fun-loving but full-on character and Owen, Anna's sensitive and adorable brother. Neither of the relationships had come to anything; Owen had landed a job a long way away, while Kyle had shown his true colours by seeing someone else behind Sonja's back. Not that Sonja could complain about that, since she was guilty of doing exactly the same thing.

Yep, Sonja decided, *Matt certainly has Kyle's swagger and humour, but at least he's more reliable. And he's as handsome and can be as gentle as Owen, but doesn't live ten trillion miles away...*

Catching herself having these strange and unprecedented thoughts about her friend, Sonja experienced something that rarely happened to her – she blushed to the roots of her honey-blonde hair.

• • •

"Did you know that if you injected the nicotine content of just *one* cigarette *directly* into a vein it would kill you?"

"That can't be true!"

"Oh, yes it is," nodded Joe seriously, wafting the smoke from Cat's cigarette away from his face. "That's why when you smoke, you're actually poisoning yourself."

"Don't lecture me, Joey! We've had a really nice night – don't spoil it," said Cat petulantly, tucking her arm more firmly through his as they strolled homeward.

"Well, don't spoil it for me by blowing smoke in my face!" Joe responded.

"You're getting very bolshy these days, Joey!" teased Cat. "It wasn't so long ago that you wouldn't have said boo to a sparrow, let alone a goose! And now, here you are, bossing me about..."

"Bossing you about?" he laughed. "Would I dare?"

"But you do seem different, Joey – what's changed?"

"I dunno," he shrugged, raising his eyebrows and shoving his hands deeper into his pockets.

Joe *did* feel different, though and he *did* know why. After years wrapping himself up in knots about the break-up of his parents' marriage, this summer he'd finally felt as though he'd come to terms with it. He was getting on a lot better with his dad and didn't feel so suffocated by his mum. That was the difference and it felt good.

"Anyway, enough about you, if you won't tell me anything," Cat flounced. "What about Kerry tonight? Didn't she look amazing?"

Joe's heart lurched at the memory of how lovely Kerry had looked.

"Mmm," he muttered non-committally.

"Although I could have done without all the mushy 'I wuv yooo' stuff Ollie was coming out with. Turned my stomach, that did."

Her comment only reminded Joe that not everything in his life was less complicated. Being crazy about your best friend's girlfriend didn't exactly rank high on the list of Great Situations To Be In.

"Hey, I meant to say," Cat continued, "I thought that compilation tape you made for Kerry was brilliant – but how did you manage to get it so right? How did you know that all those songs were her favourites?"

Joe felt a little smile play at his lips. Cat liked to shock, but how shocked would *she* be if he came out with the truth?

"Well, Cat, I know all Kerry's favourite records because I make it my job to know everything about her."

"Why's that?"

"Because I'm totally and completely in love with her."

"You're what?!!!"

Joe smiled again as he ran the imaginary conversation in his head.

"Oh, I just remembered some stuff she'd mentioned. You know how it is," he said vaguely. "So, uh, how come you were so keen to leave with me? You're never usually the first to leave a party..."

Cat threw her cigarette into the gutter and blew out a grey funnel of smoke from her perfectly made-up lips.

"Aw, Joey, I've got a lot on my mind tonight. Guess I just wasn't in the mood," she replied.

Coughing as her cloud of smoke enveloped him, Joe managed to respond, "Er, anything you'd like to share with the class?"

"Joey, darling," she grinned at him, giving his arm a squeeze, "I think I'll take a leaf out of your book on this one. I think I'll keep it to myself for a bit."

• • •

"Come on, there's one shot left – it's a shame to waste it," Maya cajoled the others as they stood shivering in their summer clothes in the cool evening air.

On her instructions, Ollie and Kerry snuggled up – with their backs to the window of the Kamil Tandoori restaurant and the glances of the curious waiters inside – while Anna stood to their left, and Sonja and Matt posed to their right.

"Son – budge up to Matt! I can't get you all in!" Maya waved over at them, her face obscured by the camera.

"C'mere, you!" said Matt, boisterously pulling Sonja in close to him.

The heat from his body so close to hers burned through Sonja's thin cotton dress.

"Matt!" barked Maya, dropping her camera down. "What on earth have you got stuck to your lip? Is it a bit of nan bread you were saving for later?"

"Huh? Where? Son – check it out for me!" said Matt, turning to Sonja.

With one finger, Sonja reached up and brushed the bit of bread away from his lips, wondering for a fleeting moment what it would be like to kiss them...

CHAPTER 3

•••••••••••••••••••••••••••••••

CAT'S CHANGE OF PLAN

"...Oh, yes. Kiss were a brilliant band. They wore the most amazing black and white make-up – were never photographed without it. And the outfits! They'd come on stage in these enormous platform boots—"

"Like the Spice Girls?"

"Er, not quite. The lads from Kiss were a lot louder and rockier than the Spice Girls."

"What – Kiss were *boys*?"

"Well, of course! Top blokes. One of the best bands I ever worked with."

"But they were *boys* and they all wore *make-up*?"

"Yeah, well, lots of bands have worn make-up: like Sweet and the Glitter Band in the '70s. And in the '80s all the New Romantic bands wore make-up, and even in the '90s you've got bands like Placebo. I remember—"

"But *boys* wearing make-up? I thought just ladies and girls wore it! Like Catrina – *she* wears make-up."

Nick Stanton nodded in agreement. "I suppose it is mostly ladies and girls who wear it, but some of the bands I used to work with—"

"Catrina wears *lots* of make-up. I think she looks like a—"

"Hey, Lewis! *You're* not bugging Nick I hope?" Kerry called across the café, losing the expression of amusement she'd been wearing as she observed her little brother's conversation with the ponytailed older man.

"I'd better rescue your Uncle Nick from his babysitting duties," she said hurriedly to Ollie, leaving him standing behind the café counter where they'd been idly chatting. Of course, what Kerry really wanted to do was stop Lewis in his tracks before he went any further with this conversation.

"Room for one more?" she asked almost breathlessly, sliding into the red banquette beside her brother.

Lewis looked daggers at his sister. He'd obviously been enjoying his man-to-man conversation with Nick, Ollie's uncle and the owner of the End-of-the-Line café. Nick, for his part, seemed a little disappointed to have to curtail telling all his old rock'n'roll stories to a captive audience. Even if that captive audience was only six years old.

"Well, guess I'd better get back to work," Nick sighed, easing himself out of the booth. Lewis watched in fascination as Nick's beer belly squashed against the table.

"Thanks for being patient with him, Nick," Kerry smiled at the café owner, knowing that he was just as glad for an excuse to sit down and take it easy as Kerry had been to have a few minutes alone with Ollie. Lewis adored Ollie and Kerry wouldn't have got a word in edgeways if Nick hadn't offered to keep her little brother company for a while.

"Pleasure," Nick replied, rubbing at the dark stubble on his chin. "Bring him through to the record shop when I'm there and I'll dig out a copy of a Kiss album so he can see what they look like. OK, Lewis?"

"Cool!" Lewis responded with his favourite word of the moment, feeling full of self-importance.

He watched as his friend Nick ambled off towards the kitchen, his cowboy boots clattering loudly on the tiled floor.

"You all right, Lew? Do you want another drink or something?" Kerry asked, happy to pacify her brother now that she knew the danger was over. "We won't stay for too long – I just want to see my friends for a while. And Maya might bring Ravi along."

"Cool! Could I have another Fanta, please? And a packet of Quavers? And some money for the jukebox?" Lewis asked, wide-eyed and innocent, and not above taking advantage of his sister's generosity.

"Right, here's some change..."

Kerry scrambled in her pockets and clattered a few coins on the table top. She didn't suppose Lewis would recognise too many of the records on the ancient jukebox, but at least it stopped him from being bored while they hung around and waited for the others.

"Can I get you something, Madam?" Ollie joked as Lewis barged past him.

"More Fanta and more Quavers for His Lordship, please," Kerry smiled up at him.

"Nick was fine looking after him, you know – you didn't have to drag him away. It's not like we're busy today."

"I know," shrugged Kerry, unwilling to admit why she'd interrupted them. Quickly, she changed the subject. "Wonder where everyone is?

I thought they all said they'd be here by around two."

Above an old Abba track that had sprung from the jukebox, a piercing shout interrupted them.

"KERRYKERRYKERRY!! Look – crossing the road! It's CATRINA THE CLOWN!"

Kerry glared over at her loud little brother, only half aware, in her embarrassment, of the guffaw of laughter coming from the kitchen.

Nick tolerated Cat because of her friendship with his nephew, but he didn't have much time for her, not after the grief she'd caused him in the past. He'd dated her mother briefly at the start of the summer and, out of jealousy and spitefulness, Cat had insinuated to her friends that *she* was the one Nick was *really* after. Right now it sounded as if he'd quite enjoyed hearing Lewis's tactless comment.

"*What* did Lewis say?" asked Ollie.

The bell above the café door tinkled as Cat walked in, and Kerry hoped frantically that both Lewis and Ollie would shut up. She didn't really want to explain to the world – and Cat – what her kid brother called her.

"Hi, guys!" trilled Catrina, slithering into the seat opposite Kerry. "What's new?"

Kerry flicked her eyes up towards Ollie and saw the wicked grin on his face. He had obviously realised what Lewis had shouted and, unfortunately, Cat's liberal application from her make-up box kind of proved Lewis's point.

"Um, the streak in your hair – it's, uh, it's nice," waffled Kerry, saying the first thing that came into her head.

Raising her heavily mascara'd eyelashes upwards, Cat tried to focus in on the chunk of hair that had been ruby red the night before at the restaurant.

"Mmm. It's supposed to wash out, but when I dried my hair this morning it had just faded to pink. Quite like it though. I decided to make it my theme colour for the day."

Kerry was suddenly aware of Lewis's presence at her side. He stood seriously and silently staring at the confection of pink that was Cat.

"Recognise the lipstick?" Cat asked, leaning forward and pouting her candy coloured lips at Kerry.

"Em, no," she flustered, noting that this close up it was easy to see where the layers of foundation smothering Cat's face met her real, unadorned skin halfway down her neck. "Should I recognise it?"

"Yeah – I bought it at your shop a couple of weeks back. Special offer? Remember?"

The vision of the basket full of loud and

unsellable coloured lipsticks and eyeshadows popped into Kerry's mind. It had been Kerry's boss's idea to finally get rid of the old stock at the chemist's.

"Oh, yes," she nodded. "Lewis, why don't you go up to the counter with Ollie and help him get our order together?"

"So, Kerry," said Cat, adjusting the straps of her pink vest top and unaware of Ollie winking as he led Lewis off. "Enjoying your two weeks' holiday before term starts?"

"Sort of. I mean, after working the whole summer, it's nice to have a break, but I wish Ollie had some time off too."

"Well, don't feel like you've missed out," yawned Cat, slowly tapping her taloned pink nails on the Formica surface. "None of us has been away anywhere exciting this summer, have we?"

"Ollie was speaking about that last night after you and Joe left, actually," said Kerry, trying not to get wound up by the fact that, out of the corner of her eye, she could see Lewis whispering in Ollie's ear. "He was saying that we should have a day trip to the seaside a couple of weeks on Saturday."

"Nice idea," Cat enthused. "But why can't we do it sooner?"

"'Cause Ollie wants time to charm Irene and

Dorothy into covering, so him and Anna can both take the day off," Kerry began to explain. "And it would also be something to look forward to – you know, after the gloom of starting back at St Mark's that week."

"Well, not all of us..." drawled Cat.

"What to you mean?" asked Kerry, confused.

"I'm not going back. I've finished with school."

CHAPTER 4

CLEAR AS MUD

Lewis and Ravi, Maya's little brother, had been offloaded to a neighbouring table and were now having a who-can-stuff-the-most-Jaffa-cakes-in-their-mouths competition. The only other people in the End-of-the-Line café at half past two on this Wednesday afternoon were Ollie and the rest of the gang.

All of them (apart from Kerry and Ollie who'd heard Cat's pronouncement already) sat with their mouths hanging open in surprise.

After a moment's stunned silence, Sonja was the first to speak. "Cat, when did you decide all this?"

"This morning. I rang to accept the college's offer of a place just before I came along here," Cat explained brightly, loving the sensation of having all eyes on her.

"But you never said anything!" Sonja continued. "Where did all this spring from?"

"Well, like I told Kerry and Ollie, Winstead College of FE had an ad in the paper last week for late applications..."

"Was that the thing you said you were thinking about last night?" Joe interrupted, remembering Cat's unusually reflective mood as they walked home from Kerry's night out.

"Uh-huh. I went to the college and saw them on Friday, then got a letter yesterday to say the place was mine, if I wanted it. I just had to decide overnight if I did."

"But why? What are you taking a beauty therapy course for? What do you plan to do with it?" questioned Sonja. She had to hand it to her cousin – Cat had well and truly managed to surprise her this time. Matt, Maya and Joe looked just as gobsmacked.

"I'm going to be... an actress!"

A hush fell around the table. Everyone's brains were whirring madly as the friends (including Kerry and Ollie who hadn't heard this snippet of information before) tried to make sense of what Cat had just said.

"Whoa – wait a minute!" said Matt. "You've just told us that you've enrolled for a *beauty* course at college. Where does acting fit in?"

"Well, the thing is, I know I want to work in TV or film—"

"Cat!" Maya burst in. "Why aren't you going for a *drama* qualification, if acting's suddenly the thing you want to do?"

"It *isn't* a sudden thing! I've always thought I'd be a good actress!" Cat said, petulantly sticking out her pink bottom lip. "And anyway, I'm trying to explain, if you'll let me!"

Maya rolled her eyes. "This I've got to hear..."

"It's like this," Cat began, slapping her manicured hands palms down on the table for emphasis. "I *could* stay on at St Mark's and do A levels and apply to drama school – but they all try and get you into theatre and Shakespeare and stuff, and I'm just not interested in that."

"That's like saying you want to be a vet but you're not interested in animals!" Ollie tried to reason.

"Don't be silly," Cat retorted. "Do you think all the actors in *Sunset Beach* or *Home and Away* did Shakespeare?"

Even Maya was stuck for an answer to the skewed wisdom of what Cat had just said.

"So from what I've read, contacts are what *really* counts."

"Cat, I'm lost," said Ollie, speaking for all of them. "What are you on about?"

Cat sighed dramatically. "Think about it: what am I good at?"

The others all stared at Cat, uncertain of what to say. Flirting, showing off, manipulating and lying were just a few of the less flattering but accurate characteristics that sprang to mind.

"Well?" she asked, looking round expectantly at her friends. "Isn't it obvious?"

They watched blankly as she pointed to her face.

"Make-up!" Joe blurted out suddenly, realising what she was trying to signal to them.

"Exactly!" Cat nodded at him. "I'm good at make-up."

Sonja grimaced inwardly as she remembered the make-over Cat had given her a couple of weeks before; Sonja had felt like the victim of an explosion in a glitter factory.

"So my way of thinking is this: I do a beauty course; become a make-up artist down in London; work on TV and film stuff; make contacts; get offered acting work!"

Kerry instinctively felt that Ollie and Matt were on the brink of either laughing or saying something that they thought would be hilariously funny but Cat wouldn't.

"What does your mum say about you changing your mind so late in the day?" she asked quickly as a means of deflection. Cat's mum Sylvia was a pretty frightening prospect to all the friends – even Sonja, who was related to her. Sylvia Osgood was a self-made, high-flying, short-tempered business woman, who had little time for half-baked ideas or crazy notions.

"Um..."

"Cat..." Maya started dubiously. "What do you mean 'um'? Isn't your mum flipping out at you? What does she think about all of this? Does she agree that it's the best route into acting?"

Cat just fumbled with the daisy clasp on her pink, fun-fur handbag and batted her eyelashes furiously. It was pretty obvious to the others that Cat hadn't yet let her mother in on her little secret...

CHAPTER 5

JUST ME AND YOU (AND EVERYBODY ELSE)

Matt walked in the room and immediately felt a mixture of awe and intimidation. He always felt like this when he came across the females of the Harvey family gathered together.

Especially when they wolf-whistled at him.

"Don't do that, Karin dear, it's so vulgar," said the fortysomething woman dressed casually in a denim shirt and jeans, who was sitting chopping vegetables at the kitchen table.

"Aww, he loves it – don't you, Matt?" grinned Sonja's big sister Karin, stretching out in her high-backed, wooden chair and running her hands through her hair.

"Just ignore her, Matt. It's lovely to see you!" crooned Sonja's mother in her husky, slightly Swedish-accented voice.

Hearing the others greet him, Sonja's eldest sister Lottie turned from the cooker where she was stirring something and gave him a beaming smile. "Hello, gorgeous!"

Matt felt flustered under the piercing, blue-eyed gaze of Sonja's mum and big sisters, and just managed a grin and a grunt in response. Sonja on her own was fine – he knew she was attractive, but she was just his friend, so he was never anything but relaxed with her.

The trouble started when he saw them altogether: all three girls were like mirror images of their mother – tall, slim, with honey-blonde hair and those pale, pale eyes... it was totally unnerving. Matt was rarely fazed by good looks – he was too confident in his own natural charms for that – but the Harvey women left him virtually speechless every time.

"Off to the End, are you?" asked Karin, with a white-toothed smile, before adding sarcastically, "Again?"

"Yeah, um, that's right," Matt bumbled, aware that he sounded as nervous as Joe often did in front of girls.

"Now, Matt – what do you want to go and hang out with a bunch of kids and grannies in that grotty café for? Hasn't a handsome boy like you got better things to do?" chipped in Lottie.

Matt knew that the teasing was partly for the benefit of their little sister, but it didn't help him feel any less humiliated. At twenty and twenty-one, Karin and Lottie were only a few years older than Matt, but they seemed a world away from him in maturity and confidence.

Sonja, who never took her sisters' wind-ups to heart, laughed along with them as she scooped up her bag from the back of a chair.

"C'mon, Matt – let's get going. We don't want to take up any more of Karin and Lottie's precious time," she jibed, pushing Matt ahead of her. "See you, Mum! See you, ugly sisters!"

Stepping out into the sunshine, Matt felt relieved to be out of the clutches of Karin and Lottie. After all, *he* was the chat-up king; *he* was the guy with the flirty one-liners – having two gorgeous older girls do it to him was totally disconcerting, especially since they were only having a laugh. And especially since he quite fancied both of them.

"Did they freak you out, babe?" Sonja said, rubbing his back comfortingly. "Those full-on sisters of mine?"

"A bit," he acknowledged with a grin, pointing the bleeper on his keyring and automatically unlocking the car doors.

"Anyway," Sonja began, slithering her long,

tanned legs into the passenger seat, "how come we're going to the End? I thought we were going straight to this record fair you were on about..."

"Yeah, but Ollie wants me to look out for some records for him. He asked me to drop by and pick up the list he's put together," Matt replied, easing the car along the road for the short journey round to the café.

"Wow, this is going to be an exciting afternoon – watching you go through racks and racks of records. It's going to take hours if you're looking for stuff for Ollie as well as yourself!"

"Well, I did tell you that you'd find it pretty boring. So why did you want to come?"

Because it's my only chance to be with you on our own – so I can figure out if there could be anything between us or if this whole idea is just a mistake... Sonja's thoughts raced.

"Dunno. I'm just bored, I guess, and fancied doing something different," was what she actually replied.

"Oh, speaking of different," Matt interrupted, "I'm DJing at the opening of the new fitness centre on River Road on Saturday. Fancy coming along and keeping me company?"

"Mmm... well, OK," Sonja said as casually as she could, although she couldn't help feeling that fate had stepped in and given them yet another chance to be together, without the rest of the crowd hanging round.

Sonja had kept Matt company on a few occasions when he'd DJ'd – they all had, together or singly – but this time... This time maybe it wouldn't be just as someone to help him carry his gear and fetch him drinks. Maybe this time he'd come to the same conclusion as Sonja had and look at her with new eyes.

• • •

"You know arranged marriages..." Sonja began, looking earnestly across the table at Maya.

Maya wondered where this sudden change in the direction of the conversation had come from. A minute ago – before Matt went through to the kitchen to gossip with Ollie about the record fair – the three of them had all been talking about the trouble Cat was going to be in if she didn't tell her mum about college soon.

"No, not really," shrugged Maya in response to Sonja's statement. "It's not something my family are into."

"Yeah, I know that," nodded Sonja, oblivious to the fact that she'd got Maya's back up a bit.

Maya's pet hate was that, because of her family background, plenty of people expected her to be some expert on Asian culture when, in reality, she knew more about McDonalds and the Body Shop than peshwari nans and bindis.

"What are you on about then?" asked Maya.

"Well, everyone in the West has a kind of downer on the idea of arranged marriages, but plenty of them work, don't they?"

"I guess so," Maya shrugged. The only people she knew who'd had an arranged marriage were her grandparents on her dad's side, but she couldn't say whether their marriage was a good one since she'd never got to know them properly. In fact, it was her own father's wish *not* to have an arranged marriage that had led to the family bust-up between him and Maya's paternal grandparents.

"What I mean is, the principle is that a couple is matched because their families think they've got a lot in common, right?" Sonja tried to explain herself.

Maya gave a grudging nod.

"So, the couple start off as just friends, then fall in love as time goes by!" Sonja proclaimed, holding her hands out in front of her as if she'd just said the most profound thing in the world.

"I guess that's the theory..." Maya answered dubiously.

"But it's an interesting idea, isn't it? 'Cause

when you think about it, most of us fancy someone, fall slap bang in love and then find that it doesn't work out. Whereas..." Sonja wriggled in her seat and continued excitedly, "...you put two friends together, who already know and like each other, and why shouldn't that make for a more solid, real love?"

"What – like Kerry and Ollie?"

"No, not exactly. They were both in love with each other for ages before they got round to admitting it out loud."

Maya was feeling really uncomfortable with this conversation. Sonja would hate to hear it, but she could be very like her cousin sometimes: just like Cat, Sonja had a habit of being transparent when it came to scheming.

"*What* then?" asked Maya impatiently. She was hoping Sonja wasn't about to hassle her some more about how she should seriously think about Billy – her friend from photography club – as serious boyfriend material.

"I mean, friends who aren't in love but are fond of each other – they should maybe just give it a go. Y'know, try dating and see if anything happens," said Sonja dreamily. "It could work out brilliantly."

"Why are we talking about this?" Maya asked bluntly. She wished Matt would hurry up in the kitchen, and come and drag Sonja and her fantasies away.

"Uh... I– I–" Sonja stammered, coming back from dreamland with a bump. To Maya, it looked as if Sonja had suddenly realised she'd said too much.

"I just saw the end of a documentary about arranged marriages the other night..." Sonja waffled, hoping Maya wasn't about to ask for times and dates.

A rumpus from the kitchen and a booming voice distracted them before Sonja could tie herself in any more knots.

"Oi, Matt! *This* kitchen – *you* customer! Stop distracting my staff and get out front where you belong!"

"Sorry, Nick!" Matt laughed as he found himself being good-naturedly pushed through the doorway between the kitchen and the café's front counter.

"Sorry, nothing!" Nick replied, following him out. "Breaking health and safety rules by leaning on a work surface when I don't know where your hands have been; distracting my nephew when there's customers to serve—"

"Nick, the lunchtime rush is over – there's only Maya and Sonja out here!" Ollie protested, close on his uncle's heels.

"But it *could* have got busy!" Nick persisted, trying to sound like the boss for once.

"Yeah, and what if it had been busy? Where were you the last twenty minutes?" Ollie counteracted, enjoying baiting his uncle.

"You know I had to nip next door to the record shop for change!"

"Nah – you went next door for a yak with Bryan and a read of the NME!"

Ollie knew he'd hit a raw nerve when even Nick's bald spot went red.

"Anyway, Matt was telling me about something you'd approve of – there's a record fair up at the Balinard Hotel this afternoon."

"Is there really?" Nick nodded thoughtfully. "Maybe I should pop up later and have a look for stock for the shop..."

Ollie rolled his eyes as he recognised Nick spotting another opportunity to skive off.

"Speaking of the fair, I'd better get going," said Matt, glancing at his watch. "Still coming with me, Son?"

"'Course," Sonja replied, sliding out of the booth. "Someone's got to stop you going crazy with your credit card!"

Matt winced – Sonja was only joking, but his father hadn't been when the hefty statement on Matt's card arrived the week before. Threats of cutting up cards and sharp scissors had been mentioned.

"Oh, Matt! I forgot—" Maya exclaimed as her two friends stood poised in the doorway. "On Saturday night, is it OK to, uh, bring a friend to this fitness centre opening?"

Maya glanced at Sonja and wondered why her face had suddenly fallen.

And Sonja – trying to swallow her disappointment over the fact that Matt's invitation had been an open one and not for her alone – wondered why Maya looked so sheepish.

CHAPTER 6

MATT MISSES THE POINT

For the fleeting moment that they passed over the railway bridge, Sonja peered down at the track and the river that ran along beside it. She loved looking out for the families of swans that lived on that stretch of water.

She found it strangely comforting to know that swans had nested in the same spot in Winstead for centuries: Ollie had told her that his mum and dad's pub, The Swan, was named after the town's favourite residents and the pub itself was nearly two hundred years old.

"Look!" Sonja gasped as she saw two huge swans glide into view.

"What, the train?" said Matt, his eyes flickering away from the road for a second and spotting the 2.45 coming in from the city.

"God, boys! What are you like?!" sighed Sonja. "I could probably stick you in front of the Mona Lisa and you'd say 'Nice frame'!"

"*Mona Lisa*? That gangster movie with Bob Hoskins?"

Sonja spun around in exasperation at his ignorance, then saw the grin on his face.

"Oh, you!" she laughed, slapping him lightly on the arm.

"The swans are beautiful and the Mona Lisa's very nice, but there are paintings I like better. Now, do I pass for an OK human being? Horrible boy that I am?"

"Of course," smiled Sonja, adding another couple of humour plus points to her mental list of Matt's virtues.

They were companionably quiet for a minute or two as the houses thinned out and the road became leafier.

Now, thought Sonja, *now is the time I should get him round to a more romantic topic of conversation...*

"It's so sweet about Billy and Maya, isn't it?" she began.

"Uh, did I miss something?" Matt replied, shaking his head slightly in confusion. "Didn't she just ask to bring him along as a friend on Saturday?"

"Yes," said Sonja patiently, "but we all know what that *really* means!"

"Well, maybe I'm just being thick here, but I thought that because he's her mate from camera club, she thought this'd be a good chance for us, her other mates, to meet him properly."

Sonja bristled. Getting Matt to see the romantic side of life obviously wasn't going to be that easy.

"Matt, Matt, Matt! However much you boast about them, you've got a lot to learn about girls!" she exclaimed. "Don't you see? If she wanted us to meet him as a friend, she'd have just told him come into the End one day. But Saturday, that's like a proper night out. Like a date!"

"She went on one of those when she first met him and it didn't work out. Why would she risk it again?"

"Because she realises she feels more for him than just friendship..."

Sonja's loaded comment went straight over Matt's head.

"And she's told you this for a fact, has she?" he smirked, stealing a quick glance at Sonja's agitated face. He loved the way they could take the mickey out of each other and have a laugh about it.

"Well, no – but you know how private Maya

is about a lot of stuff," Sonja answered defensively, unaware of Matt's teasing smile.

This isn't a very good start, she thought. *How do I move on from here? How can I push this on a stage?*

"I know what this is all about..." said Matt suddenly.

"Oh yeah?"

"Yeah. After your recent pathetic attempts to have a relationship, you're looking for love somewhere new..."

Her heart lurched in shock.

"...which is why you're so keen to believe Maya's got a bit of a love thang going with her mate Billy."

Sonja managed a breath again.

"I don't think you're on to a winner there, but never mind," said Matt, grabbing her hand and bringing it up to his mouth. "*I* love you, babes."

His lips touched the back of her hand and Sonja's heart-rate shot off the monitor.

• • •

Cat hitched her tight skirt up higher.

"Cat! I don't think the entire population of the park wants an unhindered view of your pants!" snapped Maya, who'd propped herself up on her elbows to see why Cat was wriggling so much.

"Oh, shut up, you old nark!" Cat retorted, feeling satisfied that she'd got maximum exposure for her legs.

Maya sighed and flopped back down on the grass. It was pointless trying to get Cat to cover up when she didn't want to.

"Don't worry, there's no one around – only a few ducks are getting an eyeful," Kerry announced, lifting her head just high enough off the ground to check out their surroundings.

"Pity..." Cat murmured.

The three friends fell silent and let the sun warm their skin. Only the sound of children playing and the distant growl of traffic intruded on their individual thoughts.

"So, Cat," said Maya finally. "I know this is a stupid question, but have you told your mum about college yet?"

"No," mumbled Cat sulkily. "But don't nag me. I will tell her."

"What – *this* year? *Next* year..."

"Maya, get off my case!"

"Well, when then? You start in a week and a half!"

Cat was irritated, but still too lazy to move from her comfortable sunbathing spot. If it had been a different season and colder weather, she might have stomped off in a huff to avoid this awkward line of questioning.

"Yeah, so I start in a week and a half, so I've got plenty of time..."

"So? Are you thinking of leaving it till the night before?" niggled Maya. "Or maybe just the day you're due to start, as you're walking out the door?"

Cat turned her head and glared at Maya.

"Don't get all high and mighty at me about keeping secrets from parents, when you did exactly the same thing yourself not so long ago!"

Maya stayed silent and squinted at the thin wisps of cloud in an otherwise blue sky. It was true – she had lied to her parents about joining the photography club, but only because she knew they wouldn't approve.

Cat sensed she'd hit a sore spot and couldn't resist needling Maya some more.

"And you don't have to take it out on me, just 'cause you're all in a tizz about Billy."

"I'm not in a 'tizz'! Billy is just coming out with us on Saturday night, end of story!"

"Well, why were you all flustered about it when me and Kerry arrived at the End?"

"Because Sonja started to make a big deal out of it before Matt dragged her away – Maya's already explained that," Kerry interrupted, leaping to her friend's defence. Kerry was all too aware of Sonja's overeagerness in the matchmaking department. Sonja had done the same to her and Ollie, but at least they actually had genuinely wanted to go out together.

"Where were Sonja and Matt going anyway?" asked Cat, whipping her head around to stare at Kerry now.

It's amazing the way she can pick up and drop subjects just like that, thought Kerry, as she came under Cat's scrutiny. *Actually, she probably will make a good actress...*

"Some boring record fair," Kerry answered, reaching into her bag for more sunblock.

"What did Sonja want to go to that for?" Cat quizzed her, wrinkling up her nose in disbelief.

That's what I want to know, Kerry mused to herself, instinctively sensing that her best friend wasn't telling her everything.

CHAPTER 7

ON PLANET HOLLYWOOD

"Look, Joe! Just look at them!"

Joe leant forward and felt his chest constrict with nerves. Or possibly he'd forgotten to breathe for a few seconds.

"Er, yeah, there's a few more," he acknowledged, looking at the sprinkling of freckles across the bridge of Kerry's nose.

"But it's not fair! I put plenty of sunblock on yesterday and I *still* get more freckles..."

"Yeah, but they look... nice," he tried to say encouragingly. They looked beautiful to him. He wanted to stay this close to Kerry for ever...

"Ollie! Joe's telling me lies!" she yelled over the café to her boyfriend, moving away from Joe and breaking the spell.

"Oh, yeah?" said Ollie, ambling over with an

empty tray in his hand and a less-than-shiny-clean dishcloth over his shoulder.

"Yep," Kerry nodded, her hazel eyes wide and childlike. "Joe's trying to tell me these hideous freckles look nice and that can't be right, can it?"

"Well, I'm on Joe's side." Ollie grinned his lopsided grin and bent over to kiss her on the offending nose.

A clattering of dishes from the kitchen seemed to remind him that the End was pretty busy this Friday morning and he made to move off. But an approaching vision caught his eye.

"Uh-oh – check this out..."

On the other side of the road, passing the parade of shops, was Cat, sashaying along in a deliberate, sexy, slow manner, red lips pouting and her shoulder-length blonde hair artfully tousled. She was wearing a teeny-tiny red slip dress and matching strappy high sandals.

"She reminds me of someone," Joe mused aloud as Cat sauntered past the launderette.

"Cameron Diaz in *There's Something About Mary*," said Anna succinctly, coming over to see what they were gawping at after dropping off a couple of milkshakes. "That's exactly how she was dressed in the posters for the movie. Remember?"

"Ah, of course – now that she's decided she

wants to be an actress, she's going to dress the part, isn't she?" Ollie grinned. "Doesn't look like Vera's too impressed though..."

They all peered over and watched as Mad Vera, the bonkers old lady who ran the launderette, came out on to the pavement and started mincing after Cat, mimicking her hip-thrusting walk.

Cat must have heard laughter emerging from the open doorway behind her – from their vantage point in the window booth, Ollie and the others could all make out the amused expressions of the launderette's clientele – and she spun round, catching Vera on tiptoe with one hand on her overalled hip and her nose in the air.

"Oooh!" the friends all drew in gasps as Cat temporarily lost her cool and nearly her balance, stumbling on her pinheels.

Then, seeing their friend haughtily turn towards the kerb and prepare to cross the road, they leant back from the window as one so that she didn't catch them spying on her.

"God, that woman!" snorted Cat, breezing into the café. "Isn't it about time she retired?"

"What and leave the customers with no entertainment?" said Ollie, strolling back over to the counter. "I think half of them only come to see what Vera's up to."

Cat snorted derisively.

"I haven't seen you wear that dress before," said Anna, without bringing up the Cameron Diaz connection.

"Yeah..." drawled Cat. "I only bought it the other day."

"You look nice," Kerry smiled at her friend, although she couldn't help noticing that Cat's bare shoulders were a more ferocious red than her new dress. It looked as though Kerry hadn't been the only one who didn't slap on enough sunblock the day before in the park.

"Thanks, hon," said Cat airily. "You guys wanna cappuccino? I'm buyin'."

Kerry and Joe both nodded, then exchanged glances as Cat's heels click-clacked over to the counter.

"Was that supposed to be an American accent?" Kerry whispered.

"I s'pose," Joe hissed back, sounding dubious. "What do you reckon she'll do next? Change into an Edwardian frock in the loos and come back quoting lines from *Titanic*?"

Kerry burst into stifled giggles and Joe felt good. He'd made her laugh.

Over by the counter, Cat made herself as comfortable as she could in her thigh-skimming frock. A couple of twelve-year-old boys sitting with some girls at the table by the jukebox gaped open-mouthed, visibly transfixed at the sight of all this leggy foxiness at eleven o'clock in the morning.

"It's OK, Cat," said Ollie, setting up crockery and cutlery on a tray ready for Anna's next order, "I'll bring your drinks over."

"Nah, it's all right, I'll wait," said Cat, reverting to her normal accent for Ollie. "I wanted to ask you something."

"Fire away," nodded Ollie, still busying himself.

"Ollie, what did your parents say when you told them you wanted to leave school? I mean, I remember you telling us at the time, but..."

"...but you weren't that interested back then. And now, when you're wondering how to break the news to your mum, you're suddenly keen to hear my story again – is that about right?" Ollie quizzed her, above the noise of the gurgling coffee machine.

"Well..." purred Cat coquettishly.

"I'm not going to be much help to you, Cat. My folks knew for a long time that I didn't want to go on at school. And they were fine about it. Their only stipulation was that if I didn't get work, I should go to college to get some qualifications. Anything, so long as I didn't just leave school to bum about on the dole."

Cat watched idly as Ollie filled two cups from the hissing taps on the cappuccino machine and plonked them on Anna's tray.

"So they didn't flip out at you?"

"Nope," Ollie shook his head. "But if you want my advice Cat, when you do tell your mum, don't let on all that stuff about it being your way into acting – she'll just think you're wasting your time. Or that you're off your trolley. Or both."

"Ollie! Don't you think it's a good idea?" said Cat, genuinely hurt that her friend thought so little of her new career plan.

"Cat, to be honest, I think it's one of your crazier ideas," he said, leaning on the counter and staring seriously at her. "But then, I've never known anyone more determined than you, so it wouldn't really surprise me if I saw you serving behind the bar in the Queen Vic in a few years time."

"That long?" Cat grinned back at him, happy that he wasn't scolding her too badly.

"Sorry to spoil your fun, but is that pizza ready?" Anna interrupted them.

"Jeez, I forgot..." yelped Ollie, running back into the kitchen to check the order with Irene.

Anna perched herself wearily on the stool next to Cat. It had been a frantically busy morning and she couldn't wait till twelve when Joe officially came on for his shift. He'd been a brilliant extra pair of hands through the summer holidays; he was a lot harder working and less easily distracted than Ollie, and she dreaded what it would be like in the End once he was back at college.

Still, she comforted herself, glancing round at the crowded tables, *half the customers will be back at school too.*

"So, are you coming out to play tomorrow night?" Cat asked Anna. The waitress's quiet, knowing expression sometimes freaked Cat out, but she liked Anna's dry sense of humour and was quite pleased to see her become a member of the extended crowd.

"This thing Matt's DJing at? Yeah, it sounds good," Anna replied flatly, absently rearranging the cutlery on the tray in front of her.

"Wow – don't sound too excited!" Cat said with a hint of sarcasm. She thought Anna would have jumped at the chance to get out to a do like this: it wasn't as if she had millions of friends and a dizzy social life to distract her.

"No, it's not what you think," Anna tried to correct herself, realising that it seemed as if she was unenthusiastic and ungrateful for the invitation. "It's just– it's, well, just..."

"What?" whined Cat, who had the patience of a gnat.

"You lot look so good when you get all dressed up – like the other night at the Indian restaurant," Anna blurted out. "I don't have anything apart from a couple of pairs of jeans and I never know what to do with this..."

Anna held up the long, dull brown ponytail of hair that hung down her back and gave it a contemptuous look.

When she glanced back up, Cat was wearing that expression which her other friends knew signalled danger.

"Never you mind about that," she nodded conspiratorially. "Your Auntie Cat will sort you out. Leave it to me..."

Anna – who never wore any make-up apart from a smear of lip balm and a slick of clear mascara – looked at Cat's inch-thick foundation and heavy-duty lipliner and inwardly gulped.

CHAPTER 8

WHO'S THAT GIRL?

Cat pushed the heavy green wooden door closed behind her. She'd tiptoed carefully along the alleyway between the second-hand shop and the café – she hadn't wanted the pitted tarmac to scuff her new, pale blue leather ballet pumps.

Running quickly up the metal stairs that led to Anna's flat, Cat shuddered. Even in the warm, late summer twilight the alley and the yard were full of shadows.

Doesn't it creep Anna out living here? she wondered as she pressed the doorbell, imagining the blackness of the alleyway come wintertime.

The bright glare of a light and the thump of some reggae music made her glance over to Nick's flat on the opposite side of the yard, and once again she gave an involuntary shudder. Everyone thought she'd shrugged off the whole episode with Nick; that she'd managed to forget how she'd lied about going out with him as an elaborate means of getting attention.

But as bright and breezy as she was around Nick, she was still mortified every time she came near him. It had been a spur-of the-moment thing for her to claim to her friends that she was seeing him, but the repercussions looked as if they'd last for a very long time; both in the guilt and regret that Cat felt and the barely concealed dislike that the formerly amiable Nick had shown towards her ever since.

And let's face it, thought Cat, turning her gaze away from his window, *if I had to make up a pretend boyfriend, I could have done better than to say it was some beer-bellied, ponytailed, boring old rocker...*

"Hi!" said Anna brightly, pulling open the front door and beckoning Cat inside. "You just caught me – I finished up in the café two minutes ago."

"Joe still there?" asked Cat, padding past Anna into the small flat.

"Mmm," nodded Anna, closing the door. "But I feel guilty 'cause he's clearing up all on his own. Nick disappeared to put the takings into the safe about twenty minutes ago and hasn't been seen since."

"I looked over at his window just now," said Cat. "He's got some music on, so it doesn't look like he's in a mad rush to get back."

"Just as well there's not much left to do then," Anna shrugged.

It had been uncharacteristically quiet in the End all day, which hadn't done Anna any favours. Mooching about half bored, her imagination had run riot over what Cat might inflict on her, but she'd ultimately decided that to refuse Cat was to insult Cat. So here she was, like a lamb to the slaughter, leaving her fate and her face to Cat's mercy.

"Cat, you look... um... *short*," Anna said as they walked into the living room.

"Oooh, do I? But is that *bad* short or *cute* short?" Cat grimaced, looking down at her outfit. "It's these shoes, you see..."

"Cute short," Anna reassured her quickly and meant it. It was nice to see Cat out of her trademark skyscraper heels. She looked altogether more... delicate, Anna decided. "But what's brought on this change of style?"

"Drew Barrymore," said Cat firmly. "I've done my hair like her before – her ringlet look – but I've never gone the whole way. And let's face it: flat shoes *are* Drew."

And Cat should know, thought Anna. She'd seen how Cat sat and drooled her way through the celebrity pictures in *TV Hits* and *B* in the café downstairs.

"Well, I think you look lovely like that," Anna complimented her, taking in the rosebud-edged, powder blue top and nearly knee-length, layered chiffon skirt. Suddenly, Anna felt a little less stressed about her upcoming make-over.

"Enough about me – let's get started on you," said Cat, thumping a holdall and her ominously large make-up box on to Anna's throw-covered sofa.

Cat was all of a sudden very proud of herself. Here she was, coming to the rescue of a friend in need, *and* she was resisting the urge to nosy her way round Anna's sweet little flat which neither she – nor anyone else in the crowd for that matter – had ever been in to before. And for Cat, resisting the urge to snoop was very, *very* hard.

"Right, I brought a few bits and pieces of clothes," she said, hauling out a dazzling array of brightly coloured materials from the holdall, "and we'll decide what to do with your hair and make-up once we've chosen those."

"OK," squeaked Anna and prepared to surrender.

• • •

In a move reminiscent of their slinky Burmese cat, Marcus, skinny, long-limbed Sunita slithered through Maya's open door and posed silently against the wall.

Aware that she was being watched, Maya turned away from her old-fashioned dressing table mirror – mascara wand still in hand – and focused on her staring sister.

"What do you want, Sunny?" she asked brusquely.

In her experience, her younger sister never came by just for a chat. She always wanted *some*thing, whether it was help with her homework (which their parents always expected Maya to give) or to pick up any information that she could store up and use later. (Why her sister felt the need to spy on her, Maya couldn't figure out.)

"Who's your new friend?" asked Sunny.

"Who do you mean? Anna?" Maya replied, wondering how Sunny could know that she was now part of their crowd. Sunny would have seen Anna down at the End when she was there with her own little gang, but there was no way that she'd have linked her to Maya and Sonja and the others.

"No, it's definitely not that waitress girl."

"Who are you talking about then?" said Maya irritably. She didn't have time for her sister's stupid riddles: it was Saturday night and she was busy trying to get ready to go out.

"The girl downstairs," Sunny replied flatly. "The one that arrived with all your other friends..."

Maya suddenly realised the implications of what Sunny was saying.

"Everyone's here already? I didn't hear the doorbell! Why didn't you just tell me my friends had arrived straightaway instead of mucking around?"

"I'm telling you now," shrugged Sunny, following her sister as she dashed out of her room and down the stairs.

Maya peeked her head round the living room door and found Sonja, Kerry and Cat making polite conversation with her parents. And, sitting quietly on the sofa stroking an enamoured Marcus, was the mystery girl.

"Oh, my God..." gasped Maya.

CHAPTER 9

•••••••••••••••••••••••••••••

MATT GETS ZAPPED

"Oh, my God..." gasped Ollie.

Joe stared wordlessly at Anna and tried to force his brain to come up with something appropriate, but it let him down. When he'd last seen Anna a few hours earlier at the End, she certainly hadn't looked anything like she did now.

"Put your tongue away, Joey," Sonja teased him, then regretted it as soon as she saw the colour flood to his cheeks.

"Oh, my God..." Ollie repeated, struck almost as dumb as Joe at the sight in front of him.

"That was Maya's reaction too – isn't it brilliant? Managing to shock Maya, I mean!" smirked Cat, clapping her hands together in excitement.

"Anna, you look..." Ollie struggled for the word.

"...beautiful," Joe chipped in, finally finding his voice.

"Thanks," Anna smiled, shuffling from foot to foot, furiously embarrassed and furiously thrilled in equal measure at the reaction to her transformation.

She'd been utterly awestruck herself when Cat had finally let her step in front of the full-length mirror that she'd brought through from the back of the bathroom door. ("The light in there is too harsh," Cat had informed her. "It's much more flattering through here in the living room.")

Instead of her ever-present jeans and T-shirt, Anna found herself wearing a long, sleeveless, slinky black dress. It was the same dress that Cat had poured herself into for one of Matt's parties back in the spring; the dress she had worn the night she'd decided to go after Ollie.

But without Cat's ample chest straining the neckline, it now looked more elegant than glam. Even the side split looked less sexy and more stylish worn with Anna's own strappy, flat, Roman sandals, instead of the teeteringly high shoes Cat had originally teamed with the dress.

At work, the only jewellery that Anna wore was a tiny cross on a chain – a present from her mother on her twelfth birthday. Tonight, she'd swapped that for a chunky amber pendant. The dark strands in the amber, worn high at her throat, seemed to intensify her dark brown eyes. And as for her eyes, her face... Anna could hardly recognise herself.

Cat had smudged a nut-brown eyeshadow above and just below her eyes, so they looked enormous and doe-like. The mole on her cheek had been highlighted with a brown pencil and was every bit as striking as the one that Cindy Crawford sported. A soft brownish lipstick accentuated Anna's small but full mouth, and a tinted moisturiser disguised the dryness and blotchiness which her skin tended to suffer from after a hard day working in the steamy café.

But it was Anna's hair that surprised her most. Longish, brownish, dullish: that's how she normally thought of it, and normally she did the simplest thing she could with it – pulled it back into a ponytail. But Cat had turned it into something that wouldn't look out of place in a hair magazine.

Parting it in the middle, she'd combed serum through to give it shine, then slicked her steam straightener over every lock for an immaculate look. Finally, Cat had worked in two tiny plaits, tied tightly and invisibly with dark brown thread, which hung down on either side, framing Anna's face.

"Maya's little brother said she looked like Pocahontas!" Sonja laughed, enjoying the boys' reactions. "And Sunny didn't even believe it was the same girl from the End!"

"Where is Maya? Didn't she come with you lot?" asked Ollie at the mention of Maya's name.

"Yes, but she's outside, waiting for Billy," Kerry told him. "She said she'll come and find us."

"Come on – we'll show you around," said Ollie, motioning the girls to follow him out of the plush reception area of the fitness centre and through to the huge, atmospherically-lit room beyond, where music was already booming from Matt's decks. "We had a good nosy around after we helped Matt get set up. This place is really flash!"

"Lot of yuppies, though," Joe noted, looking round at the designer-dressed, champagne-sipping throng in the main room.

"Well, it would be, wouldn't it," shrugged Ollie. "That's the whole point of tonight – get all the eligible, well-off potential punters along; let them see the place, ply 'em with some free drink and then hope they sign up and stump up a nice fat joining fee!"

Kerry huddled close to Ollie; she needed his confidence. She was uncomfortably aware that they were the youngest people there, and no matter how they'd dressed up, it felt patently obvious to her that they were there under false pretences. She glanced back to check that her other friends were still with them and saw Sonja and Cat's beaming faces as they stared round at the party set-up. They were in their element. Of course.

"Let's go over and see Matt first," Ollie grinned back at the girls over his shoulder. "I'm dying to see the look on his face when he spots Anna!"

• • •

"This... beats jogging round the park... on a drizzly morning," panted Ollie.

"Are you allowed to do that?" asked Maya. Ollie was thumping away on the running machine, his eyes glued to the screen above his head that was showing MTV.

"'Course," he said breathlessly, slowing his pace. "Everyone's... allowed to try... the equipment."

"Potential clients are meant to *look* at the equipment, I think," Maya contradicted him. "You aren't a potential client – not on your wages – and you're not meant to use gym equipment without a proper instructor around. Especially after you've knocked back a few free champagnes..."

"Oh, Maya," Ollie grinned as he leapt off the machine, "what would we all do without you looking out for our welfare?"

"I dread to think," smiled Maya, leaning casually against the wall with her arms folded across her chest.

Ollie had appointed himself tour guide of the fitness club and was on his second lap of its facilities. He'd ambled round with Kerry and the others earlier and now it was Maya's turn.

"I like Billy," said Ollie out of the blue, parking himself on an exercise bike while he got his breath back.

Maya felt a wave of pleasure. She appreciated Ollie's straightforward opinion. The girls, she knew, were looking at Billy purely from the point of view of a potential love interest for Maya, no matter how much she protested that he wasn't.

"He seems pretty sorted. He was telling me that he wants to be a professional photographer, after winning that competition," Ollie continued.

Again, Maya felt a wave of pleasure wash over her. Billy had won the photography competition at the art gallery in town with a picture of her; a candid shot she hadn't even realised he'd taken. She'd tried to play it down ever since, but couldn't deny to herself how flattered she'd been.

"Is he going to be all right out there on his

own?" Ollie asked, nodding in the direction of the general party.

"Of course!" Maya replied slightly indignantly. It wasn't like a date, where Billy might expect to have her undivided attention. She'd brought him along to meet her friends and that was exactly what she'd left him doing when she went off snooping with Ollie. "He was talking to Anna, remember?"

"Is that wise?" laughed Ollie, standing up and falling into step behind Maya, who was heading towards the exit.

"What do you mean?"

"The way Anna's looking tonight, is he going to be able to resist her?"

"He can do what he likes," Maya shrugged. "He's a free agent."

"Sure about that?"

Maya was ready to bite Ollie's head off after that last comment. Then she spotted his ear-to-ear grin.

"Was that your impersonation of Cat or Sonja?" she laughed, linking her arm with his.

"Take your pick," he answered as they headed out into the corridor. "But are you sure it's OK to take my arm? Won't Billy be jealous?"

Then he yelped as Maya pinched him.

• • •

Sonja tapped Matt on the shoulder and passed him a pint glass of orange juice.

"Thanks, Son, I'm dying of thirst," Matt barked above the music.

"Pleasure," she smiled back.

A little shiver of excitement ran down her spine as their fingers brushed round the glass – but it was more to do with the look in his eyes than the physical contact.

Gone was Matt's laid-back, hooded-eyed gaze. His eyes were wide, glinting with excitement, the black pupils enormously large, even in the subdued lighting. If she didn't know him better, she might have supposed he was on drugs. But she had read once that when a person is attracted to someone else, their pupils do dilate, for some strange hormonal, chemical, unknown reason.

Could there be something in that? she wondered.

Matt switched his gaze away from Sonja. He felt, bizarrely, that she might be able to see through his eyes to the thoughts behind them; instead he looked out over the room.

He was relieved that the last couple of tracks had finally got people up and dancing. That was always the yardstick he measured himself by: if he was doing his job well, and matching the right type of music to the crowd in front of him, then they'd shake off their shyness and get up on the dance floor pretty early in the evening.

Tonight, they'd taken so long that he felt as if he was losing his touch, but then, if he was honest, he hadn't exactly had his mind on the job over the last couple of hours.

Matt was too conscious of the hammering in his heart and the hairs on his neck standing up.

He was too busy trying to work out if he was having a heart attack, or if he was suddenly head-over-heels, flat-on-his-face in love...

CHAPTER 10

TROUBLE IN PARADISE

In the still of the night, Ollie, Kerry and Joe stood in the middle of the bridge and gazed down at the black water of the river below. Three luminously white shapes caught their attention.

"Look, there they are!" said Kerry excitedly, pointing at the swans roosting for the night by the bushes that lined the riverside path. "Don't they look beautiful in the moonlight?"

"Not as beautiful as you..." Ollie replied, pulling her closer to him, his arm round her waist.

Kerry felt fleetingly irritated. His supposed hug felt more like a clumsy tug and, apart from that, did he have to say slushy stuff like that in front of Joe? *It's as if Joe isn't here,* she thought uncomfortably. *As if Joe's feelings don't count or don't matter...*

"Can you make them out, Joe?" she asked their friend, trying to include him in the conversation and hopefully make some subtle point to Ollie.

"Uh... think so. Those white shapes, yeah?" Joe nodded. "'Course, at this distance, they could just be white plastic bags that have blown into the bushes."

Kerry found herself laughing far too loudly at his not-particularly-funny observation, still over-compensating for what she saw as Ollie's thoughtlessness.

"You know," she began conversationally, watching the reflection of the moon wobble gently in the water below, "I still can't get over what a brilliant job Cat did on Anna!"

"Well, yeah, that's true," Ollie agreed, "but don't let that put any ideas in your head!"

"What do you mean?" Kerry quizzed him.

"I don't want you offering your services as a guinea pig! I don't want Cat changing one thing about you..."

Ollie leant forward and affectionately pecked her on the cheek. Involuntarily, Kerry shivered. He'd done it again.

"Cold, babe?" Ollie asked, misinterpreting the gesture. He cuddled her closer. Kerry felt more stifled and more annoyed for Joe's sake.

A car horn blared on the road behind them and

all three spun round to see Matt and Sonja waving from Matt's Golf. Reinforced boxes containing speakers, lights and records were piled to the roof in the back seat, as well as the hatchback's boot.

"They managed to get that lot packed up quickly enough!" observed Joe. Tonight they'd all done their share: helping Matt set up and then packing most of his gear away while the others – with the exception of Sonja and Kerry – drifted on home as the party at the fitness centre fizzled out.

"Yeah, it was good of Sonja to offer to help with last of the stuff and let me and you off the hook," Ollie said to Joe. The two boys tended to be roped in to do Matt's donkey work pretty regularly when he was gigging.

"She probably just offered 'cause she knew it meant a free lift home," Joe pointed out.

"What?" Ollie pretended to be hurt. "And turn down the chance to walk home with me and Kerry?"

From the bridge, Ollie could have taken the road straight along as far as the top of the park and been home in minutes, with his friend and neighbour, Joe. But, of course, being the caring boyfriend that he was, he'd be taking a twenty-minute detour, down the west side of the park, past the station and the darkened End-of-the-Line café, and on to the enclave of streets where Kerry lived.

"That's probably why Sonja held out for a lift..." Kerry muttered. However nicely Sonja had put it, she'd let Kerry know clearly enough that Kerry'n'Ollie's cosy coupledom could get a little nauseating for the rest of them sometimes. Kerry had felt hurt at the time, but she had to acknowledge that her best friend had a point.

"What?" asked Ollie, trying to make sense of what his girlfriend had said.

"Nothing," replied Kerry, shaking her head.

• • •

It wasn't because she felt she'd be number three in Kerry and Ollie's crowd of two that Sonja had hitched a lift.

After seeing that certain sparkle in Matt's eyes tonight when he'd looked at her, Sonja wanted yet another chance to be alone with him.

As she'd carried the last of the leads and cables to the car, her mind had raced with things to say *("You looked... different tonight. Something on your mind?")* or things to do (lean her head on his shoulder as he drove) that might help move things along between them, if her intuition was right and Matt felt something for her.

But now, driving along, aware of his presence so close to her, Sonja decided on a different tactic – she was going to shut up. She'd done nothing but chatter when they'd gone to the record fair together on Thursday and nothing had happened.

Now Sonja was just going to stare wistfully and silently out of the window and give Matt the chance to say or do something. Something that might shed light on whether they had a chance together or not...

Sonja was quiet, Matt noticed. But he liked that; the fact that there could be comfortable silences between them. That was what made Sonja so special – what made him feel closest to her out of all the girls.

But now, tonight, something totally unexpected had happened and he didn't know how to put these sudden, new, scary feelings into words.

He glanced out of the corner of his eye and saw Sonja staring sleepily out of the passenger window.

God, I wish I could tell her! he thought, his emotions making his head throb and his senses ache. *But how would she take it?*

• • •

"Are you OK?" Ollie asked.

The three of them – Kerry walking in the middle of the two boys – were approaching the turning by the park that Kerry and Ollie would head down, leaving Joe to his own devices.

"Yes, of course – why are you asking?" she snapped back.

"Well, because you've been a bit... offish tonight."

Some sixth sense of Joe's, tuned in for so long to Kerry's every move and mood, was aware of her tensing up as she walked beside him.

"Offish? What's that supposed to mean?"

"Like – like, I don't know, a bit snappy or whatever," said Ollie, an uncertain note creeping into his voice.

"Listen, I'm off," Joe interrupted, turning towards the pavement and making to cross the traffic-free main road.

"Yeah, OK, see you, Joe!" Ollie called after him with artificial breeziness.

"Bye, Joe!" called Kerry softly.

As Joe reached the pavement on the other side of the road, he could make out the tone, if not the actual words, of his friends' continuing exchange – it sounded like bickering.

And Joe realised he was glad...

CHAPTER 11

WILL SHE? WON'T SHE?

Cat curled up on the sofa and gave her mum a sideways glance.

Sylvia Osgood sat in a large, cream-coloured, comfy chair, a long-stemmed wine glass in her hand and her concentration directed at the documentary on the TV in front of her.

Frantically chewing at the skin inside her mouth, Cat tried to work up the courage to say what she had to say.

Suddenly, an ad break came up and Cat knew it was time to launch in. Sort of.

"Mum?"

Sylvia Osgood turned to face her daughter. Her perfect bob seemed unruffled, despite her earlier hour's worth of aerobics at the tennis club exercise suite.

"Mmm?" she responded flatly, assuming that the questioning note in Cat's voice meant only one thing: she wanted something. Probably an advance on her allowance, since that was the norm with Cat.

"Mum – one of my friends—"

"Which one?" her mother butted in. She was a stickler for precision and couldn't stand people faffing around and obscuring the issue. Which was unfortunate, considering it was one of her daughter's major talents.

"Um... Maya," Cat burst out, fixing on the one friend who was in the same year as her and, like Cat, was supposed to be transferring to the sixth-form college of St Mark's at the end of the summer break.

"Yes, what about Maya?" asked Cat's mother, appearing slightly more interested now that she thought that money probably wasn't the issue for discussion.

"Uh, well," Cat tried to begin, now realising that Maya wasn't a good choice to pick on for the 'what if...' scenario she was about to put to her mother. But she'd started, so she was going to have to finish... "Maya was thinking of packing in school – 'cause she's seen a course she wants to do at college and they're accepting late applications..."

"Maya? Maya wants to leave before she's done her A levels?" queried Sylvia Osgood. "But what on earth does she plan to do at college with no A levels?"

Cat hated her mother's snobbery, which was the whole reason she'd dreaded telling her anything about her own plans.

"I, er, don't know," Cat waffled, not having thought out her strategy clearly enough for this conversation. "I haven't spoken to her myself – one of the others told me. But what do you think? Do you think it's a terrible idea? Or do you think it could work out, if it's something she really wants to do?"

"What do *I* think, Catrina?" Sylvia widened her eyes at her daughter. "What do the Joshis think, more like! I mean, *I* think Maya's making a terrible mistake, but *they're* both doctors. They're not exactly going to jump for joy over the fact that their daughter wants to leave school with practically worthless qualifications and go in for some half-baked, dead-end college course, are they?"

"But if she knows what she wants to do and the course leads to that, why waste time doing A levels?" Cat flared momentarily. But she was immediately cowed by her mother's steely glare.

"Uh, well, it's not definite – she was just

thinking about it," Cat waffled some more. "Oh, look – the programme's started again."

As her mother's attention was diverted back to the documentary, Cat sank down deep into the overstuffed sofa, knowing that in a roundabout way, she'd confirmed what she suspected her mother's feelings were on leaving school to do a beauty course, which only *might* lead to an acting career.

And it wasn't looking good.

• • •

From his sprawled position on the vast, grey leather sofa, Matt watched his father tighten up his golf club tie in front of the huge antique mirror above the fireplace.

"No work on tonight then?" asked his elegantly grey-haired and not so elegantly portly father, conversing with his son through the reflection in the mirror.

"Nope," Matt replied, twirling a coaster from the coffee table around in his hand. "Bit of a dry spell at the moment."

"Hmff," grunted his father, straightening the lapels of his blazer.

On the one hand, he wished his son had embarked on a more stable, respectable career, while on the other, he was too busy and didn't have the inclination to try to confront him about it.

If the truth be told, Matthew Ryan senior also suffered from a certain amount of guilt when it came to his only son. Guilt about sending him to a boarding school; guilt about his marriage breaking down; guilt that Matt's mother was too busy with her new family to bother with her eldest child; and guilt at the amount of time *he* spent away from home, because of work commitments. Added together, these had a lot to do with why he didn't hassle his eighteen-year-old son about getting a 'proper' job.

"What's the plan with you tonight then, Dad?" Matt asked, in a disinterested but dutiful tone of voice.

"Dinner at the club. Going to chat to Dean and Stan and some of the others about investing in this leisure hotel complex up in Scotland. Think they'll bite."

Matt stared dully up at his father as his well-fed frame came into view. He knew the names of all his property developer father's friends – might even recognise a few of them if he ran into them – but frankly, he didn't have the faintest interest in his father's dealings.

"Don't wait up," Matthew Snr joked feebly as he headed out of the door. The bachelor lifestyle he shared with his son in this vast house didn't sit on him all that comfortably at times.

"Yeah, whatever. Have fun," muttered Matt.

Twenty minutes passed and Matt found himself vacantly flipping through terrestrial and cable channels with the remote set to mute.

His head was whirring loudly enough to compensate for the lack of sound on the TV. Thoughts were in there that had been bouncing off his cranium since Saturday night.

It was now Wednesday. Should he call her? *Should* he?

Matt's eyes flipped from the stultifyingly dull images on the screen to the phone on the table by the window.

Do it, said a voice in his head. *What are you waiting for?*

Because I feel weird, like I've never felt before – and I don't know if that's a good thing, came another, more cautionary, voice.

Well, if that's the way you feel, teased the first voice. *If you're too scared, then don't do it. Who cares if you just passed up the love of your life?*

With two bounds, Matt propelled himself off the sofa and over to the phone. He didn't have to look up her number – he knew it off by heart.

"Hello?" he said, breathlessly as he heard her answer at the other end of the line...

CHAPTER 12

NIGGLES AND NEW STARTS

Ollie woke up to the sound of the phone instead of the trill of the alarm clock. Dozy and lazy, he stretched out in the bed, blew some ruffled strands of floppy brown hair off his sleepy face, and luxuriated in the knowledge that it was his day off.

He loved it when he got Fridays off. They were his least favourite, most hassled day at work, mainly because it was the time of the week when the massed ranks of mother and baby groups descended on the café, filling it with the ear-splitting sound of wailing as one baby set the others off every few minutes.

Apart from that, there were copious demands from mothers for bottles of milk to be heated (Ollie could never get the temperature quite right) and tables, chairs, floors and often walls to clean of strange gooey food substances after they'd left. It wasn't that he disliked kids – he loved them – but he preferred to come across them one or two at a time and not have to deal with a lorry load all at once.

Even though his curtains were closed, the intensity of the sun was apparent, seeping brightness through every woven fibre, sneaking in shafts along every edge. It made Ollie feel ridiculously happy, on top of knowing he had a baby-free day.

Then, in a flash, the light dimmed as if someone had switched off a light bulb. An unseen cloud had drifted across the sun and Ollie felt his mood slump. The nagging thoughts that had dogged him and kept him from falling asleep for ages the night before now came flooding back in full force.

What's wrong with Kerry? Why has she been so distant the last week or so? It's as if every time I try and touch her she stiffens up. What have I done? Ollie tortured himself again.

More thoughts from the night before followed on.

Maybe I'm over-reacting... Maybe she's just having a bad week. People have bad weeks. Maybe she's dreading starting back at sixth form.

Maybe I should talk to her about it – or maybe I should just give her a bit of space...

A thumping of footsteps along the hall followed by a thumping at his bedroom door disturbed Ollie's train of thought.

"Ol – you in the land of the living?" asked Stuart Stanton, peeking round his son's bedroom door.

"Yeah, sure," yawned Ollie, pushing himself upright. "What's up?"

"Your favourite girl wants to talk to you..." his father said cryptically, walking over towards the bed and holding out the white cordless phone.

Kerry? Ollie thought quizzically, scratching his head with one hand while he reached out for the phone with the other. *Why's she phoning? We're seeing each other this afternoon – or is she blowing me out?*

"Kez?"

"No – it's Tasha, you moron!" his twin sister's voice came down the line.

"Tash!" Ollie exclaimed, bouncing out of bed. "How are you? *Where* are you?"

"Oh, keep up, for God's sake!" she chastised him amiably. "I'm in Sydney! I *told* you I was going last time I spoke to you!"

"Wow, yeah! Sydney – amazing! I totally forgot you were going there!"

"Obviously..."

"Well, what's Australia like? Is it totally amazing?"

"To be honest, I haven't seen much yet – we only arrived last night and so far today I've been in taxis, the model agency office and the hotel restaurant. That's it."

"So why are you phoning now?" Ollie started being cheeky back, now that he'd woken up properly and got over the surprise of hearing Natasha's voice. "Surely you could have waited a few days till you had something interesting to tell us..."

"I'm phoning because... because I suddenly wanted to hear all your voices," Natasha explained, her tone revealing the hint of a tearful quiver. "Well, not yours, of course."

Ollie ignored her last token dig and felt genuinely touched. It wasn't often that super-confident, super-successful Natasha let down her defences and admitted any emotional wobbles to her family.

"But what's brought this on? You've lived away from home for more than a year now and you've jetted off on jobs all over the place."

"Yes, but when I'm in London it's not that far away for me to come home—"

Ollie had to laugh to himself at that comment.

She didn't seem to bother herself about popping home *that* often.

"—and the jobs abroad have just been Europe so far, apart from that one in Japan. And that was so completely brilliant I didn't have time to be homesick."

"Aww, Tasha, so do you miss your darling, wonderful brother?" he asked in as annoying a voice as possible, in an effort to get her laughing instead of blubbing.

"God, I'm not *that* lonely!"

"Well, what can I do to help? Do you want me to keep you posted on what's happening in the soaps?" he joked, knowing that Natasha had too full-on a social life back in London to bother with anything as dull as telly.

"No, thanks! No, just distract me – tell me what's been going on in your life."

"Not much. Working away with Nick the slave-driver. Still trying to get my clapped-out Vespa to work."

"Oh, that makes me feel better. I'm not exactly missing much, am I?"

It was a standard brother/sister dig, but Ollie couldn't help thinking of the difference between their lives. Natasha was earning bucketloads at the age of seventeen, had a passport full of stamps for countries Ollie had never been to, and a flatshare with other models in London's trendy Notting Hill.

By comparison, Ollie worked long hours for low pay at a small café by a train station (when he wasn't helping out at his uncle's dusty, damp, second-hand record shop next door) and he still lived at home with his parents, in the flat above the pub where he and Natasha had grown up.

He was happy with his life, but Ollie sometimes did see that it could seem pretty one-dimensional compared to his sister's.

"What, Vespa maintenance doesn't interest you then?"

"Nope. How's Kerry? Still in love?"

"She's great..." *just not right at this moment,* he thought, "...and yes, I'm still in love."

"What about your mate Matt? Is he still as creepy as ever?"

"He's not creepy, Tash! I told you all that stuff was just a misunderstanding."

Natasha and Matt had had a brief flirtation during one of her infrequent visits home, and their one proper date had lasted all of ten minutes after Natasha had misinterpreted something Matt had said and decided he was a creep of the highest order. No amount of explanation on Ollie's part had ever managed to change her mind.

"Hmm, well, I'm not so sure... Anyway, how's the band going?"

"It's not, really. Me and Joe keep meaning to—"

"What? Oh, Ol – I've got to go, that's my agent at the door. But listen, Dad said Mum's out shopping. Get her to give me a call back later, would you?"

"Sure," Ollie reassured her, but the phone was already dead.

Ollie stared at the receiver for a moment, lost in thought, then thumped some numbers out.

"Hey, Joey!" he yelled down the line.

• • •

"'Guitarist: looking for a band who are into spiritual sounds, mellow vibes and good times.'"

Ollie dropped his finger from the card he was reading from and turned to Joe. "Sounds like this guy wants a girlfriend, not a band."

"I can't see any ads for bass players," said Joe, scanning the message board in Central Sounds music shop, "but here's another one for a guitarist..."

"'R U ready for the heavy metal revival?'" Ollie read. "'Then I'm the guitarist you're looking for!'"

"Oh no, you're not, mate," muttered Joe.

"'Ambitious, talented guitarist with great

image, looking for like-minded people to take it all the way to the top!'" Ollie intoned off another pinned-up card.

"Kinda shy, that one, isn't he?" said Joe, mentally taking note of the guy's name, so that if they ever came across a guitarist called Aaron in a local band, they could put a face to this less-than-modest ad.

"Look – this one sounds quite good. 'Guitarist available (17), influences: indie stuff, old and new. Call Will on...' – Joe, pass me that pen."

Joe handed over a black ballpoint and watched as Ollie scribbled the name and phone number on his hand before Joe had a chance to dig out a notepad from his pocket.

"Could be our man, Joey! This could be the start of The Loud getting back on track!"

Enthusiasm shone from Ollie's eyes. His conversation with Natasha this morning had made him feel flat at first, then given him the kick up the bum he needed to start getting back to his long-time love: music. That's why, right after he'd taken her call, Ollie had pestered Joe into getting down to Central Sounds and checking out potential new members for their band.

"Right, I've really got to go, Ol – my shift at the End starts in twenty minutes..." said Joe, glancing down at his watch.

"Come on then," Ollie nodded towards the door, "I'll walk with you – I'm going round to Kerry's."

"Uh, everything cool?" asked Joe vaguely as they stepped out of the fluorescent-lit shop on to the sunshine-splattered pavement. What he was referring to was the state of Ollie and Kerry's relationship, but he couldn't bring himself to ask too bluntly.

"Um, I s'pose," Ollie shrugged, distractedly kicking the ring-pull from a can into the gutter. "But Kerry's just been a bit... funny with me lately. Have you noticed?"

"No," lied Joe, remembering how she'd snapped at Ollie during their walk home the previous Saturday night. But long-buried loyalty to Kerry would not allow him to criticise her in any way.

"Oh, it's nothing, I guess," Ollie shrugged again, thinking of Kerry's sweet smile and the way her freckle-covered nose crinkled when she laughed.

"Y'know what Matt would say," said Joe, who was also visualising Kerry's sweet smile.

"What's that?" Ollie asked seriously, keen for any light to be shed on his worries.

"He'd say it was her period."

"Yeah, he would," grinned Ollie, thinking of

their friend's legendary tactlessness. "A girl doesn't laugh loudly enough at one of his rotten jokes and he'll put it down to PMS..."

• • •

Kerry opened her front door out of breath. The faint, dusty pawprints on her white T-shirt and the barking and shrieking drifting through from the garden indicated to Ollie that he'd interrupted some serious silliness going on with Lewis and Barney.

Ollie gazed at Kerry's exploding halo of browny-red curls – complete with blades of grass randomly entwined – and his heart melted.

"What's going on?" he grinned.

"Barney's got the Furby and he won't give it back," she gasped. "He seems to want to kill it or bury it or both."

Ollie burst out laughing as he stepped into the hallway.

"C'mere, you..." he said warmly, wrapping his arms around her and nuzzling into her neck.

Kerry put her hands round the neck of the boy she loved and couldn't help that feeling of suffocation rise in her chest again...

• • •

Joe walked towards the End-of-the-Line café, his brow furrowed in anger.

How can I be this disloyal to my oldest, best friend? How can I be pleased at the fact that something's not quite right with him and Kerry? he questioned himself. *And what the hell chance would I have with Kerry even if something happened and they did split up?*

Just as Joe was about to shove open the café door, some posters newly plastered up on the window caught his eye and made him stop mid-step.

"Where did Nick come up with *this* stupid idea..." Joe muttered, shaking his head.

CHAPTER 13

NICK'S BIG IDEA

Nick's inspired scheme for boosting his Monday evening business had met with groans from his three younger members of staff as he'd spelled out his plan to them one by one.

"A Back-To-School night? Who wants to be reminded that they're going back to school next day?" Joe had pointed out.

"Nah, it'll be great! Last chance for kids to let their hair down before getting back to the grind!" Nick had tried to explain.

"I'll have to wear *what*?" Anna had gasped when she heard.

"Just school uniform. Y'know, like St Trinian's – school skirt, short as poss..." he'd fizzled out when he clocked her horrified expression.

"So if it's a themed night, are you doing up the

café or what?" Ollie had quizzed his uncle when he'd turned up for work on Saturday.

"Um..." Nick had mumbled, not really having thought his idea through particularly clearly. "I just thought I could make a tape of school-related tracks, like *School's Out*, y'know, by Alice Cooper."

"Nick," Ollie had looked wearily at his uncle, "no one's ever going to have heard of a crumblie old rocker like Alice Cooper. *I* only know about Alice Cooper because you forced me to listen to one of his albums last time I worked in Slick Riffs."

"Well, you know what I mean," Nick had waffled. "Maybe you and Matt could come up with some appropriate stuff..."

And after the initial moaning and groaning, everyone had got into the spirit of it: Ollie recycling his old uniform from the loft; Joe borrowing Maya's little brother's school cap for the evening; and Anna buying a pair of boy's grey school trousers out of Oxfam as an acceptable compromise.

On Monday evening, as the last of the coming-home-from-the-city commuter customers left the End, and the evening contingent began to filter in, Ollie ducked behind the counter and slipped the tape he and Matt had made up into

Nick's state-of-the-art ghetto blaster, dragged down from his flat next door.

Over at the window booth, Kerry and Sonja stared at the one-off photocopied menu that Nick had devised and winced.

"'Two times table MATHS burger, with ENGLISH mustard' – that's just the double-decker burger, right?"

Kerry shrugged.

"'GEOGRAPHY pizza (ITALIAN sauce, FRENCH cheese, GREEK olives)'," Sonja continued reading, "– that'll be the normal cheese and tomato pizza with a couple of olives chucked on top then."

"Oh, no – look," said Kerry, pointing to something further down the list. "'SUNDAE SCHOOL SURPRISE'. What's the surprise? That it's just the usual ice-cream sundae with a stupid name?"

"Jeez, it's just *so* not funny," Sonja shook her head. "You can tell Nick came up with this sad lot, and not Ollie or any of the others."

"Too right," nodded Kerry, staring over her friend's shoulder at the blackboard where the specials were usually chalked up. Instead, there was a caricature of Nick bursting out of a kiddie-style school uniform, his waistline oozing over a pair of unflattering shorts.

Now that *is quite funny,* she thought, marvelling at Joe's previously unknown and unseen talent for cartoon drawing.

"Kez?" Sonja hissed over at her, distracting her attention from Joe's artistic efforts. "Can I ask you something?"

"'Course," she nodded, wondering why Sonja was whispering.

"What would you think of me and Matt?"

"You and Matt what?" At the back of her mind, Kerry knew she'd noted warily how often Sonja seemed to be tagging along with Matt lately, and how Sonja's normal banter with him had begun to look more like flirting from where Kerry was standing.

"Me and Matt! As an item!" Sonja's eyes gleamed.

"Has something happened?" gasped Kerry in confusion.

"Not quite, but I think I'd like it to," Sonja grinned.

"Since when? You've never said you fancy him!"

"I don't," Sonja answered simply.

"Son – you're not making any sense!" Kerry was more confused than ever. What was Sonja on about?

"Well, I mean I've *tried* to imagine myself

kissing him and stuff, but I don't, y'know, get that tingly feeling when you fantasise about someone you really do fancy," Sonja tried to explain.

"And that's supposed to be a good thing?" said Kerry incredulously. "That's supposed to mean he'd make a perfect boyfriend for you?"

"Yes! It's my new theory – I think it could really work between us because we *don't* fancy each other. I think the fact that we get on brilliantly is all we need. I think the fancying each other bit would come with time—"

"Hold on!" Kerry interrupted. "Is this something to do with the mess you got into after falling for Owen *and* Kyle?"

"No!" said Sonja defensively. "I just think that love built on friendship could be more important than love built on lust."

"Well, to a certain extent you're right," Kerry hissed, trying to control the volume of her voice now that she was truly irritated by Sonja's stupid notion. Luckily, Ollie was cranking the music up pretty loudly in the background. "Friendship *is* important. But you can't suddenly turn your spotlight on Matt because you're on the rebound!"

Sonja's jaw dropped. She hadn't expected Kerry to blast her latest daydream so determinedly. It wasn't like Kerry at all. She'd wanted her friend to giggle with her, be pleased for her, and help her plan how to engineer the whole romance.

"But you and Ollie—"

"—were both crazy about each other before we got it together!" Kerry interrupted again. "It's not the same thing! You're sounding so... calculating and cold-blooded about this. I mean, has Matt given you any indication about how he feels?"

Before Sonja could answer, Anna appeared by their side and pointed out of the window.

"Looks like Cat's got into the swing of tonight's theme," she said.

Sonja and Kerry put aside their strained conversation for a moment and stared out of the plate glass at an approaching Maya, dressed in a plain black T-shirt and jeans and looking tight-lipped and ever-so-slightly mortified. Alongside her was Cat, who was decked out in shiny patent, stack-heeled ankle boots, laced-topped black hold-ups, an expanse of white thigh, a microscopic Lycra skirt, a button-popping, tight white shirt and a school tie, slung down loosely enough to accentuate her cleavage.

"Whoa!" yelped Ollie from behind the counter as Cat and Maya strode in. "What have you come as, Cat? A schoolgirl or a lap-dancer?"

Cat stuck her tongue out at him and slithered

into the booth beside Kerry.

"Oh," she said flatly, gazing at Kerry and Sonja. "You didn't get dressed up either."

Maya rolled her eyes. "Cat, I *told* you. Only the staff were dressing up. Customers don't have to."

"Hmphff," huffed Cat, gazing around the slowly filling café. "Doesn't look like Anna's made much of an effort with those boring trousers. But at least she's been doing her hair like I told her..."

All four girls gazed over at Anna, who was taking an order from a crowd huddled round a table at the other side of the cafe, and all nodded their silent agreement. Anna had still pulled her hair back in a ponytail for efficiency's sake, but it looked glossier, darker and more luscious now that she'd taken to slapping on the products Cat had recommended. And the soft, natural brown shadow that she'd started using on her eyelids every day made her eyes look more alert and animated than they ever had before.

"Cat," Maya began, "you really made a difference to Anna. I'm sure you'll do really well with the course tomorrow."

"It's not just make-up, remember!" twittered Cat. "I'm going to be learning a whole load of beauty therapies like massage, aromatherapy, electrolysis—"

"Cat!" Maya tried to reign in her friend's

attention. "Cat – you *still* haven't told your mother yet, have you? How can you expect her to take this well when you're going to spring it on her at the last minute?"

Cat flushed pink under her blusher. But just as her bright red, lipsticked mouth was about to form itself into the word 'no', she was saved from humiliation by the arrival of Matt.

Sonja's face burst into an ear-to-ear smile as he came through the door, which faded bit by bit as her gaze dropped to his arm, and on to his hand, and on to the hand that gripped his...

...and on to the stunningly pretty girl it belonged to.

CHAPTER 14

TO BE BOTHERED, OR NOT TO BE BOTHERED...

"S'cuse..." said Sonja, squeezing past Maya and heading off towards the toilet.

Matt watched her walk away across the crowded café with some disappointment. More than any of his friends, he'd wanted Sonja to meet Gabrielle – the girl who'd occupied most of his thoughts since he'd spotted her at the fitness club on Saturday. The girl who'd scribbled her phone number on a tiny scrap of paper and handed it to him shyly and wordlessly over the DJ console later that same night, after much mutual eye contact.

It had burnt a hole in his pocket and in his brain – where he'd stored the six digits after looking at them zillions of times – until he'd finally got in control of his emotions long enough to call her on Wednesday night.

"Cat... Kerry... Maya..." he pointed out to Gabrielle as she waved hello to each of his girl mates in turn and smiled broadly. "That was Sonja on her way to the loo – but you'll meet her later – and over there is Anna, serving, and there, that's Ollie by the coffee machine. Joey – that's my mate Joey fiddling with the tape deck."

Gabrielle Adjani turned her charming smile from his friends back to Matt and he felt his insides turn to mush.

Once, way back sometime in the misery of his boarding school years, Matt remembered an unspectacular visit his class had made to an art gallery up in the city. In among drab portraits, bland landscapes and indecipherable modern art doodlings, only one thing had grabbed his attention – an abstract statuette of a girl, crouched down, her head hidden in her arms.

Carved out of a dark amber-brown marble, Matt had found himself inexplicably drawn to its smooth, lustrous surface, his fingers itching to run the length of the figure's rounded back, to feel the cool stone on his skin. Only the rope that kept the public away, the sign saying 'Do Not Touch', and the watchful eye of the art teacher stopped him from doing it.

It was a brief moment in an otherwise uneventful outing and he could safely say that it wasn't something he'd dwelt on. Until he'd seen Gabrielle at the fitness club opening night. Wearing a short, strappy summer dress, her long arms and bare shoulders and the soft, dark brown of her skin made the long-buried memory of the marble statuette come flying smack bang into his mind. Only this girl was more beautiful, especially since – unlike the figure – he could see her long neck, her heart-shaped face, her huge, dark-fringed eyes.

Like the sculpture, he found himself drawn to touch her. When they'd met earlier in the park, it had been all he could do to stop himself reaching over the picnic table and stroking her satin-smooth cheek, or letting his fingertip follow the line of her thick but perfectly arched eyebrow.

He couldn't, of course. It was only the first five minutes of their first ever date and he didn't want her to think he was too full-on, or to see just how besotted he was after one brief meeting the previous weekend and one conversation on Wednesday over the phone.

Luckily for Matt, Gabrielle had seemed as smitten he was. She laughed loudly and unselfconsciously at everything he said, the silver beads tied in the ends of her braids catching the light of the late evening sun every time she threw her head back. She had even gone so far as to reach down for his hand as they left the park gates and headed for the End.

He was still holding her hand now – her tiny, delicate little hand with its nails like pale slithers of pearl against her brown skin.

"Come on, I want you to meet the lads properly," he smiled at her, with complete, unadulterated adoration.

"Who was *that*?" asked Cat incredulously as the cosy couple walked off towards Ollie and Joe.

"Gabrielle, he said her name was," Maya reminded her.

"I recognise her from the party the other Saturday," added Kerry.

"No, I mean who was *he*? That big slush-bucket wasn't our loud and lairy Matt!" Cat said jokily, leaning out of the booth for a better snoop's eye view of Matt and his gorgeous new girlfriend.

"Back in a second," Kerry excused herself, heading off to the loos in search of the missing Sonja.

"Wish Matt had looked at me that way when *we* were together..." Catrina muttered to Maya.

"Does it bother you?" her friend asked, aware that this was the first girl (apart from Ollie's sister,

Natasha) whom Matt had brought on a date since he broke up with Catrina earlier on in the year.

Cat stuck her bottom lip out as she considered the point, her eyes glued to the lovey-dovey twosome.

"You know something?" she said after a moment or two. "It doesn't bother me. Not now."

"That's good," Maya smiled at her. She'd had her suspicions in the past that Catrina still had a great big, soggy, soft spot for her ex deep down in that hard old heart of hers.

"Yes, it is, isn't it?" beamed Cat.

• • •

Sonja stared into the mirror above the sink and tried to will tears to come. But they didn't.

"Who is she?" she spat out.

Kerry had taken long enough to follow her into the Ladies. She must have been trying to find *something* out before she came to comfort her best friend.

Kerry leaned against the sink and shrugged.

"Don't know exactly," she replied, "but I remember seeing her at the party at the fitness centre. You couldn't really miss anyone that stunning."

"Gee, thanks. Rub it in, why don't you!"

snapped Sonja, not at all pleased with her so-called friend's unloyal response.

Kerry folded her arms across her chest and said nothing. She could see that Sonja was suffering from a bad case of hurt pride rather than bruised heart.

"Just when I thought I'd found the Right One..." Sonja sighed dramatically. "God, I can't believe my luck!"

"I think your luck's just fine," answered Kerry. "I think it saved you from doing something you'd really regret."

"Don't go all preachy on me, Kerry Bellamy!"

Sonja's flushed cheeks told Kerry all she needed to know.

"Don't be embarrassed, Son," she said calmly, not taking on board any of her friend's barbed comments. "We all make mistakes and at least I'm the only person who knows about this particular one."

"Me and Matt *could* have worked!" Sonja protested.

"Yeah? Well, with that logic me and Joe could work, or Maya and Ollie could work... except that'd never happen. We're all *friends*, Sonja, and that's it. You and Matt are brilliant together – but as *friends*. Don't go spoiling that."

Sonja stood with her lips pursed, silently

fuming. She was angry because Kerry was so right and she'd been so wrong. No matter how much she *wanted* to want Matt, Sonja couldn't quite convince her heart or her head that she'd ever be able to make the leap to loving him as anything more than a mate.

"Honestly, I do think it's a rebound thing," said Kerry, a little more kindly. "You fell for one boy and found out he was a rat; you fell for another and he moved away... I think you just fancy the idea of playing safe and trying for someone you already know and trust not to let you down."

"Who have you been taking lessons from – Maya?" Sonja asked, her voice now sounding sheepish rather than snarling. "Or is it Anna? She's into all that analysis stuff!"

"Well, some of it's bound to rub off," smiled Kerry, unconsciously lifting her hand to play with the tiny stones on the chakra round her neck. "But don't you think there's *something* in what I'm saying?"

"Mmm, I s'pose," Sonja replied, her voice tinged with regret.

"I mean, really, truly – does it bother you? Seeing Matt with another girl?" her friend asked.

Just as Cat had done, Sonja stuck out her bottom lip as she thought hard.

"You know something?" she said after a moment or two. "I don't think it does bother me. Not really."

"Good!" Kerry hadn't wanted her best friend to make a fool of herself over something that was just a fleeting moment of madness.

"You know..." said Sonja suddenly, changing the focus of the conversation from herself to Kerry, "you were very sharp with me out there when I tried to tell you about all this. That's not like you. Is there something up?"

"Me? No!" Kerry shook her head, playing more frantically with her chakra.

If there was one thing Kerry couldn't stand, it was having to lie.

CHAPTER 15

WHERE THERE'S A WILL...

"Joey – get us a coffee, hon!"

Joe gazed up at his friend. She'd developed an orange tan overnight and had blow-dried her hair into a shaggy style parted at the side. She was obviously meant to look like someone but he couldn't put his finger on who it was.

"Cat," he began as she made herself comfortable across the table from him, "I'm not working here any more. I'm back at sixth form as of today, remember?"

"Sixth form?" she answered vaguely as if such a juvenile concept was impossible for her to imagine. "Oh, yes, of course. I forgot. Hey, Ollie – get us a coffee, would you?"

Ollie came back over to the booth with a bottle of tomato sauce swiped from behind the counter.

"Cat – look. No apron," he said, turning from side to side like a catwalk model. "Does that tell you something?"

"Surprise me," she drawled, reapplying her Very Berry lipstick in the pocket mirror she'd pulled from her bag.

"I'm here as a customer, not a worker, today," Ollie spelt out, lifting the top of the bun in front of him and squishing red sauce on top of his burger.

"Who's serving then?" she asked, staring impatiently around the café. "When's a hard-working college girl like myself going to get anything to drink?"

"Ah, *I* get it," said Ollie, catching on. "OK then – how was your first day at college?"

Cat gave him a simpering smile and Joe suddenly realised who she'd modelled herself on for her first day on the beauty course. It was ex-*EastEnder* Michelle Collins, who was no stranger to make-up herself.

"Amazing – absolutely amazing!" she gloated. "It's just going to be fantastic – lots of practical work instead of just books, books, books like at school. I'm so glad I decided to do it! Honestly!"

Her gushingly over-the-top proclamation could only mean one thing as far as Joe was concerned: the course hadn't been what Cat'd expected and she was worried that she'd made an awful mistake. But Joe wasn't about to go bursting her bubble by pointing that out.

Before Cat could enthuse any more, a babble of voices and the ping of the bell above the door heralded the arrival of Maya, Kerry and Sonja. Anna came bustling out of the kitchen, pad in hand.

"How was the first day back?" she smiled as the girls all settled themselves around the table.

"Oh, not bad. But then the first day's always like a honeymoon, isn't it?" said Sonja, squashing in beside her cousin, her natural honey-toned skin clashing with Cat's out-of-a-bottle colouring. "The teachers are nothing but nice – then they get nastier as the week goes on and that's when they start heaping on the work!"

"How do you like sixth form? Is it better than school, Maya?" asked Ollie through a mouthful of burger.

"I like not having to wear a uniform, that's for sure," she smiled.

"I know what you mean," said Anna. "Getting back into a school shirt and tie last night was enough for me!"

"Just keep your fingers crossed that Nick doesn't get it into his head to do it again, seeing how successful his little idea was," Ollie grunted.

"Yeah, it was mobbed, wasn't it?" said Sonja. "Did he take a lot of money then?"

"Did he!" laughed Ollie. "Just stick your head through the kitchen door and check out the grin that's been glued to his face all day!"

Through everyone's giggles, a determined cough could be heard.

"Are you all right, Cat?" asked Kerry worriedly.

"Yes, she's fine," grinned Ollie. "I think she just wants to attract your attention, don't you, Cat?"

"What, me?" she replied wide-eyed.

"Oh, Cat – sorry!" Maya jumped in. "Well, how did it go today?"

"Absolutely brilliant! It's going to be a hundred times better than staying on at St Mark's. And there's going to be so much practical experience, so I'm going to need lots of volunteers!" she said brightly, glancing round at her friends.

"Victims, you mean," Ollie teased, and got a kick under the table for his trouble.

"So, you're sure you've made the right decision then? Still think it's going to be your ticket into showbiz?"

Cat ignored the sarcasm in Sonja's voice and carried right on with her glowing descriptions of everything from the college canteen to the potential hunk material on the electrical engineering course. All the while, she made a concerted effort to avoid Maya's gaze.

"So," Maya butted in when Cat finally drew breath, "how did your mum take it in the end?"

"What's that...?" Cat asked vaguely, furrowing her brow as if she had no idea at all what Maya was getting at.

"Your mum," said Maya firmly. "What did say she about you going to college?"

"Oh, that!" Cat blustered, getting up from the table. "Fine, fine. Well, moaned a bit at first, y'know what's she's like... S'cuse, please – got to nip to the loo..."

Maya stared dubiously at Cat as she shuffled past, but no one else seemed to pay any attention to her hurried explanation. Instead, her speedy exit just gave them an opportunity to change the subject and mull over the latest exploits of the absent member of their crowd.

"He kept that one quiet, didn't he?" said Ollie.

"So you guys didn't even know about Gabrielle?" Maya asked with surprise. "I can't believe Matt didn't let it slip to you or Joe."

"I know – he's not exactly shy when it comes to boasting about which girl's got the hots for him, is he?"

"Well, it's obvious that the poor, deluded girl is mad about him," joked Ollie. "But it was pretty amazing to see how crazy he seemed to be about her!"

"Yes, it was," Maya agreed. "Still, she does seem really lovely. Very friendly and natural."

"Yeah – you said the same, didn't you, Joey?"

"Uh-huh," nodded Joe. What he'd particularly liked about Gabrielle when they'd been introduced was that she'd specifically double-checked whether he preferred to be called 'Joe' or 'Joey'. It was a long-term problem for Joe that nearly all his friends had a tendency to add a 'y' to the end of his name which he detested. He was also really irritated with himself for not pointing it out a long time ago – but it felt far too late in the day to make a big thing of it now.

"Did you get a chance to talk to her, Son?" Ollie asked, aware that Sonja was probably Matt's best mate out of all the girls and was keen to hear what she had to say. It hadn't escaped Ollie's notice that so far she'd been uncharacteristically slow to chuck her opinion into the conversation.

"No, I didn't actually. But then our Matt didn't stay too long, did he? Too keen to be on his own with this Gabrielle," Sonja answered, as non-committally as possible.

It wasn't that she was hurt – it was just that she'd spent the night lying awake realising what a stupid mistake she could have made if she had pursued Matt. How right Kerry had been when she'd said it was because Sonja was on the rebound that she wasn't reading her emotions right! If Sonja was quiet now, it was more to do with feeling embarrassed when Matt's name was mentioned than wishing she could swap places with Gabrielle. That *and* the sudden realisation of just how absolutely cringeworthy it would have been to end up dating the same boy her cousin had...

"Well, good luck to him!" she smiled brightly, trying to be her old self. "At least we've got someone else to rival Ollie and Kerry in the gooey couple stakes!"

"Never!" Ollie protested and attempted to prove his point by throwing his arms around Kerry and kissing her in front of the others.

"Oi, no!" Kerry laughingly protested, trying to slither out of his embrace. "You taste too much like a burger!"

For half a second Ollie looked slightly hurt, before letting her go and turning his attention to Joe.

"What time do you make it, Joey?"

Pushing the floppy undone shirt sleeve away from his wrist, Joe glanced at his watch. "About time that guy showed up."

"What's this? What guy?" asked Cat,

returning to her seat, her boy antennae tuned in as always.

"Well, hopefully a new guitarist for The Loud. We saw his ad in Central Sounds last week and he's supposed to be meeting us here today for a chat."

"Wow, that's brilliant, Ollie!" Sonja exclaimed enthusiastically. "It's about time you boys got it together again!"

"Yes, I loved coming along to your gigs," added Maya. "They were always a laugh."

"And such a good place to spy hunky guys!" Cat chipped in.

"So who's this person, Ollie?" Kerry asked him. "You never mentioned him to me..."

Ollie was aware of the slightly surprised hurt in Kerry's voice. But then she'd been so distant with him the last few days, he didn't feel too guilty for forgetting to mention the ad and the plan to reform the band. And he was still smarting at the way she'd pushed him away just now, even if it had been done in fun.

"Don't know any more than was on the card in Central Sounds, really," he shrugged. "He's seventeen, his name's Will and he said on the phone he played in his mate's band for a bit."

"Ooh, new blood!" Cat cackled, rubbing her hands together. "I wonder if he's cute!"

Cat didn't have to wait long to find out. The door of the End tinkled open and a dark-haired boy came in, casting his gaze around the crowded room, his guitar case clattering against the door frame.

The first person he seemed to recognise was Anna – and his eyes lit up when he spotted her.

Anna gazed up from the cup she was filling at the sound of her name and gave the boy a friendly smile and a wave.

"Hey!" gasped Ollie. "Look who it is!"

CHAPTER 16

MIXED FEELINGS

Maya swivelled round in her seat to see who Ollie was talking about.

The boy with the guitar turned his gaze to where Anna had pointed – over to the crowd at the window seat.

"Billy!" she gasped.

"Maya!" he smiled in delight. "What are you doing here?"

"This is just where we... hang out, I guess!" she waffled. She only ever saw Billy at her photography club evening class – apart from taking him along to the party the Saturday before last – and she felt a little disorientated having him turn up here, unexpectedly, in her world. "What are *you* doing here?"

"Answering our ad, if that guitar case is

anything to go by!" Ollie exclaimed, laughing at the coincidence. "But since when have you been called Will?"

"And since when did you have a band?" Billy grinned back, walking over to join them. "Maya never told me!"

Maya bristled. Just because he was a friend from one part of her life, it didn't entitle him to an entire history of all her long-term mates.

"Yeah, me and Joe have been trying to get The Loud back on course since our original guitarist and bass player left to do other stuff," Ollie filled him in. "But come on, you still haven't explained the Will thing!"

"Billy's what I got stuck with at school, but at home I've always been Will," he explained. "I don't mind, though – I'll answer to whatever!"

"God, this is brilliant, isn't it?" Sonja yelped. "Maya's boy– er, Maya's friend being in Ollie and Joe's band!"

Maya threw Sonja a thunderous look for her near slip.

"Well, you might be jumping the gun there, Sonja," said Billy, pulling his guitar case round in front of him. "I mean, Ollie and Joe haven't even heard me play yet!"

The boys were pleased to hear him say that. As soon as the words were out of Sonja's mouth, they'd both instantaneously changed from being chuffed to see Billy, to panicking that he'd think he was automatically in the band, just because he was a mate of Maya's.

"Look, my uncle says we can go next door to his record shop and talk," said Ollie, getting to his feet. "He's got an old amp in his back office so we can hear what you do at the same time."

"Fine," nodded Billy. "Right, I'll see you tomorrow night then, Maya?"

"Sure," Maya replied, watching the three boys get up and make their way out of the café.

"'See you tomorrow night then'!" mimicked Cat as soon as the door had shut behind them. "How cosy, Maya!"

"Cat, I hate to spoil your romantic delusions," Maya snapped, "but Billy was talking about photography club. It's Wednesday tomorrow, remember?"

Cat's face fell.

"Oh, yeah..." she muttered. Cat still hadn't got her head around the fact that Maya hadn't fallen for Billy, especially after the business of him taking her portrait. To Cat, that was just the most romantic thing she had ever heard. She'd have given anything for someone to take a picture of her like that...

"And *please*, Sonja," Maya said to her other

friend, "don't come out with stuff like 'boyfriend' in front of Billy again – he'll get the wrong idea. He'll think I've been talking to you about him that way!"

"I know, I know – I'm sorry," Sonja cringed. "It just slipped out. I'm a moron. I'm a tactless moron."

"But why did you invite Billy to the party the other week?" Cat persisted.

Kerry rolled her eyes to the ceiling. Cat was unstoppable.

"Because," sighed Maya, "he's pretty sporty and he mentioned that he'd love to have a chance to check out the fitness centre, even though he could never afford to join it. So, as a *friend*, I thought it would be nice to give him that chance!"

"So, you really, *really* don't fancy Billy?" asked Cat, pushing the point just that bit too far.

"Cat – how many times do I have to tell you?"

"No, hold on, Maya – I just wanted to get that straight for a reason," Cat said placatingly.

"What reason?" asked Sonja. She half expected Cat to say that if Maya didn't want Billy, would she mind if she could go after him? It was just the kind of stunt Cat would pull...

Cat looked at Sonja as if she was a naive child.

"Anna, of course!" she exclaimed, turning her hands palms outward. "Billy couldn't keep his eyes off her at the party and look how he smiled at her when he walked in here! What I mean is, if Maya doesn't want him, the way's open for him and Anna!"

The other three girls all stared disbelievingly at Cat.

"You've got some imagination, Catrina Osgood!" Sonja said finally, dropping her voice, since Anna was still pottering about from table to table. "You've always had a talent for sniffing out romances that don't exist!"

Cat looked hurt at the dig.

"It's true..." she mumbled. "He *was* talking to Anna for ages that night."

"He talked to *all* of us, Cat – you included!" Sonja pointed out.

Before anyone said anything else, Maya decided to leave for home. She wasn't in the mood for any more nonsense.

• • •

Hanging up her jacket in the hall, Maya caught sight of the black and white portrait of herself that took pride of place on the living room wall.

After seeing Billy's winning photo of their eldest daughter in the gallery competition, her parents had asked him to print another copy for themselves. Seeing it now made Maya feel irrationally irritated again, and she'd only just walked off her last bout of annoyance in a quick stride from the End to her front door.

Hearing laughter coming from the kitchen, she walked in to join her little brother Ravi and Brigid, who looked after the family until Maya's parents got home from work in the early evening.

"Now, would you be looking at your sister's face?" said Brigid, nudging Ravi. "You can tell she didn't have as much fun as *you* did on her first day back at school!"

"It wasn't school," sighed Maya, flopping down on a kitchen chair. "Sixth form was OK."

"Well, what is it that's bothering you, Maya love?" Brigid asked, drying her hands on a towel.

But that was the problem: Maya couldn't fathom why these great clouds of gloom had settled over her. Yes, it was annoying when her mates – Cat in particular – tried to read more into her friendship with Billy than there was. And yes, she knew she felt a little bit weird about the idea of him joining the band.

But why did it bug me so much when Cat started to go on about Billy and Anna? she asked herself – and couldn't find an answer.

• • •

Kerry flopped back on her bed and stared at the ceiling.

A dull thump, a wobble on the bed and a wet nose snuffling at her hand indicated that Barney had jumped up to keep his sad-looking mistress company.

Kerry had felt miserable since that funny incident earlier down at the End when she'd broken away from Ollie; when he'd stared at her for that brief moment with hurt in his eyes, before turning his back on her and talking to Joe.

She sighed and felt the ripples of misery rumble across her chest. Kerry loved Ollie to pieces; she had for a very long time. She loved his open face, his lopsided grin, his silly sense of humour, the way he made her feel special instead of awkward and gawky, which she always had before.

She loved that second before they kissed; that second when she could see so deeply into his hazel eyes. She loved the touch of his lips; she loved feeling his arms bundle her into his lean body.

And yet... and yet... she said over and over to herself, feeling the tears trickle from her eyes.

CHAPTER 17

CRAZY LITTLE THING CALLED LOVE

"What's up with *him?*"

"Matt?" said Ollie, looking back over his shoulder at his friend. "Don't worry, Dad – it's nothing contagious. He's just all loved up."

Stuart Stanton gave a little snort as he continued to clean the glasses behind the bar.

"Might have guessed," he laughed. "That misty-eyed way he's staring out the window; the way he's tearing that beer mat into tiny pieces; the fact that he hasn't touched that bag of nuts I so kindly chucked his way earlier... It's a sure sign he's a goner. So who's the lucky girl? It's not one of your crowd, is it?"

"Nah," Ollie replied, picking up the two pint glasses of orange juice his dad had poured for them. "It's someone he met when he DJ'd at the new fitness centre. I think she's really blown him away."

"Aww, young love. Isn't it nice to see?" said Ollie's dad with just a hint of sarcasm.

"Yeah, especially since Matt tended to be better known for young *lust* in the past..." Ollie agreed, walking away from the bar.

"There you go, mate," he said, plonking the glass down in front of Matt.

"Thanks," said Matt, eyeing the contents of the glass dubiously. "I'd still rather have had a pint of lager, though, just to calm my nerves."

"Well, you can't – not since you're driving tonight," Ollie reminded him. "And anyway, why are you nervous? You've been out on a date with her once already this week, so what's the problem?"

"The problem," grinned Matt sheepishly, "is that she makes me turn to mush every time I think of her. Look, I've got goosebumps at the thought of seeing her again!"

Ollie examined the outstretched arm. Those were definitely goosebumps. Either that or Matt was suffering from a rare tropical skin disease.

"That can't be right, though, can it? Feeling so weird like this over a girl?" asked Matt, gazing down at the hairs standing to attention on his forearm. "I mean, I've been a bag of nerves. And

I've been breaking out into a sweat when I think about her too."

"Are you off your food as well?" asked Ollie, noting the unopened packet of honey roast nuts.

"Yeah – yeah, I am!" said Matt.

"Even Pot Noodle?"

"Even Pot Noodle!" he grinned, suddenly realising that Ollie was winding him up.

"Don't worry about it, Matt. All that's wrong with you is that you're in love, and 'cause that's never happened to you before, it's freaking you out."

Matt felt a furious blush surge into his cheeks – much stronger than when he was being teased by Sonja's gorgeous older sisters.

"Wow! You're even blushing!" Ollie sniggered. "You are in love."

"Well, I wouldn't say that..." waffled Matt.

"Aw, look, don't worry about it! Just have a good time!" Ollie tried to reassure him, seeing how embarrassed Matt seemed. "Anyway, where did you say you were taking her?"

"Just this country pub Gabrielle knows of. Can't remember the name of it."

Matt glanced at his watch for the tenth time that minute.

"Are you picking her up from her house?"

"Nah, she's going to wait for me at the bus stop on the main road near hers. She said it would save time," Matt answered him, tearing the tiny shreds of ripped-up beer mat into even tinier remnants. "Listen, Ol – I meant to say: this day trip to the seaside on Saturday. It's still on, is it?"

"Yeah, too right!" Ollie nodded. "It's taken enough manoeuvring to get time off for me and Anna. Why are you asking? Do you want to blow it out?"

"No – no, not at all," Matt shook his head. "It's just... well, I know it was just meant to be our crowd going, but I– but, well..."

"You want to bring Gabrielle?" Ollie finished Matt's sentence for him helpfully. "Yeah, of course – bring her. No one's going to mind!"

"Brilliant!" beamed Matt, then glanced worriedly at his watch again.

• • •

Sitting in the garden of the country pub, Matt caught himself grinning like a buffoon at the sight of Gabrielle sitting opposite him across the white, wrought-iron table. Luckily, she was smiling back at him, looking just as happy to be with him as he was with her.

Why did I feel so nervous earlier? Matt wondered to himself. *Now I'm with her, she makes me feel so relaxed...*

"OK, Matt. Now I know all about your family and you know all about mine..."

The middle daughter of three, with cool parents, is big pals with her older sister who's got a job as receptionist at the fitness centre, which is how she came to be there that night... Matt recounted silently, memorising everything Gabrielle said.

"...and we've covered favourite music..."

She loves dance music too, same as me.

"...and what we want to do..."

Social worker or special needs teacher; she hasn't decided yet.

"...and I've met your friends and you'll meet mine really soon..."

The same group of five girls whom she's hung out with since way back in primary school.

"...but the one thing we haven't talked about yet is past girlfriends and boyfriends," she smiled. "That's traditional to talk about when you first go out with someone, isn't it?"

Matt felt his skin go clammy and cold. What would Gabrielle think of him if he told her about his past record? How, since he'd left boarding school and come back to Winstead to live, he'd made up for lost time (*and* some) by – as Cat once put it – dating anything with a pulse?

And what about Cat, for that matter? How

would Gabrielle feel knowing that he and Catrina had a past together? That he'd treated her pretty despicably too? Without realising it, his fingers began to drum agitatedly on the cool metal of the table.

"Um– er... you first!" he stumbled, trying to buy himself some time.

"Well," said Gabrielle, dropping her eyelids down over her velvety brown eyes and reaching out to curl her fingers round Matt's wildly drumming ones. "It's like this..."

She flicked her eyes back up and gazed at him.

"You're it."

"What?" asked Matt, not entirely trusting that he understood what she meant.

"You!" she laughed at his startled expression. "*You* make up my whole history of boyfriends! There hasn't been anyone before you!"

Matt gritted his teeth together and found himself speechless. He'd never been out with a girl who hadn't dated before. Of course, he *knew* girls like that – Maya had never had a boyfriend, and Kerry hadn't till she started going out with Ollie – but he'd never considered going out with one before. They'd just seemed too... well... naive for him.

And what's she going to think about my track record now? panicked Matt. *She'll see me in a totally new light – she'll think I'm a real creep!*

"Come on then," Gabrielle giggled shyly after her proclamation. "*Your* turn! Tell, tell, tell!"

There was only one thing to do, Matt decided, his heart thumping fit to bust.

Lie.

• • •

"Just drop me here, this'll be fine," said Gabrielle as Matt's car pulled up outside a terraced house.

With only the yellow streetlight to illuminate the interior of the Golf, Matt thought her skin looked even more like dark amber marble than ever.

"Thanks for tonight, it was lovely. And thanks for this too!" she giggled, touching the clematis blossoms tucked into her braids, which Matt had pinched off the tumbling vine that cascaded down the pub wall. She moved closer towards him – for only their second ever kiss – and Matt could smell the sweet scent of the flowers.

I'll remember this moment for ever, he told himself, sensing her lips so tantalisingly close to his.

Suddenly, an unwelcome thought intruded on his blissful state.

Of course, I'm also going to have to remember

to tell all my friends that I'm only supposed to have been out with two girls. Ever. And one of them most definitely wasn't Cat.

Matt could imagine – all too easily – how they'd all laugh when they heard that...

CHAPTER 18

DAY TRIPPERS

Cat leant over the back of her seat and stared down at the four people sitting there.

Kerry was leaning against the glass, gazing out at the sun-drenched green fields that flashed past the train window. The three boys – Ollie, Joe and Billy – were all animatedly chatting about whether Fender Telecasters were better guitars than Gibson Les Pauls.

How dull! No wonder Kerry's looking so cheesed off, thought Cat. *Are they going to just drivel on about band stuff all day? I thought this day out was supposed to be a laugh...*

The lads were so engrossed that they hadn't even noticed her presence looming over them, which was pretty hard to ignore. Cat had bleached her hair a lighter, whiter shade of blonde

("It's the new Nordic look," she'd explained. "And this is the old Swedish look," Sonja had retorted, patting her own natural, soft blonde locks), and pulled it into two fat little bunches, secured by bands that each had a palm-sized daisy attached.

Cat wasn't used to being ignored.

"Ollie!" she interrupted in a thin, whiny voice.

"What?" he asked, glancing up at her over Joe and Billy's heads.

"Why isn't there a buffet car on this train?" she asked petulantly.

"Cat," sighed Ollie good-naturedly, "you asked that on the train up to the city."

"But that was just the train that does the commuter run. I *thought* it might not have a buffet..."

"Well, this train only takes forty-five minutes to get down to Maiden Bay. It's probably not worth their while having one," he answered patiently.

"So why don't they have someone walking through the train with one of those little trolley things?"

"I don't know, Cat. Do you want me to find the guard and ask him?" Ollie teased her. "Or I could knock on the driver's door..."

"Cat," said Maya, who was sitting across the

aisle with Anna, "you wouldn't happen to be bored, would you?"

Cat stuck her tongue out at Maya, looking even more like a five-year-old girl with her bunches. She turned and flopped back down into her own seat, next to Sonja.

She *was* bored. Bored looking at Matt and Gabrielle mooning over each other across the table from her for the last half-hour. Not to mention the cooing they were doing on the first part of their journey from Winstead up to the city. Only then, Cat was lucky enough not to be sitting opposite them.

"We could take a walk along to the rock pools..." said Gabrielle, gazing into Matt's eyes.

"That would be brilliant..." Matt replied, smiling enthusiastically at her as if she'd just said the most amazing thing in the world.

Yeuchhh! thought Cat and glanced round to see if Sonja was as disgusted by this wanton show of slushiness as she was.

But Sonja had her headphones on, listening to the new tape she'd bought at WH Smith in the station while they waited for their connecting train. She'd opened up the inner sleeve and was engrossed in reading the lyrics.

Lucky Sonja, escaping from all this lovey-dovey stuff. It's enough to drive you mad, thought

Cat, fidgeting in her seat and tapping her platform-trainered toes on the floor under the table in irritation.

Then another more wicked thought popped into her head and a small smile flitted over her face. *Yep, these two could drive a girl mad – or bad...*

"Hey, Matt," she said sweetly. "Didn't we go up to the rock pools together once?"

Matt flashed his eyes at her and Cat knew she'd hit home. During their brief time as a couple, they had driven to Maiden Bay one chilly April day, spending most of their time at the arcade on the prom or snuggling up in steamy, cosy, seafront cafés.

"No, we didn't," he answered, trying to suggest with his eyes that maybe Cat should shut up.

Anyway, it was true – on that day out they'd never made it as far as the rock pools because Cat had been too worried about scuffing the heels of her black suede boots.

Cat shrugged in response, batting her eyelashes innocently.

"In fact, I can't remember the last time we were *all* down at Maiden Bay," Matt continued, in a desperate attempt to make out it had been a whole crowd outing Cat had been referring to, and not the romantic day out it actually was.

Seeing her ex squirm perked Cat up no end. She loved winding him up as a matter of course, but it was much more fun when it was dangerous like this. The fact that he would kill her later – especially after her promising faithfully, along with the others, that they would play along with Matt as far as his past love-life was concerned – didn't enter her mind. She was just beginning to enjoy herself.

"Why didn't you two drive up together today?" she asked, twirling her finger through one of her bunches.

"Because we thought it would be nicer to come on the train with everyone else," said Matt through slightly gritted teeth. He was obviously beginning to regret it.

"Been in Matt's car yet?" Cat turned wide-eyed and questioningly towards Gabrielle.

"Oh, yes, a couple of times," nodded Gabrielle.

"Oh, boy," Cat laughed, turning her attention back to Matt. "If that car could tell stories, eh, Matt?"

Matt gave an insincere guffaw of laughter.

"Yeah, the amount of travelling I've done in that car, all the gigs I've driven to in it!" he said quickly, trying to deflect Cat from the dangerous route she was taking.

"I was thinking more of what's gone on in the back seat..." Cat responded, still maintaining a look of absolute innocence.

"Uh-huh," nodded Matt, aware of the prickles of sweat breaking out on his forehead. Batting off Catrina's volleys was pretty hard work. "Packing all those heavy speakers and equipment in it all the time. It's a wonder the suspension's not gone."

"Mmm, *I'll* bet..." Cat replied, allowing herself a small smirk.

Matt gulped and wondered how long it would be till they arrived at the station.

Joe was oblivious to the strained conversation going on behind him, but then again, he was also oblivious to the one he was supposed to be having with Ollie and Billy. As the boys chattered on about guitars and amplifiers, great songwriters and record deals, he nodded where it seemed appropriate, grunted "yeah" or just shrugged when they needed some response from him, all the time surreptitiously studying Kerry out of the corner of his eye.

Her forehead was resting on the glass, her eyes staring blankly out at the passing scenery.

It's more than just boredom with the conversation, Joe reasoned. He was no expert at stuff like body language, but even *he* could see that Kerry seemed to be leaning as far away as possible from her boyfriend.

What's going on between them? Has Ollie done something to hurt her? Joe fretted to himself, his loyalty to his best mate wavering at the unlikely idea of Ollie doing or saying anything to upset Kerry. *But what if he has? What can I do about it without giving away how I feel about her?*

"I just remembered," Joe heard Billy suddenly say, "I don't know why I didn't think of this before, but there's a guy in our photography club who's a bass player. I could ask him to meet up with us sometime?"

"Yeah, brilliant!" Ollie enthused. "If he's any good, then that would be the band up and running!"

"He told me once that he's been playing about a year, but I don't think he's been in a band before," Billy continued. "You know him, Maya – Andy, that quiet guy."

"Oh, yes," answered Maya, breaking away from her conversation with Anna. "He seems nice."

Maya knew her voice sounded flat, but she was still vaguely annoyed at Billy's presence on her crowd's day out. It was unreasonable, she knew, but she didn't feel comfortable with the way he'd just sailed right in and fitted so comfortably in the space of a few short days, all because Ollie and Joe were so keen to have him join their band.

And she was particularly annoyed with Ollie for inviting him along today, without asking her, without thinking that Billy was supposed to be *her* friend.

I'm being so petty about this, she scolded herself. But there was no getting away from the fact that the boys seemed so at ease chattering away together, while she'd been relegated to sitting at a separate table with Anna. *My old friends are getting on so well with my new friend that they don't seem to need me...*

"Maya," Anna said quietly, touching her hand to get her attention.

"What?" Maya answered equally quietly, sensing from Anna that something was up.

"Listen..." Anna indicated with a nod of her head and a sideward glance in the direction of the seat where Sonja and the others were sitting.

Above the fragmented buzzing noise coming from Sonja's over-loud Walkman, Maya could make out a snatch of conversation.

"Has Matt told you that Ollie's a twin?" Cat was saying.

"No," Gabrielle replied. "Are they identical?"

"Oh no," Cat laughed. "His twin's a girl! Her name's Natasha and she's a model in London. She's absolutely *beautiful*. I can't believe Matt didn't tell you about her. Didn't he say that him and Natasha—"

Right, Maya said to herself, leaping to her feet. *Time to rescue Matt...*

CHAPTER 19

SEA, SAND AND SHOCKS

"OK, so that's two Soleros, two Twisters, three Magnums and a Calippo," Maya counted off on her fingers.

"No – wait a minute," interrupted Cat, pushing herself up off her beach towel. "Make mine a Mr Whippy, if they've got it."

"Make up your mind," said Maya dryly. She was beginning to wish she hadn't volunteered to go for ice cream – the others had taken so long to make up their minds.

Joe shuffled by her side, eager to get going. He hadn't been able to settle down with the others on the beach. Firstly, Cat – unlike the other girls who were dressed mainly in shorts and vest tops – had taken advantage of the blistering late summer sunshine and stripped down to an eyewaterringly tiny bikini, which Joe found far too embarrassing to sit very close to. Secondly, Ollie and Kerry had gone off together ages ago and he couldn't relax for wondering what was going on between them.

"Last chance to change your mind..." Maya looked round at everyone settled on the mishmash of towels and rugs spread out on the sand, as if she were daring them to say anything. "Right, that's me and Joe off then."

Joe followed her silently, trudging through the shifting sand with his hands wedged deep in his pockets.

"Did you hear any of what was going on in the train just before we arrived?" Maya asked as they neared the steps up to the pavement.

"Nope," Joe shook his head.

"The wicked Miss Osgood was doing her best to mortify Matt in front of his new girlfriend."

"How?" asked Joe. Cat always amazed and regularly intimidated him. The lengths she'd go to to get what she wanted, or just to amuse herself, he found astounding. To Joe, being friends with Cat was like being friends with an unexploded bomb.

"Oh, by dropping about three thousand hints about was a 'lad' he was, and stuff about him and Natasha..."

"Wow!" said Joe. "Even after Matt making us promise not to let any of that stuff out to Gabrielle?"

"Oh, yes," nodded Maya, taking the steps two at a time. She hadn't been thrilled about the idea of having to lie, but she'd said she'd go along with it if everyone else did. And they'd all said they would, even Cat – until she'd got bored and thought she'd torture Matt for fun.

"Did Gabrielle get any of it?"

"I don't think so," Maya shook her head. "I waded in just at the point that Cat was about to go overboard."

"They seem to be getting on all right now," Joe nodded back to the group on the beach.

"Mmm, well, I had a word with Cat on the way down to the beach and told her to lay off," Maya explained. "I think Matt just wants a quiet life and for Gabrielle to have a nice time with his mates, so he's happy enough if Cat's on her best behaviour. Which she'd *better* be..."

"I wouldn't put bets on how long *that*'ll last," said Joe wryly.

"No, I guess not," smiled Maya, negotiating the Saturday afternoon traffic on the main promenade. "Wonder where Ollie and Kerry got to?"

Watching for cars as he walked towards the

cafés and gift shops on the farside pavement, Joe felt his silence would go unnoticed by Maya.

Fat chance.

"What's up?" asked Maya, sneaking a peek at him once they'd stepped safely on to the kerb. "You're quiet. Is something up with Kerry and Ollie?"

Joe didn't know which was worse or more disloyal: his silence signalling to Maya that *he* was troubled by his friends' absence or that something might be amiss between Ollie and Kerry.

Unknown to Joe, Maya – her subtle intuition attuned as ever – had already spotted signs of *something* negative going on between the missing couple. She'd also sensed that whatever it was seemed to be bothering Joe...

"What would I know?" Joe shrugged, staring blindly into the shop windows filled with boxes of Maiden Bay rock and assorted tacky trinkets.

Maya could see that he wasn't ready to talk and decided to let it drop.

"Fancy a rummage about in here before we get the ice creams?" she smiled, pointing to one gaudy souvenir shop. "I'd like to get a corny snowstorm or something to take back to Ravi."

Joe was glad that she'd changed the subject, but he didn't particularly want to go and hang around in the crowded, dark store.

"Nah, you go," he nodded towards the shop's entrance. "I'll wait out here for you."

"OK," said Maya, respecting his privacy and watching him walk over to a sea-facing bench. She just hoped that Joe would feel he could talk to her, if he ever needed to.

Joe leant back on the bench, breathed the salty ozone of the sea air and cursed himself for allowing the gloom to settle over him.

Why do I let impossible dreams of being with Kerry get me down? he worried to himself. *Things are going pretty well in my life and then I let IT bother me again. I start fantasising about her... I start thinking about what's going on with her and Ollie...*

'Oh, Joe– Joey!" he suddenly heard a hiccuping cry come.

Joe glanced up quickly and saw Kerry, tears streaming down her cheeks, hurrying towards him.

Before he could draw breath, she'd landed beside him on the bench, sobbing wetly into his neck, her wild, red-brown curls tickling his face as she hugged into him.

Joe found that his arms had involuntarily encircled her, holding her protectively close to his chest. But before he could ask her what was wrong, before he could catch his own shocked breath, his eyes locked on to Maya's face as she surveyed the scene from the shop doorway.

Not knowing what to say or do, Joe shut his eyes tight and breathed in the scent of coconut that was ever present in Kerry's hair; he willed every fibre in his body to remember this sensation of holding the girl that he loved in his arms.

Finally.

• • •

Languidly drawing warm handfuls of sand through his fingers, Matt watched Gabrielle kick through the surf, the foamy droplets of water clinging to her long, brown legs.

"She's really lovely," said Sonja, sitting somewhere behind him.

"I know..." he answered contentedly.

Matt had never felt so drawn to any girl before – so in tune, so comfortable.

"She looks a little bit like Lauryn Hill," came Cat's sleepy voice.

"You *always* think people have to look like someone else," Sonja teased her. "And who've you come as today, Cat? Denise van Outen in a bikini?"

"Yeah, but Cat's got a point," Matt heard Anna say. "Gabrielle *does* look a bit like Lauryn Hill –

same heart-shaped face, same almond eyes..."

"If she can sing as well as Lauryn Hill then you're on to a good one, Matt!" joked Sonja.

But Matt had stopped listening. He was imagining how it felt to kiss Gabrielle... How it felt when she slid her arms round his back...

Everything was so wonderful, so special with her. He might have been guilty of rushing things in the past – with other girls that he cared less about – but that wasn't going to happen with Gabrielle.

She waved as she made her way towards him out of the water and up over the soft, warm sand, her perfect smile making his heart skip a beat again.

No, I won't rush anything with her, he vowed. *Everything feels wonderful with her and when the time comes for... more, it'll be more wonderful for the waiting...*

Gabrielle dropped down on to the rug, breathless and laughing.

"That was lovely," she gasped.

Just like you, Matt thought adoringly.

"See, this is the life – hanging out at the beach instead of being trapped in dusty schoolrooms and swotting," Sonja murmured.

"Too right," laughed Gabrielle, grabbing a towel and drying her legs.

"A levels – who came up with that stupid idea, eh?" Sonja continued her anti-education rant from the comfort of her horizontal position. "What do you say, Gabrielle?"

"I guess," she smiled, still rubbing her legs.

"What?" said Sonja, pushing herself sleepily on to her elbows. "Are you going to tell me that you actually relish the idea of A levels?"

"No," Gabrielle smiled. "But I guess they don't bother me, being such a long way off."

"What do you mean?" asked Sonja, her sleepiness leaving her.

"Well, I've got a while to worry about that, haven't I?"

Sonja stared at Gabrielle, casually drying herself off, and then at Matt, who wore a slightly frozen expression on his face, as he also stared at his pretty girlfriend.

"Why's that?" asked Sonja. "How old are you, Gabrielle?"

"Fourteen," she replied, smiling back at Sonja.

Out of the corner of her eye, Sonja could have sworn she saw Matt go rigid. And to her right, she could make out Cat's prone body ripple with suppressed giggles.

Sonja knew, and obviously Cat knew, what was going on inside Matt's occasionally shallow mind. How could a cool DJ, with looks that got him chatted up by women much older than him, and who was – at eighteen – legally entitled to do whatever he wanted, possibly go out with someone who was still two years away from doing her GCSEs?

CHAPTER 20

GETTING THINGS STRAIGHT(ISH)

Kerry sat on the bench, with Maya and Joe on either side, each clutching a hand.

"Kerry, you've got to tell us what happened – or we can't help!" Maya tried to persuade her.

Kerry snuffled again and tried to talk.

"It– it's just going to sound stupid."

"Try us," Maya encouraged her.

"Well, Ollie wanted to buy me this necklace we saw at a stall further down the prom and I said I didn't want it. I've got my chakra and I didn't *need* a new necklace."

Maya and Joe exchanged fleeting puzzled glances over the top of Kerry's bowed head.

"OK, but why did that end up with you running away from him and getting so upset?" persisted Maya.

"He just kept saying over and over again that he wanted to get it for me and that it would suit me, and– and I just flipped. It was like he was trying to control me or something. Trying to tell me what I should be thinking or doing!" she sobbed. "It's like that all the time just now!"

"Ollie being possessive? That doesn't sound much like him," said Maya kindly. "Are you sure there isn't something more to it than that?"

"No..." Kerry answered unconvincingly.

"No, there's nothing more to it, or no, you're not sure..."

"Oh, Maya! I just– it's all changing!" Kerry stammered out, looking directly at her friend.

Joe sat silently at her other side, leaving Maya to do all the talking. He didn't feel he had the words to help. All he could do was keep holding the hand that gripped his.

"What's changing, Kez? Aren't you getting on together any more?" Maya asked her, though she could hardly believe it. Ollie and Kerry seemed just about perfect together.

"No, it's not really about that... it's just that—" Kerry took a deep breath as if what she had to say was too painful to express, "—me and Ollie have been going out for a few months now and it's like I feel this pressure to– well, like it's getting more serious..."

Joe felt his face flush as he realised what she was getting at. Maya sussed it too and dived in to help Kerry as she flustered around for the right words. "You're talking about sex, right?"

Kerry looked away from Maya and dropped her gaze to the ground, silently nodding her head.

"Is Ollie actually putting pressure on you?" Maya asked, relieved in a way that she could see what the problem was at last.

"No, no, not really," Kerry muttered. "It just feels like it's getting closer..."

"And you're not sure you're ready," said Maya.

"No," Kerry answered in a small voice. "We're just so happy the way we are and I'm scared that, y'know, sleeping together might change everything..."

Joe felt wildly uncomfortable hearing Kerry's confession, but couldn't bring himself to speak or move; hardly even to breathe.

"Kez, have you spoken to Ollie about any of this?"

Kerry was silent for a moment.

"No," she said finally.

Maya raised her free hand and gently stroked Kerry's unruly mass of curls.

"Do you love him, Kerry?"

"Oh, yes," she nodded, gazing up at Maya again. "Of course I do!"

"Well, shouldn't you be talking to him about how you're feeling, instead of bottling it up? I mean, what do you think is going through poor Ollie's mind at the moment? He's probably wondering what he's done wrong..."

"Oh, Maya! Why do you always see things so clearly? How do you always know the right things to say?" Kerry choked out, slipping her hand from Joe's grasp and throwing her arms around Maya's neck.

"Because it's my job – I'm the only sensible one out of the whole lot of you," Maya smiled, spotting Joe's shell-shocked face over the top of Kerry's frizzy mane.

Thundering footsteps and a breathless shout heralded the arrival, through the ambling Saturday strollers, of the long-lost Ollie.

"Kez! Kez! What's wrong? Where did you go to?" Ollie gasped, falling to his knees in front of her.

"Oh, Ollie!" she gasped, transferring her arms from Maya's neck to his. "I'm so sorry!"

"She's fine – she just needs to talk to you," Maya explained, in case Ollie's imagination was working overtime. "Come on, Joe – we've got some ice creams to buy..."

Stumbling to his feet, Joe looked down at the hugging couple and once again found his mouth incapable of speech. Instead, he silently followed Maya along the pavement, his shoulders hunched with disappointment and mixed emotions.

Once the shoppers and browsers had swallowed them up and they were a safe distance away from Ollie and Kerry, Maya pulled at Joe's T-shirt, forcing him to stop.

She stared deep into his rapidly blinking eyes, then surprised him by leaning close and planting a soft kiss on his cheek.

"I know," he heard her whisper in his ear. "And I won't tell..."

• • •

"Where have you two been? We were about to organise a search party. Y'know, send out the sniffer dogs, specially trained to sniff out Soleros..."

Maya ignored Sonja's comment and began dishing out the ice creams to everyone. She noticed that Sonja and Cat were still reclining in true sunworshipper mode on the beach towels. Gabrielle was doodling words in the wet sand down towards the water, with Matt hovering – awkwardly it seemed – by her side, while Anna and Billy sifted through a small pile of shells they must have been gathering together.

How cosy... she thought, almost bitterly, then immediately got annoyed with herself. *Why does it bother me? Am I jealous? And how come I can sort out everyone else's feelings but not my own?*

Joe thumped down on the edge of a rug closest to them and Maya followed suit.

Decide! she told herself sternly. *Decide how you feel about Billy and then deal with it. Stop letting stupid feelings spoil your day.*

As she watched Billy and Anna rifling through their collection, an obvious thought shot into her mind.

Imagine what it would be like to kiss him... she thought, closing her eyes and picturing the scene, unaware that Sonja had used exactly the same tactic when it came to analysing her feelings for Matt. *Billy leaning closer to me, his hand cupping my face, his lips slowly touching mine...*

Maya felt a shiver at the image in her head; a shiver of something not far from distaste.

Well, that solves that – I don't fancy Billy, she smiled to herself, glad that her riddle had been so easy to resolve finally. Unlike Sonja, Maya used her imagination to make sense of things, not to escape into fantasy land.

What she had to come to terms with, Maya realised, was how she felt about him infringing on her crowd and how she was going to deal with that. But it was a lot easier than any romantic entanglement. That kind of emotion was something she'd never had to deal with yet, and seeing the mess her friends got themselves into when it came to love, it wasn't anything she wanted to have happen to her in a hurry.

"Hey, did you guys see Ollie and Kez on your travels?" Sonja asked out of the blue, raising her sunglasses and squinting at Joe and Maya.

"Yes," nodded Maya. "They were just mooching about up on the prom. I think they'll be down soon."

Sonja took another ice-cold bite of her chocolate-covered bar and stared at Joe. He had that same gobsmacked expression she'd seen on Matt's face earlier, when Gabrielle had blithely revealed her age.

"Joey? You OK, Joey? You look a bit... funny," she quizzed her friend.

Joe went to open his mouth, then closed it again, his head empty of excuses.

"There's something Joe feels a little weird about telling you lot..." Maya interrupted.

Despite the heat of the sun, a chill of panic swept over Joe. What was she going to say?

"He really, *really*—" Maya reached over and squeezed his fingers conspiratorially, "—*hates* being called Joey."

• • •

Cat had squealed with delight when Ollie came back with a frisbee. She'd spotted some cool lads lounging further along the beach and had been wondering how to casually get their attention. Bouncing about in her bikini chasing a piece of plastic was the perfect excuse.

With Ollie's help, Cat had persuaded Maya, Kerry, Billy, Anna, Gabrielle and a reluctant-ish Joe to make up a four-a-side team, while Sonja and Matt offered their services as impartial referees.

Sonja had quite fancied the idea of joining in when Ollie first suggested it, but an appealing look from Matt made her change her mind. It seemed as though he needed to talk.

"So, I take it that Gabrielle being fourteen came as a bit of a surprise then?" she asked as they watched their friends begin the game.

"I feel like I've just been run over by a twenty-ton lorry..." Matt mumbled.

"Is it that bad?"

"Son!" he said agitatedly, astounded that one of his best mates couldn't see his predicament. "I'm eighteen! How can I go out with a girl of fourteen?! How big a mistake would that be?"

Sonja smiled at him and thought to herself

what a berk he could be. A likeable berk, but a berk all the same. She suddenly felt so, *so* glad that she'd come to her senses about that stupid notion of him being boyfriend material.

"Matt, I know that's quite a big age gap, but really, what's the problem?" she questioned him. "I thought you were mad about her!"

"I am! I was! But I just can't..." Matt chewed his lip in consternation.

"Is this anything to do with an age of consent thing?" Sonja suggested, reading his mind.

"Yes! No! I mean, honest, Son, I was only thinking earlier how I'd never rush her – she's too... special."

"So, you hadn't planned on seducing her in the near future?"

"No!"

"And you're crazy about her?"

"Well, yes!"

"You haven't got a problem then, have *you*?" said Sonja, poking him in the ribs. "It's just about your ego – you think it's not *cool* to go out with someone of fourteen, which is ridiculous."

Matt rubbed the heels of his hands over his face. "I s'pose you're right. But I just don't know if I can handle it."

"C'mon," said Sonja, now tickling him. "Get over it. Prove to me what a mature lad you are..."

"I don't know if I am mature enough, Son," he mumbled, then caught a glimpse of Gabrielle as she sprinted easily along the sand in pursuit of the frisbee.

His heart did a quick double back-flip before melting completely and he knew the decision was made for him.

• • •

"What are those two gossiping about?" Cat asked Maya breathlessly, staring over at Matt and Sonja.

The others were in a tangle in the sand a few metres away from them, having pursued Gabrielle and ended up in an undignified, giggling pile, all trying to grab the frisbee from her.

"Don't know," answered Maya, just as breathlessly, "but I wouldn't worry about it. If I was you, I'd pay more attention to keeping your boobs inside your top."

Cat looked down and giggled when she saw one bosom had made its bid for freedom while she'd been running around.

"Oops!" she snickered, rearranging herself.

Maya took the opportunity to check out her watch while they took a breather.

"Going to have to head off soon, to make the train," she said, looking over at her friend.

Cat's face fell.

"What's wrong?" asked Maya. "Having too much fun playing with your little chums? Don't want to go home to Mummy?"

"Too right," Cat replied, a frown creasing her brow.

"Why? What's the big deal?"

Cat shot a guilty look at her friend. "Maya, you know how I said I'd told my mum about college?"

"Cat!" Maya gasped. "Don't tell me she *still* doesn't know!"

"She will by now..." said Cat, twirling one of her bunches. "I left her a letter this morning, telling her."

"You've let your mum believe you've been going to sixth form all week and now you break the news to her in a *letter*?"

"I *had* to – the college was going to get in touch with her this week about fees and stuff," Cat explained, completely missing Maya's point. "They hadn't got round to it till now since I was a late entrant..."

"Cat," said Maya despairingly, visualising the rage Cat's very scary mother would have worked herself up into by the time her daughter got home, "I think you've just surpassed yourself. I think out of all the mistakes you've ever made, this is one of your biggest."

Cat twirled her hair some more, gave Maya an embarrassed little smile and wondered if it was too late to apply for a transfer to a beauty school in Australia...

CHAPTER 21

••••••••••••••••••••••••••••••

SHOWDOWN

Cat shivered as she slipped her key into the lock. She tried to tell herself that it was down to leaving a day's worth of sun behind and stepping into the tiled chill of the mansion block's high-ceilinged hallway.

But it wasn't.

"Mum? Mum, are you home?" she called out to a silent flat.

Looking down at her watch, Cat saw it was nearly eight o'clock. She'd tried to persuade the others to stay out a little longer, to make a night of it, but everyone was too tired and lazy after their day out.

"Eight o'clock," she muttered under her breath. Maybe her mother was at the gym, but it wasn't likely – not on a Saturday night.

Maybe she's gone out with some of her boring friends from the tennis club? But a sixth sense told Cat that this wasn't the case. A sixth sense felt a cold, malevolent presence close by.

It was either a poltergeist or her mother and Cat didn't really want to make contact with either.

Tentatively, she peered around the kitchen doorway, one of her giant daisy hairgrips preceeding her anxious face.

Sylvia Osgood sat at the kitchen table with Cat's letter and what looked like a large glass of gin and tonic in front of her. She gave her daughter a long, lingering, dead-eyed glare of disgust.

"Hi!" squeaked Cat, unsure how to play things until her mother started whatever she was going to start.

"Let me ask you something," Sylvia Osgood began, picking up a smouldering cigarette from an ashtray. "That lovely little chat we had a while back. About Maya wanting to leave school to do a vocational course. I take it that was all about you?"

"Mmm," Cat nodded, clinging on to the doorway for lack of anything more constructive to do.

"Why? Why didn't you just say it was you instead of going through that stupid charade?"

Cat shrugged.

"Oh, for God's sake, sit down instead of hovering over there," her mother barked.

Cat shuffled over and sat down in a chair opposite her mum. It suddenly reminded her of the time the deputy headmistress at primary school had called Cat into her office and told her off for showing her knickers to Jeremy Smith in exchange for his Mars Bar.

"Look at you!" her mother sighed, her eyes roaming over Cat's little-girl bunches and the novelty hairgrips that kept them in place. "It's like trying to have a sensible conversation with a five-year-old!"

Suddenly, Cat knew how to play it. That comment, along with her memory of school tickings-off, inspired her to go for wide-eyed innocence instead of full-on argument.

"Are you aware of what you've done? Do you realise what a stupid mistake you've made?"

Cat pictured a sad little Andrex puppy and drew on her best acting ability to get that same expression on her face.

"Well? Speak to me, Catrina!"

"I– I just really, *really* wanted to do this course and I knew you wouldn't let me..." she said in a little girl voice, her bottom lip wobbling for added effect.

"Catrina, apart from the fact that I think it's a monumentally foolish thing to leave school before you've done your A levels," her mother said, the irritation in her voice making it sound a hair's breath away from breaking into a shout, "what I want to know is where on earth you suddenly got the idea that beauty therapy was your vocation in life? It's not one of your silly whims, is it?"

"Of course not!" Cat protested, although it was. She'd never even thought about it until she'd seen the ad for late applications in the paper and decided she was bored with school. And it had only taken another ten minutes after reading the ad for her to link it with her daydream to get on TV. "I've wanted to do it for ages, but I knew you wouldn't approve!"

Sylvia Osgood sighed again and rolled her eyes to the ceiling.

"I suppose it's a *complete* waste of time for me to try and persuade you that you should go back to sixth form and do a course like this later?" she said dryly, tapping her nails on the glass in front of her.

Saying nothing, Cat twirled her fingers through one of her bunches and nodded, her face a picture of childish contrition. At least she hoped so.

"Catrina, you're a stupid, stubborn little girl and you infuriate me!" said her mother finally, angrily stubbing out her cigarette. "Oh, I give up..."

Cat tilted her head to one side, gazing off sorrowfully into space, while letting a smile break out on the inside.

She knew she had won.

Sugar SECRETS...

...& Choices

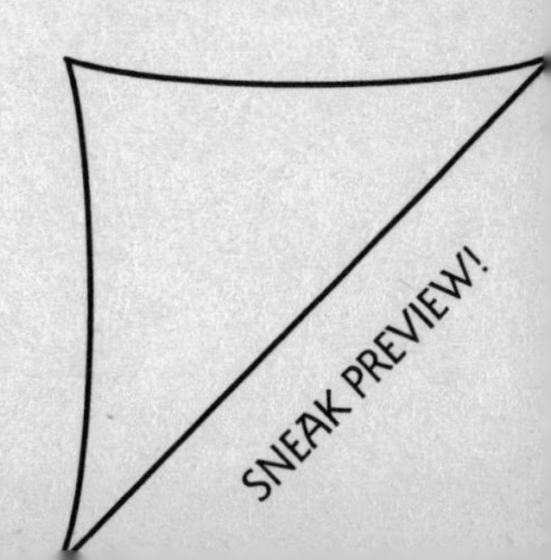

Kerry spent the rest of her Sunday striding purposefully to the phone in the Bellamy household, standing over it for a few moments, rehearsing some lines in her head as her hand hovered over the receiver, then skulking guiltily off again. However much she tried, however much she practised their imaginary conversation in her head, she couldn't bring herself to pick up the phone.

Eventually, Kerry convinced herself that it would be far better to see Ollie face to face, rather than confront him on the phone. She decided to call in on him at work on the way home from college next day and felt relief wash over her – albeit temporarily – with the knowledge that she had another twenty-four hours' grace.

Sonja Harvey – being the confrontational sort – badgered Kerry for most of Monday at school.

"Kez, after everything that we discussed yesterday," she'd sighed wearily during lunchbreak, "I can't believe you still haven't spoken to Ollie..."

"I know," Kerry had hissed back. "It's just that my parents were at home all day, so I was limited as to when I could call. And then when I could, I chickened out in case they overheard. I'll do it on the way home from college tonight. I promise."

To make sure that she did, Sonja practically

frogmarched Kerry from the college gates to Nick's Slick Riffs where Ollie was working that afternoon.

"The longer you leave it, the harder it will be," said Sonja as she stood outside the café next door. "So I'll be in here waiting for you. Stop by when you've finished and let me know how you got on."

"OK," said Kerry weakly.

She knew Sonja was right. She had to get this sorted once and for all, even though the thought of it made her feel physically sick.

Kerry walked past the poster-clad window of the record shop and opened the door. The musty smell that came from deep within the place hit her immediately, whiffed up her nostrils, rendered her immobile and brought on the biggest, most ungainly sneeze she had ever experienced.

"Aaa-aaa-aaaa-CHOOO!"

Kerry looked up from where she had found herself bent double in the doorway and saw two pairs of startled eyes peering at her in the semi-gloom. Ollie and his Uncle Nick were standing behind the counter and Kerry watched, mortified, as grins as wide as dinner plates spread across their faces.

"Great entrance, Kerry," laughed Nick as he turned and disappeared into the stockroom at the back. "Can you warn me if there's an encore? I'm not sure the old ticker will stand another shock like that."

"Oh... uh... ouff, *sniiffff,*" Kerry spluttered. She dug into the pockets of her jacket and pulled out a ragged tissue. The opening lines she had planned in her head had deserted her and she was left with the overriding feeling that she looked like a berk.

Typical, she thought. *Just when I want to be compos mentis, I end up like a bumbling twerp!*

She took a few steps forward to where Ollie was standing, still grinning.

"Um, hi, Ollie," she said, "sorry about that. I didn't mean to make quite such an entrance..." Her voice trailed off.

"That's OK," he said. "At least you woke us up. We've been catching up on paperwork for most of the afternoon and were on the point of dozing off."

"I, uh... only stopped by to apologise for Saturday night," continued Kerry. "I thought perhaps it was my turn to make the first move."

She stood staring nervously at the till for a moment, unsure of what to say next.

Then she felt Ollie's hand take hold of hers and give it a little squeeze.

"It's OK," he said softly. "It doesn't matter.

I was going to call you later anyway."

Kerry felt her heart melt. As she looked into Ollie's all-forgiving face she wondered why she'd been getting so anxious. Ollie was such a decent, caring boyfriend – he would understand once she'd explained to him how she was feeling. All she had to do was tell him...

"I'm sorry, Ol," she said, grasping his hand tightly in hers. "I've been such a misery guts recently and I've been taking it out on you. It's just that there's... there's something I need to talk to you about. It's kind of important."

Kerry looked beyond Ollie to the stockroom behind. She could see Nick's head bobbing up and down between cardboard boxes and knew now wasn't the right time to launch into what she had to say.

"Could we meet up?" she continued. "One evening this week?"

"Sure," Ollie replied. "I'm a bit tied up here tonight, but how about tomorrow night? I should get off at about six. I could meet you next door."

Kerry didn't want to talk to Ollie in the End, not when the others were likely to be in there too. If she was going to tackle the issue that had been tearing her insides out these past few weeks, she needed them to be on their own.

"Uh, I'm not sure," she replied uncertainly.

"Perhaps we could meet there, then go on somewhere else. Some place a bit quieter."

"OK," replied Ollie. "Whatever you like. I'll have a think. Maybe we could go and get something to eat in the Plaza."

"That'd be great. Um, how did the band meeting go last night?"

"Brilliant! We all had loads of ideas – it's going to be fab. I can't wait to start rehearsing again—"

"When you've finished, Ollie, could you come back here and give me a hand?" He was interrupted by Nick's voice from the storeroom.

Kerry backed away towards the door. "I'll let you get on," she said. "I'll meet you in the café just after six then."

She turned round, suddenly keen to get out.

"Kerry?" Ollie's voice came from behind her.

She turned back to face him. "Hmmm?"

"Is everything going to be OK?"

"Yes, of course it is. Look, I'll... uh, see you tomorrow." Kerry returned to Ollie, leaned over the wooden counter and gave him a little kiss on the lips. The corners of her mouth turned up into the ghost of a smile and she left the shop, relieved that at least now she'd set the wheels in motion.

ARE YOU A WORRIER?

Kerry's got a lot on her mind, but will she tackle the problem head on, or will she keep it to herself and hope it goes away?

How would *you* react in Kerry's situation? Do you get uptight at life's little niggles, or are you a laid-back lass? Answer these questions and rate your score on the stress-o-meter.

Look at the following questions and decide if your answer would be **YES**, **NO** or **SOMETIMES**.

1 Fretting about life?

- Do you get wound up by stuff really easily?
- Do you hate it when things have to change?
- Do you worry yourself silly about teeny-weeny details?
- Do you feel really tired out all day but can't get to sleep at night?
- Do you get a bit weepy (and not just when *Animal Hospital*'s on)?
- Do you ever wish you could get away from everyone and everything for a little while?
- Do you think other people are having an easier time of it than you?

2 Fretting about love?

- Does your tongue tie itself in knots when you try to talk to the boy you like?
- Are you scared he won't stay interested in you?
- Do you look for all sorts of hidden meanings in things he says?
- Do you worry that he'll think you're silly or just being a baby?
- Do you constantly analyse how you feel about him?
- Do you keep things in rather than say them out loud to him?

3 Fretting about friends?

- When you're with your friends, do you sometimes feel like a bit of an outsider?
- Do you ever imagine bad things happening to your friends or family, and get in a right old state about it?
- Do you get in a panic about saying the wrong thing in front of people?
- Do people tell you you're over-reacting when you try to tell them your troubles?
- Do you get in a tizz when people spring surprises or changes of plans on you?
- Do you think your friends wouldn't understand if you tried to tell them what's whizzing through your mind?

4 Fretting about everything?

- Do you lie in bed and dread getting up in the morning (and not just because you're so comfy)?
- Do you have zillions of things to do yet never seem to get anything done?
- Do you duck out of situations rather than face them?
- Do you find it hard just to relax and veg out?
- Do you find yourself snapping at people and you don't really know why?
- Do you ever worry about how much you're worrying?

COUNT UP HOW MANY TIMES YOU ANSWERED **YES**, HOW MANY TIMES YOU ANSWERED **NO** AND HOW MANY TIMES YOU ANSWERED **SOMETIMES**, THEN TURN THE PAGE TO SEE WHAT IT MEANS...

SO, ARE YOU A WORRIER OR NOT?

If you answered mostly **YES**:

Uh-oh, you're so stressed you could win the Eurovision Stress Contest! Everyone worries about stuff, but the reason you get it so bad is 'cause you tend to keep it to yourself and not to discuss it with anyone. Even when you do talk to friends, you don't listen to what they say and so stay miserable. The three rules are: talk, listen and lighten up – which is good advice for Kerry too, if only she'd take notice!

If you answered mostly **SOMETIMES**:

You're pretty normal; you get wound up more than you'd like to and suffer the odd stress-related twinges, but for the most part you can shake it off. You know that a heart-to-heart with your mum, or a natter and a giggle with your mates can clear your head of whatever's cluttering it up.

If you answered mostly **NO**:

Boy are you lucky; nothing much ruffles your feathers. Do a good deed and turn counsellor if you see any of your friends showing signs of stress. That's what Sonja and Maya are trying to do for Kerry – but will she listen to their advice, or carry on fretting about Ollie?

Order Form

To order direct from the publishers, just make a list of the titles you want and fill in the form below:

Name ....

Address ....

....

....

Send to: Dept 6, HarperCollins Publishers Ltd, Westerhill Road, Bishopbriggs, Glasgow G64 2QT.

Please enclose a cheque or postal order to the value of the cover price, plus:

UK & BFPO: Add £1.00 for the first book, and 25p per copy for each additional book ordered.

Overseas and Eire: Add £2.95 service charge. Books will be sent by surface mail but quotes for airmail despatch will be given on request.

A 24-hour telephone ordering service is available to Visa and Access card holders: 0141- 772 2281

THE LIFE AND L

Martin Waddell has at least two things in common with Zoë T. Curley's dad. He's a writer and, until recent years, he was an avid pipe-smoker! Widely regarded as one of the finest contemporary writers of books for young people, he has twice won the Smarties Book Prize – for *Farmer Duck* and *Can't You Sleep, Little Bear?* His other prizes include the 1989 Emil/Kurt Maschler Award for *The Park in the Dark* and the 1990 Best Books for Babies Award for *Rosie's Babies*. Among his many other titles for children are *My Aunty Sal and the Mega-sized Moose*, *The Dump Gang*, *Cup Final Kid*, *The Perils of Lord Reggie Parrot*, two collections of read-aloud stories about Little Obie, and the young adult novel *Tango's Baby*.

He also writes books under the pseudonym Catherine Sefton, including the Irish trilogy *Beat the Drum*, *Frankie's Story* and *Starry Night*, winner of the 1986 Other Award. This title was also shortlisted for the Guardian Children's Fiction Award, as was *Along a Lonely Road*, which was similarly shortlisted for the 1992 Smarties Books Prize.

Martin Waddell lives with his wife in County Down.

Books by the same author

Under the name Catherine Sefton

Along a Lonely Road

Beat of the Drum

The Cast-off

Emer's Ghost

Frankie's Story

The Ghost Girl

The Haunting of Ellen

In a Blue Velvet Dress

Island of the Strangers

The Kidnapping of Suzie Q

Shadows of the Lake

Starry Night

Under the name Martin Waddell

Our Wild Weekend

Tango's Baby

The Life and Loves of ZOË T. CURLEY

MARTIN WADDELL

WALKER BOOKS
AND SUBSIDIARIES
LONDON • BOSTON • SYDNEY

Special thanks to Dash Music Company for permission
to use lyrics on page 31.

First published 1997 by Walker Books Ltd
87 Vauxhall Walk, London SE11 5HJ

This edition published 1998

2 4 6 8 10 9 7 5 3 1

This book has been typeset in Sabon.

Printed in Great Britain

British Library Cataloguing in Publication Data
A catalogue record for this book is available
from the British Library.

ISBN 0-7445-5489-6

For Diana Hickman

This Notebook contains things which I will use for my autobiography when I have time to write it, so I will remember how I felt when I was a prisoner in Zog. No one but me is allowed to look at it so KEEP OUT.

Signed,

Zoë T. Curley

Famous Writer

Saturday 1st August a.m.
Subject:

In the Park

Today, Graham D. was in the park. He trailed us to the swings, with Merson, his dog. The light of love shone bright in his eye, Melissa says.

"Bug off and stop following us!" Melissa told him, cleverly grabbing her opportunity. "Zoë doesn't fancy you so it is no use you dragging round after us. Go walk your dog some place else."

"It's a free park, I'll walk my dog where I like!" Graham D. said.

"Not after us. Bug off!" Melissa told him. "Go chase Awful Alison."

And he bugged off with his little dog, broken-hearted ... last seen in full retreat, pausing only to use his dog scoop down by the boating lake, where Merson had performed yet again. Eeeeeeugh!

"Graham D. *definitely, definitely* fancies you, Zoë!" Melissa said.

"Not with this brace on my teeth," I said.

I hate my brace. I prefer my teeth crooked and interesting, but life has ordained it otherwise. I have to wear this rotten old brace for two years, so it will be yonks before I can kiss anybody. Up to then I am playing hard to get and keeping Graham D. interested, but I have to keep my mouth shut so he won't see my brace. Melissa is my Best Friend, so she's doing all the talking for me. Graham D. is a long-term prospect, but not a very good one.

My brace has to be mentioned because that is what this Notebook is about: me and my life. For a whole month I am going to write something every day about Zoë T. Curley: her Life and Loves. This is part of my training to be a Famous Writer. It will come in useful later, because I will have a slice of my now-feelings as a prisoner in Zog to refer to, written while I am still young enough to see things clearly.

Sunday 2nd August
Subject:

Brothers!

Zog is a life-system. Zog is also a place and a state of mind. All will be made clear in these pages.

The important thing is that I am not alone in Zog. There are other Zog dwellers, not all of whom are civilized persons. This encounter illustrates what I have to put up with sometimes.

This morning my middle-sized brother, Ob-Noxious, communicated at breakfast to my minuscule brother, Creep. I am seated between the juvenile pair, but I am not a party to their conversation. I do not talk to them. They are not to be talked to. They are to be observed as a species of Zog dweller.

"Who is that fat elderly person beside you, brother-small?" asked Ob.

"What person?" replied Creep, licking the jam off his fingers, one at a time, and then inspecting each one to see that nothing was missed.

"That spotted person," said Ob-Noxious. "The one with the big bum and the wiggly ears and the tooth brace and the dumbhead who is in love with herself, which is just as well because no one else is. Except Graham D. Batbugs, maybe, if he hasn't gone off her yet. She is crazy for him."

The Horrible Two expect a response, but I do not deign to reply.

A First Principle of mine is that I do not discuss my *amours* with children. I am there, I register disdain with an ear wiggle, but I do *not* speak. Ob-Noxious and Creep are rumoured to be my kith and kin, but I do not own them. I may have been kidnapped at birth and brought to this hovel ... nay *must* have been.

"The individual described is, however, *not* a person, my brother," Ob went on. "It is a horrible phantasm or creature from some Black Lagoon or Outer Space or Slimy Toad Hole. Graham D. Batbugs is welcome to it."

"Agreed," said Creep, stuffing his crummy little face with toast.

"We could pay him to elope with it, maybe?" Ob suggested. "Three Mars bars and some crisps? So long as he doesn't bring it back. He could ride off with it on the handlebars of his new bike, into the sunset, and then we would be free of this Scourge for ever! Or he could put it in the dog kennel with his little dog."

Both small persons are convulsed with glee at this witticism.

Assorted bow-wows follow.

At this point, with great dignity, I left the room, and retreated up the ladder through the trapdoor to my prospective Sky Cabin in the roof space (my Writer's Room-to-be!), where I now sit on my writing-cushion beneath the stars (it is morning, but stars sounds good) and communicate my thoughts, as is my wont.

Resolution One: Creep and Ob-Noxious to die Lingering Deaths ere summer is over. Well, not deaths maybe; Mum would be upset, for reasons I can't fathom, because she has had them for almost nine years (Creep) and eleven years (Ob-Noxious) and she should have seen through them by now, but she hasn't. *Something* horrible is to happen to them.

I will consider raising this matter with Melissa tomorrow morning. She had to go to her gran's today with her mum and dad, and so she is unavailable for comment, which is *dead* boring of her, but she can't help it. Her dad is a plumber and he takes Sundays off. She has to go when they go. She has no choice. It isn't fair that important matters in our lives are disrupted by mum-and-dad-type *whims*.

That is *it* for today. *Serious* writing for possible future use (when I do my auto-biography) can be very tiring when you first do it.

Monday 3rd August p.m.
Subject:

My Bluebottle Problem

My morning with Melissa was messed up by the Cyril Bluebottle Problem, *again*. The problem with Cyril Bluebottle is that he is seven, he lives next door, and I get dumped with looking after him as a free infant-minding service of one.

I protested to Mum about Cyril-minding yet again. Ob had slipped off when he saw Mum Bluebottle coming through our gate with little Cyril. Mum collared me.

"It is always *me*," I told her. "Why can't Creep do some Bluebottle-minding for a change?"

"You know Taylor is only nine!" Mum said. (By *Taylor* she means Creep. Creep was named Taylor after an honorary auntie who was good to Mum when she was small. Her name is Thelma Taylor. Guess who got stuck with the *Thelma*? She comes once or twice a year to check up on us.)

"I'm spending my *whole* life Cyril-minding for Mum Bluebottle!" I told her firmly.

"Try not to be *so* unhelpful, Zoë," Mum said. "Don't be such a grump! You know Cynthia-next-door has lots of personal problems at the moment. And you mustn't call her Mum Bluebottle. She would be terribly upset if she heard you."

Mum Bluebottle is a single mum, Dad Bluebottle having buzzed away to a new leaf. The Edict of the Mistress of Zog (Mum) is that we are to be helpful to Cynthia Bluebottle from next door at all times, because she has a lot on her plate, but I am not having my holidays squelched by unpaid little-Cyril-minding, and I told Mum so. Also I am too young to child-mind. It is illegal and immoral. The argument that Mum is always there in the background doesn't wash, as Mum is always so busy.

Mum lectured me about what she described as my "bolshie attitude" these days, with some other irrelevant (in my view) remarks about the state of my room, and my approach to life in general ... most uncalled for, given that I am the one with grounds for complaint, because I am getting older every day and the springtime of my life is being frittered away Cyril Bluebottle-minding (*unpaid*)!

After deep thought (and a lengthy consultation with Melissa at her house this afternoon) I am considering an appeal to Dad on the Bluebottle-minding issue. He may be persuaded to see it my way. He doesn't like Mum Bluebottle since she scolded him about accidentally scorching Mum's geraniums when he was doing Sausage Man at their Wrinklies' Barbecue. He has never liked geraniums. Mum does. The scorching may not have been as accidental as it seemed.

Dad is the one who thought up the Zog stuff, so he ought to stick to his own rules, and they are being *bent*, as I see it.

According to Dad, Zog is an Alien Planet where all is neat and tidy: newspapers are folded, bills are paid promptly, hens play golf all day in the bright sunshine. The Creative (Dad) maintains that our Happy Home is the Top Secret Zog Base on Earth, unaccredited to all major embassies. Mum is the Mistress of this Earth Outpost of Zog, and we are all her Minions. Her Minions are officially listed as me and Ob-Noxious and Creep and my absent brother, Turtle. Dad sees his role as Zogbudsman and Provider of All Things. Melissa qualifies for Licensed Zog Observer status, as my Best Friend, though she does not see everything. The truth is you have to *live* Zog to know it.

It is the constitutional line I am going to take with Dad. The Constitution of Zog lays down that even the humblest and most unworthy Minion (say, Creep) shall have full democratic rights and freedom of expression within the limitations imposed by the need for good government in Zog. This includes the right of appeal to the Zogbudsman (Dad) against oppressive measures – like *illegally* looking after Cyril Bluebottle all the holidays for *free*!

That is the way it is supposed to work, but it obviously isn't working. I feel there is a Zog Principle at stake, and I must take a stand somewhere. I am not going to spend all summer as Mum Bluebottle's unpaid child-minder, when Melissa and I have our whole lives to sort out, and not much time left to do it, as we are getting older every day.

As I said to Ob later, it would not be so bad if Mum Bluebottle was as saintly and misunderstood as Mum makes her out to be. Ob and I know she is not, from certain observations we have made.

Tuesday 4th August
Subject:

Bluebottle Observations

This morning Ob reported a further development on the Bluebottle front, which confirms my opinion that I am being exploited for amoral ends.

Ob and I know what is *really* going on next door. It is a disgrace and a bad example to us. Mum Bluebottle is having an affair with a Double Glazing Salesman. We have seen a double glazing car parked outside her house three times and it stayed for *hours*, twice last week, at night-time, and now last night as well. Their house is already double-glazed; enough said!

Officially, Mum and Dad do not know what is going on, so we are not supposed to know either. Ob and I think Mum *does* know, but just isn't saying. If *she* knows, it follows that Dad knows too, because they work that way on sensitive matters. They probably believe they are protecting our innocence, but it makes my negotiating position very difficult, as I am not supposed to know what is happening.

The whole thing is a come-down for Mum Bluebottle because the original Mr Bluebottle, Cyril's dad, was an Assistant Bank Manager before he was made redundant and left her to fend for herself. She is a Financial Adviser working from home, which Dad says is a way of diddling foolish people into letting her have all their money. Mum says she is an enterprising example of what a spirited woman can do when left to face the world alone.

Melissa, of course, is unaware of the Scandal-next-door. She is my Best Friend, but I have not fully explained it to her, as Melissa is not a very sophisticated person and might be shocked.

I intended to tackle Dad this morning but he is having a Creative Crisis on plot development in his scripts for "Famous Foxy". He has not heard from his Agent for days, so I am biding my time. When dealing with the Zogbudsman, timing is of the essence.

This afternoon Melissa and I had a *loud* conversation in our garden about babysitting rates and terms of employment. I am not sure if it did any good. Mum Bluebottle was doing stuff in her back garden, and she *must* have heard us, but she was pretending that she hadn't.

Also Melissa reports that Graham D. and Arnold passed her house yesterday and looked over the fence but they did not say anything to her and she did not say anything to them, so not much progress has been made with our Love Lives.

It is about time something exciting happened to us.

Wednesday 5th August
Subject:

Love-Life Developments

This Book is first with the news. Something new and exciting has happened in our lives at last... At least Melissa is very excited, but I am not so sure.

I telephoned Melissa this morning to discuss further the Bluebottle exploitation matter, hoping she could help me figure the tactics but we didn't get doing that because Melissa has informed me that new people are going to move in next door to her tomorrow and she has discovered that there is a *boy* and his name is *Rupert*.

Apparently he plays a trumpet. Melissa thinks he might be in a Rock Band, but I have never heard of a Rock Band with trumpets in it. It is probably just the Boys' Brigade, and he will trumpet all night. Melissa is naturally worried in case she won't get her Beauty Sleep. Melissa hopes he will be gorgeous, but in my opinion she is over-excited about the matter. She is *seriously* debating amending her Secret Love List to include Rupert and she hasn't even seen him yet. I have told her that our Love Lists should not be amended lightly, if we are to be True to our Hearts.

My Secret Love List (No. 2) is as follows:

Z.T. Curley's Secret Love List (No. 2)

1. *Graham Denzil Batty xxxxxxx*
2. *Tarzan (joke)*
3. *A.N. Other – probably a TV Star or a Russian Count or somebody very rich and handsome who can act as my consort when I go to big parties*

My Secret Love List (No.1) had Arnold Potts on it, but I dropped him because he chose Awful Alison for the Mixed Doubles when he could have chosen me, so I am never, ever kissing him, not ever, not even if he went down on his bended knees to me.

I have now passed Arnold on to Melissa, as he betrayed me over the tennis thing. I had Arnold on my Secret Love List (No. 1) but I crossed him off and put Graham D. on. Arnold Potts is not worthy of my love.

Melissa rang me back twice with further tit-bits about Rupert. She understands he will not be going to our school. He goes to a private school somewhere. So they must be rich.

What we don't know is why they are coming to live in the bungalow next to Melissa's if they are *that* rich. They have had a white marble bathroom installed, with gold-flecked mirrors round the walls. This is very sophisticated. Melissa's dad didn't do the installation, although he is practically the only *good* plumber there is. He is very sour about it. He says he hopes their fancy pipes burst. They have put in new central heating and he says the pipes are small bore and the whole house will rumble when they use it.

Later
Subject:

Fresh Revelations

Melissa has rung me again, very excited. It is a *two-person* marble bath, with a swirl thing. Melissa went over their fence when no one was looking and she saw it, because the bathroom window was open so the new plaster could dry out.

There must also be something else because Melissa rang me another time (that makes four), but Mum took the call and told Melissa not to keep calling when they only live one avenue away, and her dad is a plumber, and can't live with a multimillionaire's phone bill.

I was going to nip round to Melissa's house to find out what she was ringing me about but there was a Crisis in Zog so I had to stay and help Mum avert it (though we failed). The Creative had lost his pipe again and he has a deadline to meet and can't write without that *particular* pipe, apparently. He stated that he intended to be up all night at his desk puffing, so he had to have it.

Mum has pledged to wean him off the pipe, but I don't think she will succeed. She has suggested nicotine patches or chewing baby rusks, but he is not having any. I *think* the baby rusks suggestion was meant as a joke, but it didn't go down well.

She should not have risked it. Now he is sulking.

Thursday 6th August
Subject:

My Banana Plan

This morning Ob found the Creative's pipe, and put him out of his agony. Too late, of course. He claimed he was unable to work last night without it, and as a result he will earn no money and before we know it we will all be out on the street.

The pipe was found down the sofa. If it had smouldered and set fire to the sofa we would all be dead, burnt alive. Mum pointed this out to him. He was not pleased.

"He smokes far too much. It is like you and sweets," Mum said to me later. Then she read me a lecture on cutting out sweets if I am really worried about being fat all my life (which I am). I know how Dad feels. Mum suggests I forget sweets and start eating lots of fruit instead if I want to lose weight. I am sure she is right, so I will, and then I will be a new me – though still with the rotten brace. Alternatively if I ate *more* sweets my teeth would fall out and then I wouldn't *need* a brace. But I'd be a toothless hag, so you can't win.

I am starting with my Banana Plan, because I like bananas and I found some in the kitchen. The Plan is to eat at least *four* bananas per day, which will give me a healthy diet and I will be a new slimline Zoë as well (with teeth).

"Don't fret about it so much, Zoë," Mum advised me. "It is your hormones doing it. The fat will just melt away one day, I promise."

Which means she thinks I *am* fat. It isn't just me imagining it, which is what she usually says.

Writing all the things that happen to you is a very tiring business when you are young. I do not know if I can keep this up.

Later
Subject:

The Edicts of Zog

It is sad to have a dad with an addiction, but Mum is trying to cope by using caring persuasion without having recourse to the Edicts of Zog. To make this clear I will have to outline the Edicts, which are as follows:

Edicts of Zog

- ***That the Mistress is the Supreme Arbitrator on all things pertaining to Zog.***
- ***That there shall be no pleasure in Zog unpaid for by the sweat of honest toil exacted by the Mistress.***
- ***That all items of clothing stuffed down the side of the bed, left wet in kit bags, dropped in the bath or sink or left on the living-room floor rightfully belong in the dirty clothes basket and shall be placed therein by the miscreant owner thereof on pain of the Wrath of the Mistress, who, in her view, does all the washing and most of the picking up after, augmented by her tears and lamentations.***

- *That all Happiness is hereby decreed an un-Zogly thing to be set aside by the Minions of Zog as of no account if it interferes with keeping a clean house, particularly the Creative's pipe-smoking, which renders everyone else in the household probably dead if so much as a sniff of a whiff of his smoke escapes the sordid surroundings of his lair, where the satellite TV is so he can watch his football matches in comfort.*

It is noteworthy that my dad has watched a lot more football matches since the Pipe Ban went on downstairs. We think it has more to do with wanting to smoke than watching football... *Supposedly* that is what he is doing. Mum says we are not to mention that the football season isn't properly under way yet, so there can't be that many matches to watch, can there?

In keeping with her *caring persuasion* line, the Mistress didn't impose the Pipe Ban. It was part of the Iron Will campaign he came up with after he found his stomach was burnt.

Dad had tests on his stomach because he couldn't eat his dinner properly and the hospital stuck lots of tubes down him, and then told Dad he was A1, but his stomach was raw, due to smoking too much. The Creative said he would invoke his Iron Will and cut down on the pipe and there is a packet count going on. The packets are laid in a pile in his lair and he counts them once a week and gets cross at failure, so he smokes some more. In my judgement this is a pathetic performance, and I have told him so.

Mum has told him she wants to save him for the Nation and more particularly for the love and companionship he will bring her as her Golden Years approach, but Dad says she is being sarcastic, and she shouldn't joke about it, because his dirty old pipe matters to him as an Artist.

I don't think there is much that is artistic about doing "Famous Foxy" cartoon scripts for satellite TV but it does bring home the bacon ... not, as Mum points out, that he can eat much of it because of the state of his stomach. What he does eat she has to crisp so much that it keeps setting the fire alarm off.

After the hospital's pronouncement Dad had a major, *major* sulk and a week when he didn't smoke at all, and then the Iron Will wilted, and he came up with the "well, I will only smoke in my work room upstairs" alternative which is where the situation stands at present.

Mum and Ob and I have decided to ignore the fact that the pipe which might have smouldered and killed us was found down the sofa in the front room ... which is not "my work room upstairs". Therefore, it appears that the Iron Will has wilted even further, and he is sneaking puffs out of bounds.

The whole thing has to do with whether he will be able to eat the Beef Wellington he drools over when Mum makes it at Christmas, which he won't be fit to do if he goes on smoking the way he is now, but maybe he thinks Christmas is still a long way away, so he can go on puffing for a while yet.

Later
Subject:

Concerning Secret Love Lists

There was some crisis next door at the Bluebottles'. Mum went in to mop up Mum Bluebottle's tears and blow her nose for her (which always takes a a long time) and as a result I got ringing Melissa to find out what she was ringing me about last night when Mum answered the call and told her not to keep phoning.

Melissa has suggested that we put our Love Lists in a Time Capsule and bury it in her garden and when we are old (thirty) we can come back and dig it up and look at our lists to see if we married any of the boys on them. I have amended this idea by stating that we should use two Time Capsules (one each) buried separately, for Security Reasons.

Melissa's recently amended Love List (No. 3) now reads as follows:

Melissa Adams' Secret Love List (No. 3)

1. *Arnold Potts*
2. *Rupert-Next-Door (if he turns out to be gorgeous)*
3. *A.N. Other*

We plan to put our Love Lists in separate sealed tins wrapped in tin foil so that they will be preserved for ever. We are still discussing where we will bury them. Her garden has dog poo in it sometimes and my garden has Creep and Ob, who cannot be trusted.

I would *die* if Ob found my Love List.

Ob has reported to me that the car with the double glazing stickers was outside the Bluebottles' house for two hours this morning. It drove off and just after that Mum dashed in to see Cynthia (Mum Bluebottle).

Ob suggests that Mum had to dash in when the Double Glazing Man had gone so

Cynthia Bluebottle could tell Mum about it. That sounds like Melissa and me and our Loves, but Mum Bluebottle is well past it and ought not to be having *amours*, though I didn't say so to Ob, who is not yet twelve so he does not fully understand these things.

Friday 7th August
Subject:

Heartless Boys

Went boy-spotting with Melissa in the park, as the Hare family (including Rupert) have not moved in next door to her yet.

Graham wouldn't let me ride his new bike. I asked him when I had my brace out and he said, "No way, Chickadee," and rode off with Scats round the tennis pavilion. He is cruel and he loves-me-not (yet) and is heartless, or else he loves another.

But it can't be Awful Alison Bartley, can it? She is always after him. I hate Alison Bartley. She started the *Fat Elephant* thing.

Melissa and I were at the Leisure Centre and we met Alison. We were having a sort of friendly conversation (as much as it could be with *her*, because we don't like *her*) about Sonja Banjerdee's Birthday Party. Sonja was boasting about it being a real big one in the Function Room at the Manor House Hotel, all Junior Tennis Club Members invited. (So it includes us but we are not certain if we are going to go.)

I had an ice-cream cone and I kind of waved it at Alison, and some of the ice-cream *accidentally* flew off and landed on her red "I'm a Dream Girl" T-shirt. It was an accident...Well, almost, though if anybody deserves to be ice-cream spattered it is A.B.

I said, "Oh, I am sorry, Alison," very politely because I am a polite person, and she said, "You *fat clumsy elephant*, Zoë!" very impolitely.

The next thing was that she jogged my elbow, sort of, and the ice-cream cone ended up stuck on my nose. Alison said the cone was my elephant trunk. Then Awful Alison went off with her friend Sneaky Sonja Banjerdee, and they were chanting a silly song they made up. It went:

Zoë the elephant packed her trunk
And ran away to the circus,
Off she went with a trumpety-trump,
Trump-trump-trump!

Nearly everybody was laughing at me, even Melissa, but it wasn't funny.

The only one who took my side was Hopeless Hobsbawn. "You are not an elephant, Zoë," he said. "Just sort of nice-big."

And he blinked at me fondly.

The trouble is, Hobsbawn doesn't count. He wears a sunhat and a big green jersey with a stupid dolphin on it that his mother knitted for him. His real name is Hubert Vincent Hobsbawn, after his grandfather, but his mum calls him "Hubie" and everyone knows Hubie is a baby-boy name. He should have left it in his pram. His mum still keeps his pram in the spare room with his cot but she hasn't had another baby, so she goes on about "Hubie is my baby still, aren't you, Hubie?" in front of people. I could never love a boy who has a pram and a cot and a sunhat and a Mum who calls him *Hubie.*

Later

Melissa reports there is no sighting yet of Rupert, though she has hung around hoping to see him. They had zebra striped sofas and chairs delivered from Rimmingtons, which is a cheapo shop. We don't know why they have zebra striped stuff from Rimmingtons if they are rich.

Melissa and I are agreed that zebra striped sofas and chairs are *not* sophisticated. Our mums would not have them in our houses.

*   *   *

Weighed self. 55.33 kgs, so no improvement so far, despite Banana Plan.

Saturday 8th August
Subject:

Kissing

"You could take your brace out for kissing, and then put it in again," Melissa suggested this morning when we were having a serious conversation at her house, relating in part to the long delayed arrival of Rupert-next-door-to-her, and whether he is a kisser or not. "You don't have to wear it all the time, do you?"

Even my Best Friend does not *understand*! The very existence of the brace is the problem. I know it should be in even when it isn't, so the only way I can get by is to smile without parting my lips so that nobody knows my brace is there.

"Like the Mona Lisa," I told Melissa. "Enigmatic. I will be a mystery woman. Dark Lady of the Sonnets, all that stuff. Graham D. will get interested and then when my brace comes off he can solve the mystery."

"Not if you keep on calling him Blind-as-a-Batbugs the way you did when he wouldn't let you ride his bike yesterday," Melissa said. I told her Graham was unpleasant to me and therefore I was annoyed with him and unpleasant back, which puts us even. Like Mum says, modern woman must not simply sit back and take it when chauvinistic males throw their weight about.

"Well, I don't think it was a good idea calling him Blind-as-a-Batbugs if he is supposed to be your One True Love, the way you are always saying he is!" she insisted.

I told her it was nowhere near as bad as being called a *Fat Clumsy Elephant* by people like Awful Alison but I conceded that maybe she was right and I won't do it again, unless he gets me mad by acting in an unfeeling and uncaring way as if I was just anyone, as he did yesterday. The truth is that Graham D. and I have that special *electricity* between us which leads us to extremes.

I tried to explain this emotional concept to Melissa, citing many lovers from History and the Arts, such as Cleopatra and Antony and Mr and Mrs Macbeth (which is what Dad calls them when he is in his "I-don't-approve-of-Kings-and-Queens" mode) but Melissa is too immature to understand this fully, given her limited experience of adult emotions. In the end we changed the subject by mutual consent, and went on to more interesting stuff.

"I don't think I will ever let anyone kiss me!" Melissa told me. "I couldn't. But then I am me and not you!"

"You will when you fall in love," I told her, and we discussed in principle who else she might fall in love with if Arnold doesn't love another. I have Graham booked, so he is out. Hobsbawn is a no-no. She doesn't like Scats and she has now agreed to take the new Rupert off her list, as even Melissa can scarcely love someone she has never met.

We sat in the garden for a long time to see if Rupert would turn up next door to look at their new fancy bath. Her niffy old dog was sniffing round us. Melissa's *maybe* new boyfriend Rupert didn't turn up, however, and they were supposed to move in this week, so something is wrong. Maybe they are regretting the fancy bath.

"Leaving Rupert out of it until you have at least *glimpsed* him, that means you are back to Arnold the Betrayer," I told her.

"I thought he was your Reserve Lover," Melissa said, although she knows full well that I binned the list Potts was on and wrote another with Graham D.'s name as my First Love instead of Arnold's after what Arnold did at tennis, since when I have not played tennis. (Don't like it anyway, because I wind up looking fat and puffy even when I win, which I usually do because I have practised a lot with my elder brother, Citizen Turtle, who played on the school team before he left for his holiday job in the Onion Fields of Amsterdam.)

"No way. Not any more," I told her. "You can have Arnold Potts if you want." I had told her this before of course. Sometimes Melissa repeats herself on emotional matters.

We left it that Melissa is considering Arnold for her First Love, at least until she has had a look at Rupert. She is welcome to Arnold. I think she fancies him rotten but is denying it to me because she fears my heart is still with Arnold, even though I have told her she can have him. Perhaps Melissa is still too immature to know what love is.

Later
Subject:

My Own True Love

Graham D. is my True Love, but he doesn't know because I am not telling him. I am keeping him in suspense. Melissa is probably right to say that I should never have called him Blind-as-a-Batbugs in the first place, because he can't help having no-good eyesight. Arnold Potts was my Love when I thought up the name Batbugs, otherwise I wouldn't have called Graham something silly like that, but I was *younger* in July and I thought it was funny *then*.

We were watching them play football and Graham can't see the ball and he kind of misses it and lets wonky goals in, which is difficult because he is a goalkeeper ... or was. He isn't now. He doesn't play football any more, because everyone laughed at him doing it. I have agreed with Melissa that football is nothing and doesn't matter, and personally I will never go near their football again now that Graham is not in the team.

I first knew that Graham was mine when he whacked Arnold 6-0,6-0,6-0, straight sets, the day after Arnold spurned me so hurtfully, which was the day the scales dropped from my eyes and I saw clear sightedly. Graham is able to wear his specs playing tennis, so he can see the ball. It was not Love on the Rebound, as Melissa alleges, because my love for Arnold Potts was a mere passing *infatuation*, which can happen easily when you are young adults, but Melissa does not fully appreciate what this means, never having experienced the Real Thing.

I think that Graham Denzil Batty (Graham's full name) is a beautiful name. When we have Plighted our Troth I will call him "Denzil" and then the old Blind Batbugs stuff I should never have called him will be forgotten for ever. Probably he will be a real tennis player on TV one day.

Personally, I think Denzil Batty is a brilliant name for a tennis player, and Melissa agrees. He has lovely eyes behind his glasses, which are the mirror of his meaningful soul, and he pines for me, but he is afraid to admit it to himself in case I would put him off his serve.

Melissa was trying to rationalize her fear of Love when she said she wouldn't let anyone kiss her till she grows up, but plainly Melissa is jealous because Graham D. fancies me and not her, only he is keeping me a secret from his heart.

I am stopping now, because writing about Love is even more tiring than other sorts of writing. I believe it is very important to be true to oneself about Love Matters, as no one else can ever know the secrets of one's heart but oneself and one's Loved One. In my case, *probably* Graham D. I fear now lest I have hurt my love with the Blind Batbugs stuff, but True Love is like that. There are always tiffs and then you make up and it is Love and kisses and stuff, so it should be all right.

Even later

I have to report that there are *no* new

developments on the Bluebottle front. Ob and I have not seen the double glazing car all day. Mum Bluebottle appears to have absented herself, taking Cyril with her for once, which is how I was able to have a long intelligent conversation on the telephone later with Melissa about the European Community and its effects on CD prices without having to look over my shoulder all the time to see if Cyril was bluebottle-eating again. Cyril ate some bluebottles once, that is how he got his name.

Cyril did it when he was four. Mum Bluebottle had hysterics and came hopping over our fence clutching Cyril and screaming. Mum had to drive Cyril and Cynthia (Mum Bluebottle) to the hospital to see if they could get the bluebottle out. They said they didn't do bluebottles (Mum knew they wouldn't but Cynthia was insistent) and it wound up with Mum Bluebottle accusing my mum of not being sympathetic, which was unreasonable, Mum being a Trained Professional Educational Psychologist (redundant) and therefore an experienced Sympathizer. It wasn't Mum's bluebottle Cyril swallowed, as Mum pointed out. But it didn't go down well ... the remark, not the bluebottle. The bluebottle went down *excellently* and stayed swallowed, but little Cyril survived. Little Cyril is like that. Things seem to bounce his way.

In our telephone conversation, Melissa and I agreed that I am burying *her* Secret Love List in *our* back garden, and she is burying *mine* in *hers*. So mine will risk the dog poo but at least it will be safe from Ob and Creep.

Melissa and I also agreed that CD prices are extortionate. She cares more than I do because she has her own CD player and I haven't. However, we were discussing CD prices because she knows I am planning to have one for my Sky Cabin, but Mum and the Creative remain unpersuaded and keep saying, "Wait until your birthday, Zoë," which is yonks away. It is not as if we were *very* poor, and Melissa and I regard a CD player as an essential of modern living.

Melissa has promised that if my mum asks her confidentially what I would like for my birthday she will say, "A new CD player like mine, because positively all the other people our age we know have one, and Zoë has not." We doubt if my mum will ask Melissa, but she might. Meanwhile we are both dropping hints ... and Mum ought to know already, because I have told her often enough, but no dice so far.

Sunday 9th August
Subject:

Appraisal of Sky Cabin Plan

I will have to sort out the Sky Cabin thing soon. I am the one who thought of it first. My Sky Cabin Plan for the roof space is an entirely reasonable Plan, and in keeping with the good ordinance of Zog as laid down by the Mistress thereof, only she doesn't see it that way. Mum is totally against the Sky Cabin Plan and Creep and Ob-Noxious are obstructive (because of Ob's pool table obsession and Creep wanting it for his toy railway) but I will not be denied by Zog's Minions. All I need is a skylight and some floorboards and a carpet and my own TV and a sign saying, SKY CABIN, KEEP OUT. And a bed, but I don't know how we can get a bed up the ladder and through the trapdoor, let alone Ob's pool table, which there isn't going to be. Or Creep's proposed model railway, either. So there!

I have inspected Melissa's proposed Den round their back (really Cromwell the dog's dog shed), where Melissa hopes that one day we can hide from the world and discuss Life and Love, but Melissa admits her mum and dad aren't budging, so my Sky Cabin is the only realistic hope we have. Also their back is a plumber's dump, though I did not say so to Melissa. There is just a patch of grass and the dog shed and a lot of old baths and cisterns left there by her dad the Plumber. Her Den is a nice idea (potentially) but it won't happen until poor old Cromwell dies and maybe not even then, although I have not said so to Melissa, to avoid hurting her feelings.

I am now hidden in my prospective Sky Cabin writing this by torchlight, as the Creative is going round scolding because he can't get his words right, and downstairs is no place to be. His tobacco has jammed up his PC keyboard again. Apparently all the keys work except the one with the *G* on it. He is demanding that Mum takes the Hoover to it and sucks the tobacco dust out of his machine. Mum says this is arrant male nonsense, and what does he think she is anyway, his slave? She relented later, and she is going to try using the pastry brush, and if that doesn't work his PC will have to go back to the shop to be fixed, so his work won't be finished and he will go mad.

Back to my Sky Cabin Plan, which is what I thought I was going to write this entry about, but it hasn't come out that way so far. I am the same at school. I do headings for my essay paragraphs but I can never stick to them. Miss Drover says it is a bad fault, and I must concentrate. I really, *really* like Miss Drover, because she lets me write about things that interest me and not just "What I Did on Holiday" and things like that.

Back to my Sky Cabin Plan (second time). I will work on Dad when he gets over his Crisis. I will *wile* him with my *guile*. If the Creative doesn't see it my way there will be no more helping out with the grass-cuttings, no way, José, and he can look for his pipes and glasses himself. I will ally myself with my one *good* and *worthy* brother, Citizen Turtle (aged eighteen), and I am sure we can do a deal – if and when the Turtle comes home from the Onion Fields of Amsterdam, where he is reportedly processing onions to augment the Year Out funds so grudgingly donated by Mum and the Creative. The absent Turtle is a co-operative elder brother, unlike the minuscule cretins Creep and Ob-Noxious, who are beneath my contempt.

And so I leave my Sky Cabin and descend the ladder to Zog, where I will sleep in my lonely cell, dreaming of the Love that One Day will be Mine (when I get my brace out).

And ... some way of getting my own back on Awful Alison B.

Later (afterthought written in bed)
Subject:

S. B.'s Party

There will be disco dancing and things at Sonja Banjerdee's Party (August 29th) and if Melissa and I decide not to go because we don't like Sonja and Alison, then Sonja and Alison will have Arnold and Graham all to themselves, but Melissa has not thought of this. It is a good thing that I did.

For that reason I think we should go.

I rang Melissa before I came up to bed to say this but her mum said Melissa was in the bath and then going to bed and really there was no need for all these phone calls when we live only one avenue away. Melissa's mum says she is going to have yet another word with my mum about it, but probably (hopefully) she will forget.

Melissa agrees with me that her mum can be most unreasonable sometimes, but her mum insists that they need the telephone line unengaged because of urgent calls for her dad the plumber. Melissa has tried to persuade them that they should install an exclusively plumbing-only line and her mum said she would like a shot if Melissa would pay for it out of her pocket money.

I suggested that Melissa's dad should get a fax like my dad's and then we could fax each other instead of phoning.

Forgot to weigh self. Don't suppose there is any improvement. Shape still same.

Monday 10th August
Subject:

Storms in Zog

Unwisely, having been dumped yet again with Cyril-sitting, I attempted to raise the Bluebottle problem with Dad, but he was most unsympathetic. I thought I was on a good number because Mum's pastry brush efforts on the PC had got it going. One problem solved, and he promptly came up with another.

The new grouse was that his Muse had deserted him. Apparently his Muse doesn't like waiting for his Editor to ring him, and his Editor hadn't yet rung and the Creative had been expecting a call for *three* whole days. He grumbled about Editors not realizing how sensitive Creatives are. Then his Editor rang, which should have made things all right, but his Muse didn't like what his Editor said to him and after that things got bang-around-the-house-slamming-doors worse.

Mum says it is like teething with a baby, except that my Creative Dad is too old to grow out of it.

I had a further Serious Conversation with Ob in the shed, on the Sky Cabin matter. Ob now indicates that he is prepared to deal but demands concessions. I have told him that I welcome his co-operation in principle, and I will consider the pool table matter he has raised, but he must acknowledge that Big Sister is running this show, not him.

"No way, Fatty!" Ob said, which was very hurtful. Gave him an ear wiggle and departed in wrath.

Nothing much else happened. Melissa stayed Rupert-waiting all day and I refused to go round and join her, as I think this Rupert stuff is stupid, though I refrained from telling her so, as she is supposed to be my Best Friend.

Weight same, allowing for the fact that I weighed earlier in day than before, and body gets lighter (I think) through day. Actual weight on Mum's scales 55.45, but must be wrong. Maybe scales have been adjusted, or moved on the carpet or something.

I *think* I *feel* trimmer since I went on my Banana Plan, but it is difficult to be certain.

Tuesday 11th August
Subject:

My Rotten Life

After what happened today I think I will give up doing this book. I will never be famous and I will always be *fat*.

Goodbye, Notebook.
Farewell for ever.

Zoë T. Curley

Wednesday 12th August

I have nothing to say.
I am giving up writing.

Zoë T. Curley

Thursday 13th August
Subject:

NOT Being Beaten

I am not giving up writing. Although I missed doing it yesterday (and the day before really) I have decided that I am taking up my pen again, despite the horrible thing that has happened to me, because that is what a True Artist must do even when her whole life is rotten and blasted and probably over, for ever.

I buried Melissa's Love List as promised but Melissa didn't bury mine. She left the tin my List was in on their kitchen windowsill and her mum looked inside and saw my Secret Love List. Her mum knows Graham D.'s mum from their Bridge Club so she will tell Graham's mum and Graham's mum will tell Graham and he will think I fancy him and he will tell everyone and they will all laugh at me.

I hate this. I hate having this happen to me. I am really, really hurt, and I am really, *really* upset with Melissa letting me down when she is supposed to be my Best Friend. Melissa has rung me six times today trying to apologize but I have refused to speak to her, and I have come in here to mind Cyril so that she cannot find me.

I am in the Bluebottles' house now, Bluebottle-minding, unpaid, *alone*, illegally (though Mum is next door if there is an emergency) with only little Cyril to talk to. I don't think I will ever go out and speak to anybody real ever again.

Friday 14th August
Subject:

Mum's Rotten Advice

Mum spotted that I wasn't going out of the house much so she tried to talk to me today, but of course it was useless. My life is like a beautiful butterfly broken on a wheel of adverse circumstance.

Mum does not know about my Secret Love List (No. 2). She thinks I am upset because people have been calling me fat, as usual. Bad news about bananas. She says bananas are almost as bad as sweets. She says I should be on apples, but even then she says she cannot guarantee weight loss will result, as puppy fat is "a stage you're going through, Zoë. It will not last." I am really, really *annoyed* with her, because I have been eating yonks of bananas, after she, herself, *in person*, advised me to. Well ...

she didn't say *not* bananas, and now I will be even fatter.

"OK, Zoë," Mum said. "Look, I know Life doesn't seem good to you right now. And I know you are fed up Cyril-minding. But none of this will last. It is only for a little while till Cynthia gets her personal life sorted."

I could have pointed out that Cynthia's "little while" is a long time in *my* life – looks like being the whole holidays. But I care not – I have nothing to live for but Art and Literature, so I will devote myself to those.

Weighed self. 55.85. Mum's advice rotten. Am giving up weighing self. It is how one feels that counts. Which doesn't help much when one feels *fat* and one is being called rotten stupid *Elephant* names by people who ought to know better. Putting me on to bananas when bananas only make you fatter was *gross*, and I will tell her so.

I think for someone who is a Trained Professional Educational Psychologist (Redundant because of the Cuts, now writing a book about it), Mum's performance as an adviser has been *inadequate* in this instance. If she cannot *helpfully* advise her own daughter when that daughter is going through a difficult and delicate period, then who can she advise?

Later
Subject:

Forgiveness

Melissa telephoned full of *abject* apologies, which I have accepted, as I am now sure she did not intend to betray my secrets, although as I pointed out that has been the *effect* of what she did.

Melissa has made her mum *swear* never, ever to tell anyone (particularly my mum or Graham's) that she read my Secret Love List. She says her mum swore and will stick to her word. She says her mum said something like "it was most amusing". It is not one bit amusing. It is the innermost core of my life exposed to an unfeeling world. Apparently, her mum told Melissa to tell me that she would never break her Vow of Silence on the subject. Melissa's mum is C. of E. so it should be OK, but I don't know how I will ever face her mum again.

It is *really, really* embarrassing.

Melissa has her own worry and I was a big enough person to acknowledge it, though my world is in ruins. She was so upset that I went round to her house (after I'd checked that her mum would be out, because I couldn't face her) and we sat and calmly and objectively discussed Melissa's problem, because I cannot withdraw entirely from Life.

Melissa was out in the garden moping when I arrived. She was in her new jeans and T-shirt, wearing the eyeshadow her mum is not supposed to know about, but she would have to be blind not to notice. It was kind of smeared, because of Melissa sitting out so long in the heat waiting for Rupert to appear and be agog at her beauty.

Melissa is upset because Sonja Banjerdee was seen with Arnold. At least she thinks Sonja was with Arnold, although they may just have happened to be in the same place, but they were only yards apart. Sonja had her so-called sexy jeans on, the ones with the gold buckled belt that Mrs C. Banjerdee brought her from Texas, which my mum says will damage her kidneys.

Melissa told me (somewhat tearfully) that she might not mind Arnold Potts betraying her with Sneaky Sonja if she had Rupert, but Rupert has still not arrived. I did my best to take this matter seriously, out of feeling for my friend, and because S. Banjerdee really is a problem. If she takes up with Arnold Potts and A. Alison gets my Graham, then we will be right out of it, and there will be no decent boys left, unless we share Rupert between us.

"There would be Hobsbawn, I suppose," Melissa pointed out.

Neither of us is keen on Hobsbawn.

Melissa has further reason to be upset because her parents are totally unreasonable. Her mum still refuses to toss Cromwell out of the dog shed so Melissa and I can have it as a Den from which we could observe Rupert. If he is in a Rock Band, Melissa thinks we could invite them to practise in Cromwell's dog shed, and then we would be an integral part of their rise to fame, like the Beatles' auntie was. (I think it was their auntie.)

I don't think Melissa's dad would let her have a Rock Band practising in their dog shed (even if he let her have it as a Den, which seems unlikely) and I told her so. I am not having them in my Sky Cabin because that is just for Melissa and me, no boys.

I have told Melissa that we should stick to the boys we know, at least until we see what Rupert is like, but Melissa remains unconvinced.

Later
Subject:

The Bluebottle Scandal

Ob reports a further development in the Scandal next door – Creep has been going round talking about what Cyril Bluebottle's dad said to him (Creep) when he was in the next door garden killing ants with Cyril.

Of course, we know it was not Cyril's dad who spoke to Creep. It was the Double Glazing Salesman. Mum Bluebottle is apparently misleading her small child into believing this Double Glazing Man is his dad. Ob and I are agreed that this is disgraceful behaviour on her part.

"You would think Creep would remember what Cyril's dad looked like," Ob observed, but I told him Cyril's dad left more than a year ago. Creep must have forgotten, and little Cyril is probably traumatized.

How are we to explain the delicacy of this matter to little Creep? We conferred on referring the matter to Mum, but decided not to in the circs, as we are not sure how much Mum knows and we do not want to tell tales on Mum Bluebottle, even if she is the sort of woman who lies to children, as well as being mean with the babysitting money.

"The man looked like Cyril's dad," Creep

kept insisting. "And Cyril called him Dad. So it was his dad, wasn't it? Must have been."

Ob and I are agreed that this is very sad. Poor little Cyril is missing a dad so much that he might call *anyone* Dad, but we don't think he has much hope of this new one moving in. Poor Cyril...

Ob and I will keep Creep away from playing next door, if we can, at least until the Bluebottle Scandal is over.

Saturday 15th August
Subject:

Life and Loves

Melissa came round this morning, very cross. Rupert-next-door has arrived. He is only *three years old*! Apparently the private school he will be going to is some playgroup. Melissa feels we have been wasting our time... Well, she has anyway.

Rupert's dad has pots of money and three cars and his mum is small and wears a bikini. She was out in the garden playing with Rupert when she should have been supervising the men putting the furniture in her new house, which Melissa and I agree is strange, but at least she seems to be a caring mum who puts her child first.

At least that is the end of the Rock Band problem, which was perplexing us. Obviously Melissa was misinformed on this matter. It appears the new people next door once lived in Trumpington, so she says her mum must have misheard. We don't know why Melissa's mum was so firm about there being no Rock Band in the shed when Melissa asked about it, if that is true. We didn't say it was going to be Rupert-next-door's Rock Band. She thought it was Melissa and me planning to start a Rock Band ourselves. That's *stupid* because we don't play anything now, though I got stage 3 in piano before I blackmailed the Creative into persuading Mum to let me give up, on the grounds of being tone deaf and not liking old Jo-anna the Piano-Teacher.

Afterwards Melissa and I went out looking for boys, and a *horrible* thing happened.

First, Graham D. rode past Melissa and me on his bike without saying anything, which anyone would think was bad enough.

"He is just pretending not to see you!" Melissa said, trying to console me.

Graham was with Ivor Magella and Hobsbawn. They went down to the Common to play football, despite all the talk about Graham not playing football any more because he can't see. Arnold was there too, so Melissa thought we should walk past the pitch casually and we did. And we got their football, and we wouldn't give it to Hobsbawn when he ran up panting and asking for it.

"Give it back!" Arnold shouted.

"No way!" Melissa said.

"Pair of fat bags!" Graham yelled. "Give us our ball."

And Melissa did.

I was really upset.

"*You* are not fat so he must have meant *me*," I told Melissa.

"He was just shouting for something to say," Melissa said. "He didn't mean anybody specifically. He only shouted it because he didn't want to look soft in front of Pottsy. And he hadn't his glasses on because of playing football, so he probably couldn't see it was you. You know he can't see much without his glasses."

"We should chuck them in!" I told her, because I was feeling huffy all of a sudden, but we are not agreed. Melissa isn't fat. She is a thin little thing, so she wasn't hurt. And Arnold is not really her Heart's Desire, so she does not know how I feel.

I feel my world is at an end.

Later

Melissa went to the cinema at the Centre without me because I didn't feel like going. I am depressed about my Love Life and my brace and being fat. I will never go anywhere again.

Awful Alison was at the cinema but she didn't speak to Melissa. Alison Bartley is a thin, bony, knock-kneed *frimp*. (I made that word up. It is a good one. It describes her perfectly.)

Melissa reports that Graham was there, though this is of only marginal interest to me now. He was two rows back from Alison, who spent the whole time trying to attract his attention by squeaking with excitement. Arnold Potts and Scats were there too. Scats threw peanuts at Melissa and said rude things. Melissa told him where to go. She says Ivor Magella was asking after me, but I do not think I believe her, though I cannot see why my Best Friend would make up a thing like that, when she knows I care not for Ivor, but for Another. She says Graham D. heard Ivor asking, so that will make Graham D. jealous. It might do some good.

If she thinks having spotty Ivor Magella asking after me would in *any way whatsoever* make up for the bruising of my heart by Graham's cruel and casual words, then she has another thing coming. I am Inconsolable.

Alison is going round telling everyone that nobody fancies me because of my brace and being fattish, but this is not true. I had lots more boys than she did before I got my brace. Ivor counts now, because he was asking after me. And Arnold is my ex-but-one. The other one was Kirk Hamsted, but he was a mere flirtation on a summer's weekend. He borrowed Ob's skates and bust them. Arnold had my heart but he betrayed me. He took scummy old Alison in the tennis doubles practice instead of me when I was there and ready to play and everything. Mr Wapes, who coaches us, said to pick a partner and he picked Alison and she has thin little knees and no forehand, let alone a backhand. I can follow through and spin serve.

I am thinking of giving up tennis, but I will have to play in the Junior Tournament at school in September because Mum is expecting me to. I *like* tennis because I am quite good at it but I don't like people calling me names. Alison and Sonja are always doing that. They won't let me alone to play. I reckon I am better than them and so does Mr Wapes. I kind of grunt when I hit the ball hard. Melissa says everybody grunts but I think not as much as me.

Alison is an *awful,* thin, ginger-haired bat

with a sticky-out nose and she will be like that for ever. If I don't lose what Mum calls my "puppy fat" I will wait until I am rich and go to a Health Farm and melt it off, but she can't melt off her old prong nose, can she? No one could get past it to kiss her. On the other hand she doesn't have to wear a brace, but nobody would *want* to kiss her, so there!

Her ears are small too, and her mum let her have them pierced and the man didn't do it right and she almost got gangrene or something. She wears a little pearl in one because she thinks it makes her look good, but it doesn't. I call it Alison's Extra Ear Pimple.

Sunday 16th August a.m.
Subject:

Betrayal

Ob reports that this morning when he went on the bike for the Creative's paper he saw A. Alison with Graham in the park.

She was trying the gears on *his* bike.

On Graham's *new* bike, that he wouldn't let me on.

Graham D. is a Betrayer just like the rest.

My soul is in torment. I am giving consideration to being a nun but the Creative has suggested that there might be a problem there as I am not a Catholic or an Anglican but an agnostic. There must be agnostic nuns somewhere. Maybe I will be the first one.

I have discussed this with Melissa on the telephone. We could be the first two agnostic nuns, except that Melissa is C. of E., like her mum. We could give up boys and hie us to a nunnery like the Lady of Shalott. She floated about in a boat with onions. Maybe eating too many onions made her fat, and that is why she became a nun.

How will I face A. Alison, when she knows she has outwooed me?

There remains the possibility that Ob is making this up, for his own nefarious reasons, to put me off my stroke in the Sky Cabin negotiations. That would be an Ob-like manoeuvre. Ob is not to be trusted.

I *might* take my brace out and casually ask Graham D. if he has done any cycling lately, just to test it out, but I don't think it would do any good.

Later, p.m.
Subject:

Revenge of the Fish!

A fresh Crisis has arisen in Zog. The prospect of a Broken Home looms over us.

His PC being kaput (yet again) and his script deadline being in peril, my dad the Creative said some filthy words and vamoosed from his lair, taking Creep and little Cyril Bluebottle fishing ... which isn't fair because Ob was looking after Cyril, and Ob hasn't done any Cyril-minding for ages, and when he does Dad suddenly takes over.

Mum was in a foul mood when Dad marched off, and did not sympathize with me when I protested. That is because Dad had left her to fix *his* PC problem as usual. She has been doing a word processing course because someone had to, since we got the new system. He maintains that it is not his job to fix machines, ever. She is the PA and it is up to her to do it. Really it is because he loses his temper and shouts and bangs his fist on his work table, and PCs don't like that. His PC is a computer of character. I have every sympathy for it. Mum talks to it nicely in its own language and the PC works for *her*.

Creep fell in the river on the journey to where Dad fishes. The Creative dived in and heroically grabbed Creep from what Creep maintains was a deep bit, although no one believes him because there isn't one, just some mud holes.

While this was going on, little Cyril Bluebottle panicked and ran up and down the bank waving Dad's fishing net till some people came and helped them out. Dad would have got out anyway easily enough, but he does admit that little Cyril's presence *helped*, because people respond to small children in distress more than they do to damp authors being cross with their sons.

Fishing was cancelled forthwith.

"Serve you right for setting out to kill poor innocent fish!" I told Dad at the Inquest Into Events, back in Zog. Fish have feelings just like anyone else.

When Mum saw her carpet she said she would report Dad to Greenpeace for polluting her environment. That was because Dad set Creep down on the sofa when he came in. There was oil and gungy brown muck on Creep's jeans, so we now have an oiled and gungy sofa, and an oiled and gungy carpet and Mum can't shift it, so naturally she was mad and started on him.

"You forget I *am* Mr Greenpeace round here!" Dad said, in Lord-of-Zog fashion.

"Oh yes?" she said. "When did you last send them a sub?"

"I don't do the subs!" he said. "You do!"

"That makes *me* Mrs Greenpeace, so I am reporting you to me!" Mum said, joyfully.

The best bit is that Creep is in trouble and it is the End of Fishing so all the fish will be saved. Mum has so decreed. It is the Word of the Mistress of Zog. So I won't have to stick any more DOWN WITH BLOODSPORTS notices on Dad's fishing bag.

Later still
Subject:

Mum Bluebottle Strikes!

On returning from what Ob and I suspect was a further romantic engagement with her Double Glazing Man, Mum Bluebottle came over the fence in a puff of Bluebottle smoke complaining about her little Cyril being taken to dangerous places without parental consent. Dad's story was that Cyril maintained that he *had* asked for Senior Bluebottle permission and been granted it, although it is now clear that he *hadn't*.

"Are you calling my son a liar?" Cyril Bluebottle's mum asked, breathing fire.

Mum Bluebottle looked as if she was going to hit my dad with the rake, which would have been good because Dad calls himself a Theoretical Pacifist and we would have liked to see the theory tested. Dad stuttered a bit and took a tack about not wrapping children in cotton wool when the whole world is a dangerous place, but this didn't work. Cynthia went Bluebottle bananas and Mum had to intervene so she wouldn't have a pronged husband as well as a wet one.

Mum says we are to be extra polite and careful with the Wrights (that's Cyril Bluebottle's family name) till it blows over. She sent Ob round with a box of chocolates for Cyril. (She got them out of a cupboard where she hid them after Creep was sick all over the rug last Boxing Day.)

Mr Greenpeace, the Fish-Killer Pacifist (saved by his wife from being a perforated one), has gone into one of his sulks upstairs in his room.

Mum made him a cup of tea but he wouldn't come down.

Little Cyril Bluebottle has got rabies or something. Mrs Cynthia Bluebottle maintains Cyril got it from the river when he was saving Dad. She is threatening to sue. She says Dad can expect to hear from her solicitor.

Cyril was never in the river. Dad was, and he hasn't got rabies. Foaming at the mouth just comes naturally. He says if Mum Bluebottle goes round the town shouting off her mouth about him putting her little Cyril in danger of his life she will be hearing from *his* solicitor about Defamation of Character, because he has his Reputation as a Famous Writer to protect. He says Mum Bluebottle is a *jawbox*, but if she so much as breathes a word against him, his solicitor will have her for all she has got.

"You haven't got a solicitor, have you?" Mum asked innocently.

Dad went dignified and told her he had to have one when he was registering his book for Public Lending Right. It was done that way years ago, and you had to swear an Oath in front of a Commissioner for Oaths, and his C. of O. was a solicitor.

"So how come we never got any money out of it?" Mum said. "I bet you had to pay to have it registered, because solicitors do nothing for free, do they?" She knows and we know why. Public Lending Right is paid when somebody borrows a writer's book from a Public Library, and nobody ever borrowed his book. That is why it was his *only* book. If he had made lots of money he would still be writing books, instead of writing cartoon scripts for TV and faxing them to Newark, New Jersey, which is where the animation is done these days. He's been working on "Famous Foxy" and he has all these *disgusting* mutant toys in his room. The cartoons are only on satellite so Mum charges his satellite TV to business expenses, but really he has it for watching the football.

"If you wanted lots of money you should have married somebody else!" the Creative told her.

"Money Can't Buy Me Love!" she sang at him, pretending to be a Beatle, and she hugged him, so I suppose the Divorce is off.

Monday 17th August
Subject:

Developments

I rang Melissa this morning before breakfast to see if she had got her invitation to Sonja Banjerdee's Party but she hadn't. I haven't got mine either. We think we should have had our invitations by now. Maybe Awful Alison and Sneaky Sonja have ordered Mrs Banjerdee not to invite us because we are their Rivals in Love, which would be unfair, because we are Tennis Club Juniors and we go to the same school and everybody will be there but us. Christobel got hers and so did Lucy and Ivor Magella and *everyone* and that lot live right the other end of town, not just down the road from the Banjerdee's posh house, like us.

* * *

Dad has had an altercation with Mum over the allegedly possible drowning of Cyril Bluebottle while he was in the Creative's care.

"You are a hypocrite!" Dad told her when she was going on about how upset Cynthia-next-door was. "You know that child is a liar. I can't stand deception in a child. It says something about the lone parent-next-door. My children have been brought up to seek the Truth, and you are undermining one of the most important lessons in life we can teach them. It is a matter of principle. So much for your *professional* ethics."

Then the Mistress of Zog said something very un-Mum like to the Master of Zog and the Master stomped off up the stairs to his lair.

I told Melissa about this on the telephone later. Melissa told me not to worry: many parents are like that, and I told her I was not worrying. She is a good friend.

The Creative still wouldn't come downstairs even when Mum relented and made him tea and those little round chocolate biscuits, which usually does for his principled sulks, but it didn't work this time. I seized on this as an opportunity to start on the Sky Cabin deal. I took the cup and biscuits up to him, wearing my sympathetic and understanding smile.

He was very grumpy, but he knew he was

in everybody's bad books so he was more forthcoming than usual. It was all "maybe if we had the money some day we could open the roofspace up, I suppose" stuff, but I am working on it. I got him as far as saying, "Look, Zoë, if Ike Walensky pulls the Toons Contract for me in the States I'll look at it, really I will."

I don't know what the Toons contract is, but Ike Walensky is the Agent who lives off Dad's money and only sends Dad a fraction of what Dad really earns. According to Dad. "If it wasn't for poor Ike sweating blood in your cause, you'd all be living on my redundancy money," Mum says, and I don't know who is right.

Ike sends me a card with BIRTHDAY WISHES FROM TALENT ASSOCIATES on it every year on my birthday. We think he has got my birthday mixed up with Dad's, some way. It is not much use as a birthday card because there are no tokens in it and no money. Dad says agents never give away their own money, just other people's. Sounds like the same principle as Mum Bluebottle-next-door, though she never, ever gives me any, despite all my Cyril Bluebottle-sitting.

Returning to serious matters about Zog and my Sky Cabin: I am treating this as a positive contractual commitment, which Dad will not be able to go back on now he has said it.

Meanwhile, Melissa is working on her dad and mum too, with a view to having their shed as her *petit château*, same principle as me, only I thought of it first. It is a sort of race, but I bet I get mine before she does. All Melissa's dog shed needs is a new roof and a stove and a new door and electricity. Her dad is a plumber so none of that should be any problem, but he keeps their moth-eaten old dog in it. People were coming round the back of Melissa's house and pinching old baths and lavatory cisterns before Cromwell (Melissa's old dog) came. The back of their house is a Dump because of her dad's old stuff and Melissa has told him so, but he doesn't listen ... though Melissa reports that the new Mr Hare-next-door was seen looking over the fence at their garden and the old baths in it, so we think he will complain. That will get Melissa's dad mad.

It turns out that the Hares-next-door-to-Melissa are interesting, even if Rupert is not. Dad Hare is very young and smart-looking and smokes what Melissa's dad thinks is pot and has four sports cars parked outside in the street. What Melissa's dad calls the "Motor Show" obstructed his plumbing lorry when it came to dump more stuff in

Melissa's so-called back garden, and Melissa's dad was furious. He went to talk to Mrs Hare about moving the cars, but he came back cooing.

This is because Mum Hare walks around the garden with almost no clothes on, just a halter and teeny-tiny-teeny red silk short shorts and bare feet with her toenails painted green. And she was smoking too, but Melissa's dad didn't think it was pot. He said she was a *most charming* young woman which put Melissa's mum in a sour mood, though she got over it later.

Apparently, Mrs Hare subsequently won Melissa's mum round by entering into negotiations with her about possible *paid* babysitting employing Melissa, with Rupert coming to Melissa's house and Melissa doing the same as me (but she will get paid *yonks* of dough), with Melissa's mum as back-up if the cops come about illegal under-age child-minding.

Melissa is crowing about this, of course, and talking about buying tons of CDs for her player. I really must tackle the free-Bluebottle-sitting service with Mum. (Telling Dad has got me nowhere.) If I am going to break the law and babysit when I am supposedly too young to take the responsibility, I want to be *paid* for it. I don't see why Melissa should be a paid babysitter when I am not.

The big, *big*, BIG exciting headline news is that the new Mrs Hare is a Professional Model and she needs Rupert-sitting when she is off on jobs. Melissa and I are most impressed. So is Melissa's dad, apparently, but for different reasons. Melissa's dad made some joke to Melissa's mum about Mrs Hare and Melissa's mum went red and said, "Oh, Ralph! Not in front of Melissa!"

(Melissa's dad's name is Ralph.)

Melissa didn't hear what the joke was, but she thinks it was a rude one. Her dad is suddenly spending a lot of time counting all the old broken cisterns and stuff in his garden while Mrs H. is sunbathing in almost her birthday suit ... with no clothes on, that means.

Melissa's mum has promised him binoculars for Christmas so he can do his *bird-watching* over the fence without being so obvious about it. Melissa's mum said that to Melissa's dad, not Melissa, and it was a kind of a joke, but of course Melissa understood it immediately.

"If the lady next door doesn't want to be looked at she should put some clothes on!" Melissa's dad told her mum, and they both laughed.

Melissa has promised to show Mrs Hare round the town and I am going with them.

We are waiting to see whether she will have clothes on or not. We expect they will be lovely clothes if she is a model.

Later
Subject:

Double Glazing, Stop Press Bulletin

Mum to Dad (*within my hearing, but without their knowledge of my presence*): Did you see his double glazing van was parked there again last night? Outside next door?
Dad to Mum: Well, I'll be…
Mum to Dad: It would be marvellous if it works out, wouldn't it?
Dad to Mum: Bloody miraculous!
Mum to Dad: Cyril needs a father.
Dad to Mum (*v. sourly*): Cyril needs a kick up the backside if you ask me!
Mum to Dad: Don't be like that!
Dad to Mum: It seems to me our family life revolves round looking after Cyril while his mum is out courting her reborn Double Glazer! Just ask Zoë!

At which point they spotted me, and clammed up.

Much later

Mum has just explained what is going on next door. It is a bitter disappointment: Apparently what Ob and I thought was Mum Bluebottle's new lover is only rotten old Dad Bluebottle come back. He has re-invented himself as a Double Glazing Man and now plans to move back in with Cynthia and give their love a Second Chance. So Cyril will have a daddy after all. It appears that Mum Bluebottle has said yes she will have him back.

"Creep had it right after all!" Ob remarked to me.

I bet I still get stuck with minding Cyril, though. I bet they go off on a second honeymoon and I will get stuck with him all day, every day, for ever.

"So that is what all the to-ing and fro-ing has been about," Mum said.

"Maybe it will put her in a better temper and she won't keep persecuting Dad over Cyril nearly being drowned," I said, making the best of it.

Mum just laughed.

Tuesday 18th August
Subject:

Concerning Malicious Untruths and Brothers

I now have it on Good Authority that A. Bartley and S. Banjerdee were all morning on the Lions' Club beach clean-up on Sunday and therefore that Ob's observation of A. Bartley riding Graham's bike in the park when Ob was getting the Sunday paper for the Creative is all lies.

Thus Ob has yet again breached the Family Trust which is the ground rule of Zog, as expounded by the Master thereof. I am therefore quite within my rights to treat him as outside the Law.

I told Bouncer Higgs that Ob didn't think he could be *bothered* playing in their next match because he thinks the Man. U Red Devils (which is their park team) are crap and Bouncer is crap and so is Bouncer's dad, who runs it, and says he played for Bradford City Juniors once. (He is a little hairy man.) We don't think he did and anyway Ob says Bradford City are hopeless Div. 2 and no good.

"Tell him my dad was never going to pick him again after the last time!" Bouncer said, and he bounced off to tell all his little mates, and his fat dad.

I have met treachery with treachery. No one has the right to mess up my Love Life with Graham.

I await results with Zog-like aplomb.

Wednesday 19th August
Subject:

Our Boy-Deal

Mrs Hare the Professional Model pulled out of being taken round the shops by Melissa and myself, so we went swimming instead. We will take her shopping next week and show her the sights. I saw her and she had quite a few clothes on and wasn't smoking pot or anything else, so I think Melissa is making it up for dramatic effect, following her disappointment over Rupert, though Mrs Hare was certainly very model-looking in her tight pants and flared top.

When we know her better, Melissa and I are going to ask her advice on how young girls become Top Models. Won't be much use if I go on being fat the way I am. I have weighed myself three times since the Banana Plan backfired and I haven't taken any weight off, although I haven't touched a single banana.

* * *

Melissa and I walked past Graham D.'s house on our way to the pool. Melissa said we might spy on Graham D. in his garden so we went the long way round. Melissa had some eye-shadow. We put it on standing in the hedge so no one would see us doing it.

Graham D.'s mum was in the garden. She had a green jungle hat on and she was talking to a woman and waving a lobster. At least it looked like a lobster. She saw us when Graham's dog Merson barked. I don't know why he barked. We were not doing anything dog-objectionable whatsoever, to my mind or Melissa's.

Graham's mum said "Hi!" and I heard her telling the woman she was with that we were two of Graham's "little friends" from the Tennis Club.

The Battys must be very rich. They have a double garage.

The Big News today is that Melissa has finally and conclusively decided that she absolutely *does* fancy Arnold more than any of the other boys. She has told me so, and we have firmed up our Boy-deal.

"You help me get Pottsy and I will help you cut out Alison," Melissa said and that is our Boy-deal. She will talk to Graham for me (because of my brace) and I will tell Arnold that Melissa is a Krazy Kisser and stuff like that to get him interested.

Melissa thinks Alison is after Graham D. *and* Arnold. Alison is sex mad, which is odd for someone who wears little white ankle socks with bunny rabbits on them. We are Women of the World and she is a mere child when it comes to men.

Later
Subject:

Sky Cabin Plan Progress Report

My perfidious brother Ob claims he has broached the subject of the Cabin in the Sky. (Pool-Table-version ... I will have the pool table removed or neutralized when my Plan is realized.) He tried it on Dad, and Ob reports that it was not turned down out of hand. Ob took the line that Dad himself might like to play pool on the *putative* table, which is contrary to my line, as it would introduce parents, pool table and the filthy pipe to my sanctum, three things devoutly to be avoided. Nonetheless, I feel Ob's intervention could be helpful if properly controlled. Dad was in a looking-for-pipe-storm at the time, so he may not have heard Ob properly.

"Still, we're making progress," Ob told me.

"The Sky Cabin is my idea!" I said. "Keep

your nose out."

"You need me, or it will never succeed," Ob said. I gave him my ear wiggle. I have never heard of a Top Catwalk Model wiggling her ears. Maybe some of them could when they were young and gave it up later.

I will try not to wiggle my ears while we discuss our future modelling career prospects with Mrs Hare when we take her round the shops. She might know someone who could put us in touch with an agency and then we would be snapped up and before anyone knew it we would be on billboards all over the world.

That would show Awful Alison and Sneaky Sonja who is Big Cheese and who is not.

Thursday 20th August

I *hate* A. Bartley and S. Banjerdee. What they have done is mean and unfair and nasty and designed to show me up in front of my mum and dad and everyone I know, and there is nothing I can do about it, because Mum has already seen it.

We were having breakfast yesterday and the post came and there was a letter in it for me, second-class post, and I opened it in front of Mum and that is how she saw it.

This is my *rotten, stupid* invitation to S. Banjerdee's *rotten, stupid* party, with what they wrote on it.

> *Mrs Crystal Banjerdee is*
> *delighted to invite*
>
> Fat Elephant
> ~~*Zoë Curley*~~
>
> *to SONJA BANJERDEE'S*
> *BIRTHDAY PARTY*
> *at the Richmond Function Room*
> *Manor House Hotel*
> *Saturday, August 29th, at 7.30 p.m.* *R.S.V.P.*

It will be a rotten stinking show-off Birthday Party at the Manor House Hotel, which her *stupid* old show-off mum has hired because she wants to show everybody that the Banjerdees have more money than anyone else round here. It will be a *rotten, stupid* disco with snacks and Melissa and I were not going to go but now it looks as if I will have to go to the *rotten, stupid* thing, because this has happened. It is all down to Awful Alison because she must have got Sneaky Sonja Banjerdee to let her fiddle with the *rotten, stupid* invitation. She knew my mum would see it. She knew what would happen. She wanted it to happen, so I would be embarrassed in front of my mum.

I opened my invitation in front of Mum and Mum saw it and there was nothing I could do.

"Fat Elephant?" she said. "Oh, Zoë!"

"It's her nickname," Ob butted in. "*Everybody* calls her Fat Elephant, because she is one."

So I went off upstairs to my Sky Cabin.

It is bad enough having a *rotten, stupid* brace without being called Zoë *Fat Elephant.*

Mum came up after me about twenty minutes later. Usually, she just shouts up, but this time she climbed the ladder and put her head and shoulders through the trapdoor.

"Zoë-Zog?" she said. "Are you all right?"

"I'm quite all right," I said, coolly and calmly. "Why wouldn't I be?"

"Look at me," she said.

So I raised my head and looked at her.

"Zoë?" she climbed into the roof space on her knees, and then she stood up and came over to me. I was on my cushion, in front of the water tank, where I do my writing.

"Hi," I said. "Welcome to my Sky Cabin to-be."

"You don't have to pretend to me, Zoë," she said.

I didn't say anything.

"There isn't a lot I can do," Mum said.

"If you wanted me to I would speak to Mrs Banjerdee, but I don't think that would do much good, do you? Parents interfering always washes back on the kid concerned."

I shook my head.

Mum hugged me.

"Just have a good cry," she said. "If you want to, that is. That will get it out of you." Then she stood back and said, "It isn't true, you know. You are a fine big girl and you are going to be a real wow with the boys when you are a bit more grown up. You wait and see."

"I'll *always* be *Fat Elephant* now," I said bitterly.

"Yes, well, you're not," she said firmly. "Not in this house, you're not. And I have told Colin (that's Ob-Noxious) that he is never, ever to call you that again. And Taylor (that's Creep) too. You are *not* fat and I will not have people in this house going round making jokes about it when they know you are sensitive on the subject."

"I *am* fat," I told her. "I am *rotten, stupid* fat. You are only saying I'm not. If I wasn't fat I wouldn't be sensitive about it, would I?"

"Oh, Zoë, you're *not*. You must know you're not. Look around you at *really* fat people. People with gland trouble and stuff like that..." Mum said, but it tailed off.

"I *am* fat *and* I have to wear a brace on my

teeth," I said, straight out, daring her to contradict me.

She went on a bit about it, but she didn't help. And now everyone knows. Mum and Dad will be having conferences about me, and Creep and Ob will tell all their sneaky little friends and I will never, ever live it down, not in a hundred thousand years – if I live that long. I will be Zoë *Fat Elephant* for ever.

Mum said she would try to sort a diet out for me, if I liked, although it really wasn't necessary, but if it would make me feel better she would do it.

I told her, "No."

Awful Alison and Sneaky Sonja would find out about it and they would go round all their stinky *rotten, stupid* little friends and make more jokes about me and I would have to live with all that every day.

I don't think I will write any more in this Zog Book. Nothing is happening in my life that I want to write about.

Friday 21st August
Subject:

Me

Hello, Book. This is me, Zoë, back!

I am not letting them get to me, no way, because that would mean they win.

I am going to Sneaky Sonja's Party with my head up and I will show them that I don't care what they call me because I know I am all right inside, even if I am fat and I have a brace on my teeth.

The Creative is right.

He said that this is what I must do so I am doing it, but not because he says so. I am doing it because I am a mature person who can laugh off stupid childish stuff. So I will go to the party and they will all see I am above their little game and the laugh will be on them, not me.

Mum and Dad are being good about it. They took counsel with me and as a result haven't said a word to Mrs Banjerdee or her sneaky awful daughter, because, like Mum says, they know that would do no good.

Mum is taking me out for some new trainers and we will get the new Sponbloom Super Trainers that are on TV, which are probably the best trainers ever made. And I am not giving up tennis either, because that would just suit them. So I am going to be back in there fighting my corner and Sneaky Sonja and her Awful friend Alison can call me any names they like and I will show them I don't care.

The Good News is that Mum and Dad have had a conference and they are making enquiries, through a builder they know, about how much it *might* cost *if* we did it and there is a real serious *possible, maybe, probable, possible* possibility that I will get my Sky Cabin after all. (If Dad's Ike Walensky can pull it off, and Dad gets some money. No contract, no Sky Cabin is the deal.)

That is the Good News. The Bad News is that Dad *must* have been listening to Ob because he says I could not have absolutely exclusive use of the whole roof space *if* ... IF ... they do go ahead and get a skylight put in and a floor and a spiral staircase, because they have to think of Ob as well.

Ob needs a space of his own too, because Creep keeps interfering with things Ob is trying to do, like his modelling kits. But the pool table is O-U-T and Ob has agreed to that, because if they spend the money on having the roof done they wouldn't have enough money to spare to buy pool tables even if they wrote off our Christmases and birthdays.

Anyway, there wouldn't be room up there for the cues. Ob maintained that there would be room and Dad had to take him up into the roof space with a stick to act as a cue. Dad showed Ob, finally and conclusively, that there wouldn't be room, because you need the width of the table plus full cueing length either side.

In my view, Ob nearly imperilled the whole Sky Cabin negotiation, just when I had almost pulled it off, by his last stand on the pool table issue; Ob is stubborn and lacks the maturity and composure necessary when top level discussions are hammering out the fine print.

Dad has promised (creative work progress permitting) to take Ob to the Amusements once a week and play pool with him. Ob says it won't last. Probably Dad will wind up paying for Ob and his little football mates to go a few times, though I am sure Dad means to do what he says now but he gets excited about what he is working on and forgets sometimes.

Ob is glum about the failure (relative) of his pool table plan but I have told him that I have had to give up *my exclusivity* and he has had to give up *his pool table*, so we are quits. The Big Deal is that we will both have the Sky Cabin (if Dad's Ike Walensky comes up with the American cartoon dough). So we should settle for that.

I told Melissa and she was green with envy.

It is a *reasonable* deal. I have to give a bit if I am going to make any gain, which having my Sky Cabin would be. Only I don't know if they will do it yet. Mum is still wavering slightly, as she isn't sure how much the skylight would cost and what other complications there would be, but Dad insists they are *earnestly pursuing* the matter with the builder and will report progress back to Ob and me when there are developments.

What all that means is that *she* is finding out about estimates and stuff from builders. They do the deciding together, but she gets all the dirty work like ringing up builders and roofmen and electricians and painters and stuff when they need something done. And when the builders and people don't come, and he grumbles about his Creative Mood being disturbed by upset in the house ... but she is the one who finds them and *he* is the one who expects people to praise him for his nice house.

Mum says Life is like that. She would be a feminist but she is too busy baby-minding Dad to bother. She says she is a soft number. Their marriage is founded on him doing most of the talking and her doing everything else almost, if you ask me. He says that is because he is kept so busy being a Creative ... which is a brilliant excuse for anything if you ask me and one of the reasons why I am going to be a Writer.

I am resuming Life, after spending all day yesterday inside and not even going to the telephone when Melissa rang.

This morning I am going to ring her and say we should go on a Boy-hunt this afternoon on our bikes. We will go where Graham D. goes with Arnold and we will let everyone see that I don't care what names people call me.

Later
Subject:

Annoyances

I am really annoyed.

Oh woe, woe, woe!

I have had to ring Melissa and tell her I can't go out on our Boy-hunt this afternoon. I had forgotten my Honorary Auntie Thelma's summer visitation was due and now Mum has spoiled everything by announcing that the big day is tomorrow so all my plans are bust and my Life is laid waste. The Mistress of Zog has decreed that I have to tidy up my room and me, in that order, and we will go for the trainers the day after tomorrow. I had nicked some of her eye-shadow too. It is green so it goes with my Greenpeace personality. Melissa's mum's was blue. I feel I am a green person, not a blue.

This means that Alison Bartley and Sneaky Sonja will see Graham D. and Arnold because they will be out and we won't. Melissa won't go down to the park without me because she might meet Arnold and not know what to say.

There would have been a time for such a thing,
tomorrow and tomorrow and tomorrow...

as William Shakespeare puts it, but Mum says I must do it this p.m., because there may not be another time pre-Auntie, and she needs me as emergency standby back-up for cleaning the house.

Even the Creative gets roped in when *Thelma* is about to descend.

The Creative was seen to quiver at the news of her imminent arrival, and is rumoured to be considering being busy meeting a deadline. He won't get away with it. No one does when Thelma comes. We all have to be on duty, and take the abuse she delivers, and all because she was *so good* to

Mum when Mum was a baby.

Later, by torchlight in my Sky Cabin to-be
Subject:

What My Auntie Thelma Has Done to Me, and Other Musings

I am called "Thelma" after Auntie Taylor, which just goes to show the baleful influence she has had on my life. No one with a good name like Zoë should have a Thelma tacked on to it. I have disowned it, but it is on my exam passes and things. When I am famous my writing name will be Zoë T. Curley, cunningly disguising the awful truth. I will tell people that "T" stands for Titania or Toyah or something exotic, not rock-bottom old Thelma, which destroys my street cred. Even Melissa admits it.

Enough. I am going to bed in my cell down below, laughingly called a bedroom. They don't mind me staying up here during the day but Dad says they don't want me sleeping in the roof space before it is properly converted because of the fire risk. I don't see what fire risk there is, as I am not an addicted pipe smoker like some people I could name.

Saturday 22nd August a.m., pre-Auntie Visit (due at 2 p.m.)
Subject:

Matters Domestic

Dad's dive in the river put oil and gunge on the sofa but also on the carpet, although Mum didn't discover it there until she went house-proud over Thelma's coming. She found she had stood in some of it and was walking goo-smears round the house on the heel of her shoe.

She was trying desperately to get the smears off and she rubbed on some stuff from the cupboard under the sink. It was the wrong stuff and now there are bald spots on our carpet in some places, and untouched-because-she-doesn't-know-how-to-get-rid-of-it smears on other bits, where she trod it in. She says *we* trod it in, but Ob and I have shown her our shoes and there is no trace of whatever the brown mucky thing is on *our* shoes so the Mistress has had to admit it was probably her after all, and we were being wrongly accused.

The Mistress of Zog has put a woven mat on the bald bit and a new **Edict of Zog** has been proclaimed: **No one is to move the mat until Thelma has been and gone.**

The Mistress was about to put a rug and

cushions on the sofa to cover the gunge when the Creative got a fax from the US of A saying that Ike Walensky has pulled off a Big Contract. The Creative came dancing down the stairs from his room.

"Does that mean I get my Sky Cabin?" I said.

"*Our* loft room," Ob put in, being unable to cede even that much, when I would have thought it was time for clarity regarding Dad's intentions, rather than disputes over who will control the space when we get it.

But Dad was too busy whooping and waltzing Mum round the room (while she told him what a brilliant success he was) to answer properly. The Rulers of Zog do not usually pull out, but he might *renege* on the deal if he gets time to think it over, as his initial reaction to the Builder's Estimate was: "I think this is too expensive to contemplate even though you want it a lot, Zoë, but we are still thinking it over."

They were so busy telling each other how wonderful he is that we couldn't get an answer about the Sky Cabin and then he started to quiz her about what tax they would lose while they were knocking back their celebration whiskys. The result was that she wound up looking for his tax papers in the measly cubby-hole which is her office. He has a proper Creative's study upstairs over the garage. She has what should have been the place for coats, but everybody just drops coats about the place anyway and uses the fact that the coat-place is now her office as an excuse.

Being busy looking up papers made Mum neglect the apple tart she had in the oven for Thelma coming. It started to smoke and the fire alarm went off and the security company rang us. Dad swore at them and forgot the security number. They were about to send for the police, thinking he was a burglar who had set fire to our house, but Mum rang them back and explained that there wasn't a burglar only her husband, who had been celebrating a success and had drunk too much.

"That's nonsense! I'm totally sober!" he snarled at her.

"Well, I had to say something, hadn't I?" she said. "It is such a totally silly thing to do, forgetting the security number!"

He bumbled off to his lair after giving his speech again about being a Creative, creatives apparently being above such things as security numbers. (We have all had the security number drummed into us because if our alarm goes there is a line to the security firm and they ring up to ask if we are in deadly peril or being burgled, and if you don't give the security number they don't believe it is you. They believe you are being held ransom for your pearls and they call the police and the police come and arrest the intruders. That is the theory. We only have this sytem because of his computer set-up for doing his cartoons, which costs us zillions on insurance and makes us high risk, so the insurance company said we had to have it.)

Meanwhile, Melissa has rung to say she has something urgent to show me and it is important I come now. She sounded very excited, so I am going ... if I can escape without Mum seeing me. Out of this Sky Cabin-to-be, down the stairs, through the back door, across the garden, over the fence into the Bluebottles' garden-next-door and out their front so she won't spot me. All this because of a totally unreasonable Edict about me staying in the house until Thelma comes, when she won't be here till this afternoon.

Later, but still pre-Auntie
Subject:

An Unpleasant Interlude with Melissa

I have just returned from Melissa's and escaped up to my Sky Cabin to-be. Mum never noticed I was missing, so that is one to me, and shows how silly the Edict was.

I am disappointed in Melissa, although she is my Best Friend. When I got to her house she was waiting for me in the front garden, looking kind of smirky.

"Listen, Zoë," she said. "You need not think you are the only one who can pull stuff. Come round to our back and have a look at what I have got."

She took me into what has previously been known as the dog shed because smelly Cromwell hangs out there.

"Welcome to my new Den!" Melissa said, proudly holding open the door.

There were two old car seats, each with a faded cushion, and a wonky old table with a tea tray with orange juice and chocolate biscuits on it. She had put a mouldy old curtain up on hooks to cover the window. Her CD player was also on display, but as there is no electricity in the dog shed I deduce that it was there to demonstrate that she has one and I haven't, which I know already, although I have high hopes of having one installed in my Sky Cabin.

"Isn't it lovely?" Melissa said.

I said it was lovely.

"I knew you would like it," she beamed. "Now we can meet here every day."

"What about him?" I said, pointing at Cromwell. Niffy old Cromwell was firmly plomped in situ, on an old rug Melissa had put down on the concrete floor. His dog basket was tucked under the table.

"The deal is the Den is mine during the day and Cromwell sleeps in it at night," she said. I pointed out that it was day and Cromwell was still here.

"Well, he is old, and doesn't move much," Melissa pleaded. "The deal is I don't disturb him if he is sitting in here, but when he goes out I am allowed to close the door so he can't get back in. So I have the place to myself. Unless it rains. Then I let him back in because he has rheumatism."

"And he is a bit niffy," I pointed out.

"Not very," Melissa said.

"Well, yes. I think your Den is very nice," I said. "Wonderful. I am so happy for you! I *love* it."

"You don't love it," Melissa said suddenly. "You wiggled your ears when you said that, the way you do when you don't like something or somebody. You don't *want* to like it, do you? You are jealous. You can't stand me getting my Den first!"

I thought about that. The truth is, Melissa's Den is really a niffy old dog shed, the way it always was; two chairs and a table don't make that much difference. Not with the dog feeding bowls and dog smell all over the place, not to mention the dog, which I prefer not to mention. Cromwell is old and bad tempered and a droopy kind of dog. We don't get on, poor old Cromwell and me.

"I think you are the one who is being jealous," I told her. "Just because I have won through in my Sky Cabin negotiation and will have my Sky Cabin beautiful soon."

"Everybody knows how you did that!" Melissa said cruelly. "You were weeping your eyes out because Alison and Sonja called you Zoë Fat Elephant and your mum and dad gave in to the Sky Cabin idea to shut you up. The whole *world* knows that!"

"That isn't true!" I told her.

"Yes, it is," she said. "Your brother Ob told me. He says they were probably going to ask the builder about it anyway but you jump-started them by going round the house for hours weeping your eyes out because you are a Fat Elephant! He says you blackmailed them into doing it, by making a whole fuss about nothing."

"Well, if I am so fat and jealous you won't be coming to visit me in my Sky Cabin, and I am certainly not staying here to be called fat!" I told her, and off I went, boiling.

I tackled Mum when I got home.

"Melissa says you only gave in on the Sky Cabin deal because I was upset about the thing Sonja Banjerdee wrote on her rotten party invitation. Is that true?" I demanded.

"Well, sort of true," Mum said. "Why

not? It seems as good a reason as any to me. We knew you wanted it. We *hoped* we could do it. So why shouldn't we do something to cheer you up? We are your *loving* parents after all, Zoë-Zog."

So it is true!!!!!

Ob has been going round telling people that I am a cry-baby who weeps over being called fat and has to be *patronized* and *made* up to. I am mortified. I will probably hand over the entire Sky Cabin deal to Ob.

No, I will not do that!

Ob is the Ob-Noxious person who has been spreading lies about me to my friends, saying I am a cry-baby as well as fat and elephant-like. He will never have my Sky Cabin for his pool table even if I vow never to use it myself, because I will not be treated like a child and *cheered up*. I am grown up, almost. They ought to know that. I do not care how much they plead. I am having nothing to do with the rotten Sky Cabin ... except if Ob thinks he is getting it all for himself, I will start talking to Mum and Dad in a rational and adult way about letting Creep have it for his model railway instead. I will probably never speak to Melissa again. I will certainly never speak to Ob again. I may never speak to my mum again.

Well, I will have to when Auntie Thelma comes, because I will not disgrace Mum in front of her... But after that I aim to maintain a cool, dignified and adult silence in the face of all provocation and bribery and attempts to butter me up.

They will be sorry when they see they have hurt me so.

Later
Subject:

There Is Justice!

Brilliant! This day will echo in the Annals of Zog, as long as there is a Zog to echo it in. The slimy and reprehensible Ob-Noxious has earned his chips with nobs on ... if chips have nobs.

Picture the scene: My Auntie Thelma has arrived. She has false teeth that click and a *nasty, nasty, nasty* habit of enquiring after one's personal life while she peers over her glasses. Thelma has already worked her way round the rest of the family with varied abuse. Now Ob enters the scene, disinterred by Mum from the bathroom, where he has been hiding, but forty minutes is enough for any physical function, and he can't stay hidden for ever.

"Colin!" cries Thelma, and she embraces him.

Ob-Noxious, all done up in his best jeans and Man. U shirt, winces.

"Goodness me, Mummy Myrtle!" Thelma exclaims to Mum, adding in a voice of coy amazement, "is this Great Big Man the Little Colin that I used to bounce on my knee?"

Ob does not speak. Ob glowers.

"Yes, it is!" says Mummy Myrtle, breaking the silence that follows. (Thelma habitually calls Mum "Mummy Myrtle" in our presence, hugely to Mum's discomfort and the Creative's delight. About the only delight he gets when Thelma visits.)

Ob scowls. I note *something* is up with Ob, but I know not what it is ... I should have wotted. He had just heard he'd been dropped from Man. U Red Devils and couldn't figure why, though I could have told him, being instrumental in it ... about which I now feel no regrets, after the cry-baby stories he has been telling my erstwhile Best Friend, Melissa Adams.

Out comes the *photograph*. Dad winces. Creep grins. I smirk. We have all seen it before, at roughly biannual intervals. It is little Colin in his birthday suit, grinning inanely up from a rug by the fire. Mummy Myrtle is beside him.

"What a nice little body," Thelma clacks. "His little bottom looks so sweet!"

The colour rises to Ob's face and he goes a kind of pink, which probably designates a rush of blood to the head, and he says *something* in a furious mutter, no doubt intended not to be heard above the chink of the cups, but heard it is.

Auntie Thelma Taylor gasps. Mummy Myrtle pales. Dad perks up and then remembers to look shocked. Creep's mouth drops open. I come awake with the crash of Auntie's cup as it drops from her gnarled fingers.

"Colin!" cries Mum, aghast, victim of perfect hearing and undivided attention.

And Ob *repeats* what he has just said, with Ob-knobs on! This time I *do* catch it. All of it. In glorious stereo sound, for Ob has lost his head. He is determined to be heard.

I will not record the words my now-about-to-be-deceased brother let rip – such words would not be seemly; they would not grace these pages; suffice to say they were short and pithy; an anatomically comical description of Thelma.

Exit Thelma, furiously proclaiming that never has she been so insulted by a foul-mouthed child, and never will she return to a house where such obscenities are even *known* to a boy of that age ... somehow implying along the way that defective parenthood is responsible. Mummy Myrtle pleads with her, trying to avert the storm ... but Auntie Thelma Taylor is gone, gone, gone. And the best bit is, as I pointed out to Dad later,

Thelma sat on the sofa where the gunge was. Mum never got round to putting a rug on it because they started celebrating Dad's contract!

Hopefully Thelma will not notice it when she gets home and she will sit on her chintzy sofa she is so proud of and she will get it gungy and mucky, and then she will be so cross that she will keep her word and *never, ever* come to see us again.

Sunday 23rd August a.m.
Subject:

More Zog Troubles

This morning Ob still lies a prisoner in his room... Well, not a prisoner really, but he reckons it is better to stay up there until Mum is over it and has stopped scolding Dad. That is because Mum has accused Dad of grinning about what Ob said to Thelma.

The conversation between them became quite heated and he had to apologize and act the outraged Papa with Ob, though we suspect his heart wasn't in it. Mum and Dad are at present having a conference in their room (sometimes known as the Passion Pit) about whether Ob has to be made to apologize and if so, how.

I have attempted preliminary discussions with Mum about the Sky Cabin Plan, but this was a mistake. This important matter is now on long-term hold, which is little short of a disaster in my eyes and all rotten Ob's fault too. I bet he never wanted me to have it because of the Pool Table Exclusion Clause that we all agreed to, and insulting Auntie T. was just a clever way of smashing my plans, just when I had everything fixed and they had made some money and could afford it.

"You are an ungrateful pack, the whole lot of you, you included!" Mum said. "You were all so rude to your Auntie Thelma, even *him*, and he purports to be grown up and should know better. I don't see what is funny and amusing and admirable about a small boy insulting an old lady who has been kind and good to me all my life. Nobody is getting any favours out of me today, or probably ever."

Things have reached a pretty pass. She refused to make the Creative any breakfast. "If he is so bloody creative, he can do it himself!" she said.

We have really upset Mum. Something will have to be done about this; Mum out of orbit is contrary to the Principle of Peace in Zog, which is central to all our hearts ... and indeed our doings.

I will approach the Creative with a view to holding an Emergency Zog-Dwellers' Conference in his lair. Subject: how to get Mum back to earth.

All Minions will have to pull together on this, even Creep and the deeply and direly disgraced Ob, who will have to emerge from his bedroom some time. The sour old Creative will have to do his bit too and stop complaining about everything all the time. I will ram this home to them at the Emergency Meeting, as I am the one with the clearest vision and someone must give a lead.

Later

Have held a prelim discussion with the Creative. He is weak minded. He proposed flowers and a cake with *Sorry, Mum* on it. His plan was that this would be presented to Mum by Ob. I pointed out that Ob had no money to go buying cakes. He said he would fund it, if only to get a bit of peace so he can write. *Self-centred* as usual, as though nothing but his work matters, when the whole basis of the Zog World is threatened.

Later still
Subject:

Melissa

Melissa rang me to apologize for yesterday, practically sobbing down the phone.

"I'm awfully, awfully sorry about yesterday, Zoë," she said. "I need to speak to you. Can you pop round to our house, like soonest poss? Like now, *this minute*, because it really is important."

I told her that was quite all right and that I supposed I would see her around *some time*, if I was out, but that I was very busy at home these days, owing to difficult domestic circumstances, and would therefore not be able to *pop* round.

"*Please,* Zoë! Like *now*, Zoë," she pleaded. "I really, really need you *now* because you are my Friend and something *awful* is happening. And I am sure your Sky Cabin will be zounds better than my old dog shed, but it was all I could get out of Mum. And I shouldn't have said rude things about you which just aren't true."

At last, somewhat reluctantly, I relented in the face of her repeated *grovelling* apologies. I told her it takes a big person to apologize and I was sorry too and I would come at once, as she obviously needed me. I also lied, but it was a white lie told to save my friend from feeling pain, so it doesn't count. I told her I really like her Den, despite the dog. That is what friends are for.

After our phone call I went round to Melissa's and we sat in her so-called Den, after we had lured the old dog out with dog biscuits. Cromwell is a nice enough dog, if he didn't niff so much. It means Melissa's Den niffs too, but on this occasion I was diplomatic and pretended not to notice, while we discussed the matter which had distressed her so greatly … and which is, in truth, *deeply* distressing to me as Melissa's Best Friend, because I feel a duty to help her when she is upset by the unreasonable and unpleasant behaviour of others.

It transpires that Melissa, alone of the Tennis Club members, has *not* been invited to Sonja Banjerdee's birthday party which is being held in the Private Function Room of the Manor House Hotel. We don't know why. The story was that all the Tennis Club would be there (even me, because Mum and Dad persuaded me to go, not because I want to) and Melissa is in the Tennis Club but her invitation has *not* arrived.

I told Melissa that I felt not inviting her was very mean and a typical Sneaky Sonja action, no doubt egged on by Awful Alison.

"Sneaky S. Banjerdee doesn't like you,"

Melissa mumped. "But *you* got an invitation. I didn't even get that!"

"Yes, well..." I said. "But you know what Sneaky put on my invitation!"

The problem is everybody else we know will be there, even people like Ivor Magella and Shirley Ogle, who are not even *supposed* to be friends with Sneaky like we are, and are not in the Tennis Club, but their mums know Mrs Banjerdee. Of course, we don't like Sneaky S. Banjerdee and she doesn't like us, but that has nothing to do with it. As far as the mums are concerned, we are all *friends* from the Tennis Club and it was to be an all Tennis Club binge. Arnold will be there and so, of course, will Awful Alison, who will doubtless make use of her opportunity to cut Melissa out of the Arnold picture; and *naturally* Sneaky Sonja will make eyes at Graham – not that I care about that.

Melissa is my friend. It takes a big friend to apologize the way she did this morning and I feel I have to show solidarity with her, and that is all there is to it. Friends are friends, and my friend's enemy is my enemy.

"Well, I'm not going to Sneaky's Party on 29th August if you are not invited!" I told her. "We will both not go, and then nobody will know it is just you that didn't get invited."

Melissa says I am her True Friend. We are

still hoping maybe her invitation has got lost in the post because everyone else has had theirs, so we are going to see if it turns up before I tell anyone I am not going, in case Melissa *has* been invited, in which case we would both go just to annoy them, but also because we do not want to let Sneaky nab Arnold off Melissa.

Meanwhile, I have agreed to go out with Melissa tomorrow, accompanying Mrs Hare from next door to the shops, as Mrs Hare is new to the town and needs guidance.

Mrs Hare is a brilliant Top Model, according to Melissa. We are going to ask her for advice on our Top Model Careers. I am going to find out if she ever had to diet, and if so how old she was when she started, and whether or not it has weakened her bones. I shall ask *discreetly* of course, as a Top Model might not want to own up about having done stuff like diets, and once being fat. I expect many Top Models had puppy fat like mine once. Well, some of them anyway. It melts off as you grow. I hope.

Later note
Subject:

Bluebottles

Dad Bluebottle has returned next door. Ob saw him playing in the garden with little Cyril.

Little Cyril was being his usual horrible self, but Dad Bluebottle was coping. That is the good news. The bad news is that Dad Bluebottle has lost his double glazing job, and we think that he has come back to sponge off Mum Bluebottle. He has had to hand back the keys of his double glazing van to the company.

Dad Bluebottle gave Mum Bluebottle a big kiss and she was all smiles welcoming him home and little Cyril was delighted, so all the rotten stuff next door has ended. Well, for now. Hopefully this ought to ease the load on their *unpaid* minder (ie, me). Perhaps Cyril will form a bond with his dad and become less ghastly. Some hopes!

Even later

Arnold and Awful A. and Graham Denzil Blind-as-a-Batbugs Batty saw me this afternoon.

Graham shouted, "Here comes Fat

Elephant!" at me as I was coming away from Mr Hunter's Sunday paper stand, and Mr Hunter heard.

"How very rude!" he said, and he told them to go away.

"Yah, bug off!" Arnold said, and they ran off shouting, "Fat Elephant! Fat Elephant!" so the whole street could hear but probably most people didn't know it was me they were shouting at. I hope so, anyway.

That is what Hobsbawn says.

I was walking down the street upset and he came up to me and put his bike across in front of me so I couldn't move, and I thought he was going to "Zoë-Fat-Elephant" me, but he didn't.

"I think they are really mean, Zoë," Hobsbawn said. "My mum says you are not fat, and she can't understand why people say you are. She says they are nasty for picking on you."

So Hobsbawn's mum knows. I suppose they all know, all the mums. And they have all been talking about me behind my back.

"Who told your mum people were calling me names, Hubie?" I said.

"Melissa's mum told my mum," he said. "Melissa's mum was very cross about it. And my mum told me I was to make sure I stood up for you if I heard anybody calling you names, so I am. I am on your side, Zoë.

And I am called *Vince* now. I am telling everybody to call me *Vince* because I am fed up with being called Hubie. *Vince* is a much better name, and I was Christened it so I am not cheating."

I thanked Vince very politely (because I am a polite person, however much my feelings may have been hurt). I suppose the new Vince Hobsbawn was trying to be good like his mummy told him to in the days when he was in his Hubie-mobile, which is what Vince's mum called his precious pram. My mum thought this was a funny name and she told some of the other mums. She should *not* have done this. I see now that it can be very hurtful and distressing for a person to find out that other people's mums are laughing at you, so I can understand from *personal* experience why Hubie is now calling himself Vince.

"You are not a cry-baby either," he said. "I know that. And I told my mum so."

I am really fed up.

I might just leave home and start a new life but I wouldn't give them the satisfaction and the worst thing of all is that by now all the mums must know about the Fat Elephant thing and me having no friends, and that includes my mum.

As far as I am concerned that is the end

of Batbugs Batty, the toad, and Arnold and everybody in that lot, except maybe Hobsbawn. I suspect Vince only said he was standing up for me because his mum told him to, after all the other mums had been telling each other I was a cry-baby Fat Elephant who blackmailed my mum into letting me have things my own way.

On my return to Zog, I rang Melissa to tell her I would not be coming out with her to walk Mrs Hare round the shops tomorrow, as *people* have been spreading stories about me and I do not want to see anybody just now, or ever again probably.

"Oh, yes you are!" Melissa said.

"Oh, no I am not," I said. "You don't know how it feels."

"You *must* come, Zoë!" Melissa said, very seriously. "If you do not you will just be letting Alison and Sonja and Pottsy and Batbugs think they have you *beaten.* And they have not and I am not letting you be beaten, because I am your friend. And what is more I am knocking Arnold Potts off my Love List because he did that to you."

I think that is very big of Melissa.

I have told her I may reconsider going out, but at the moment I do not feel like it. The truth is I do not want to meet Melissa's mum and have her saying nice things about me because she is sorry for me. I am very much afraid that Melissa may have said something to her mum which has started the mums talking. So it would all be Melissa's fault. Although I suppose Melissa meant well if she did say something to her mum.

Melissa rang off, after insisting that she was coming round to collect me first thing tomorrow, because I *was* going out, even if she had to drag me.

"Anything the matter, Zoë-Zog?" Mum said when I came off the telephone.

"No," I said.

"You look a bit upset," Mum said.

"I am not upset," I told Mum.

And I have made up my mind.

I had a think about it, sitting alone on my cushion in the Sky Cabin to-be.

I *am* going out with Melissa tomorrow because I am *me*, Zoë, and I am not a *Fat Elephant*. I am not going to let Alison and Sneaky and Arnold and Blind-as-an-old-Batbugs or Melissa's mum think I am when I know I am not, and they are the ones who should be ashamed of themselves. I suppose that's not true about Melissa's mum. She has hurt me by discussing my problem with other mums behind my back, but she was trying to help me so I cannot hold that against her. I just wish she hadn't done it.

I shall say nothing of this matter to Melissa. No doubt she meant well.

Monday 24th August
Subject:

Best REVENGE Ever

I was *right* to come out with Melissa this morning because the best REVENGE ever has just happened to the person I HATE most in all the world, who is mouldy old Graham D. Can't-see-a-sausage-Batbugs!

Graham D. Blind-as-a-Batbugs was in the park, walking Merson, thinking his little thoughts and humming his little hums like Winnie-the-Pooh and hugging his little poop scoop to his podgy and undesirable person.

Towards him strode Melissa's new neighbour, Mrs Hare, with no clothes on. Well, she was in the silk shorts and her halter top, not having bothered to change from her Private Garden Wear for the trip Melissa and I had promised her round the shops. They are short silk shorts. A strip of red adorns her upper person and she has a gold chain belt swinging round her waist, in collision with her belly button.

Behind her trot Melissa and I, as kind of Maids of Honour.

Stinky old Graham D. Batbugs takes in this vision.

Stinky old Graham D. Batbugs is mesmerized.

Stinky old Batbugs lets us pass, then he follows ... but Merson does not. Merson is not in the least interested in Mrs Hare (Tina), as she traverses the park. Merson has doggy priorities in mind.

Batbugs wanders after us, with glazed and staring eyes. Merson departs into a bush.

We reach the end of the park and are about to cross over at the lights to go down to the shopping centre. Melissa is as agog as I am, and indeed as Graham D. Batbugs is.

Batbugs pauses, realizes that Merson is missing and, sticking his fingers in his mouth, Batbugs' manner, gives a loud whistle designed to bring Merson out of the bushes.

Batbugs has picked the wrong moment, for Mrs Hare (Tina) has turned and is observing him, and she has had occasion to notice his gaze fixed on her as we have been on our march through the park.

Merson is not in evidence. She has not seen Merson. She sees only an uncouth boy, apparently whistling at her. We must take it that she presumes the whistle is directed at her as a response to her garb, and we must take it that this has happened before in the life of Mrs Hare (Tina) – but not, apparently, from persons with Batbugs' lack of street cred.

"You rude little plonker!" she shouts. "Stop ogling my bum. Sod off or I'll go round and call on your mother."

Batbugs is left in no doubt as to whom she addresses.

Batbugs goes scarlet. Batbugs retreats!

All is well with the world. With any luck Graham D. will leave town, taking Merson with him. Nobody will miss him except his mum and dad and his Auntie Florence. He *is* a plonker. That will teach him to call me names.

The rest of the trip was good too. Tina (she says we can call her *Tina*, because Mrs Hare is too formal) took us into the lounge bar at the Sea Crest Hotel. Tina had a Bacardi and she let us taste it, both of us. It was not very nice. We had cokes with ice and a slice of lemon each and there were crisps and nuts.

Bum is a very rude word, both Melissa and I are agreed, but we are certain sure she said *bum*. If we had said bum out in the park and our mums had heard us we would have been in trouble, but as usual there is one rule for grown-ups and one rule for us, which is unfair.

The one disappointment is that Melissa's potential *paying* childminder-employer-next-door is not, as reported by Melissa's mum, a Top Model.

We asked her about our Model Careers over our ice-cream (I did the talking in the end, because Melissa felt shy, though Melissa claimed she was being cautious because of her future employment prospects) and it turns out that Tina-the-Top-Model was once on TV doing the Daz Whites Test but shortly afterwards she got pregnant with Rupert and this put a stop to what would otherwise have been her glittering career. She got on because her cousin knew somebody who knew somebody in the PR company doing Daz. She was never a proper model on an agency's books or anything, so she was regretfully unable to advise us on our possible careers.

We did suspect she might not be a Top Model when she said "sod off" and "bum" to Batbugs because although they are rude words they are not that rude, and we think Top Models probably know ruder ones. That is Melissa's opinion anyway.

I don't mind much. It doesn't look like I will be a Top Model when I grow up anyway, not the way things are going.

Tina not-a-Top-Model Hare did not ask us who Batbugs is or where his mum lives so we do not think she meant it about going to his house to tell his mother. After we left her Melissa and I discussed whether we would have told on him if she had asked. We think probably we wouldn't have. The good thing is Batbugs doesn't know whether we did or not. His mum would go bananas if Tina turned up on her doorstep and it would serve him just right if he thought that was going to happen, even if it wasn't.

Of course Graham D. was unaware that we had not divulged his identity to Tina, and we should have guessed what would happen: he was waiting for us when we came back through the park, having left Tina to do some shopping in the off licence. He was hiding in the hedge with his bike because he thought we would come back that way. He had dumped Merson and he was wearing his balaclava so he wouldn't be recognized if Tina was still with us. I don't think he would have jumped out on us if Tina had been there.

He put his bike across the path and he started talking to us. He was very red in the face ... at least the bit of his face that we could see.

He wanted to know whether Tina knew who he was, and whether she would really go and tell his mum on him.

"We are not saying," Melissa said, in line with our keep-him-worried decision. "We *might* have told her and we might *not* have."

"If you told on me there will be trouble!" he said, and he followed us on his bike, shouting names at us so we didn't go back to Melissa's to check out her Den; we headed for Zog instead, Zog being closer to the park.

He was mooching along behind us as we got nearer to my house, chanting, "Fat Elephant, Fat Elephant!"

"Don't pay any attention to him," Melissa told me. "Fat Elephant is the only name he can think of because he isn't very bright."

Then an amazing thing happened.

Ob came running out of our front gate and went straight past us right up to Batbugs.

Ob said, "Who do you think you are calling names?" just like that, to Batbugs.

Batbugs is older than us, and big. Ob is only eleven. Batbugs towered over him. The next thing was that Batbugs very slowly and aggressively made a show of taking off his glasses.

"I was talking to your Fat Elephant sister and her friend," Batbugs said to Ob. "What are you planning to do about it, pudding face? Want to make something of it?"

"How would you like it if people called you names like that?" Ob demanded. "You are just a blubbermouth, Batty!"

I thought Batbugs was going to hit him, so I dived in to save Ob.

"You pick on someone your own size!" I told Batbugs. He kind of shoved me and made a grab for Ob, who had gone pale and looked as if he wanted to run away but wouldn't.

Then Melissa said, "If you touch that little

boy half your size I will yell for his dad, and then you will be in Big Trouble!" and Batbugs backed off.

"You're all yellow!" Batbugs said. Then he got on his bike and said to Ob, "I'll fix you later, worm!"

"Anytime you want!" Ob said, but I could see that whatever had started him off had stopped. Ob was frightened. He must have been really, *really* pleased that Melissa said she was going to shout for the Creative to come and sort it, because otherwise there would have been a big fight, and I think Ob might have been hurt.

It is not a good idea for somebody Ob's size to go around picking fights with someone as big as Batbugs, even if the someone does wear glasses. We might have been able to save Ob because I don't think even Batbugs would go hitting girls, but Ob is a boy so I think Batbugs would have hit him if we hadn't butted in.

"Why did you do that?" I asked Ob. "You could have been in dead trouble."

"Mum and Dad told me I wasn't to stand by and let people call you names, Zoë," Ob said. "So I am not."

Ob's lip was quivering and he was kind of shaky looking, his eyes all bright and watery, though he didn't want to let on that he was nearly crying. He turned round and went back into the house without saying another word.

"Thanks, Ob! It was dead brave of you, what you did!" I shouted after him.

When we discussed Ob's bravery in my Sky Cabin later, I confessed to Melissa about getting him into trouble with Man. U Red Devils, which was really *mean* of me, though I thought he deserved it at the time. I feel very bad about that. Melissa agrees with me that it was a mean thing to do to my own brother but she says Ob was *noble* (considering he is much smaller than Batbugs) standing up for me like that.

I will have to think of some way to make it up to Ob. He has been brave and may have got himself into long-term trouble with the bigger ones, on my behalf. Ob has to live in the same town with Batbugs and Arnold and Scats, who go round together. I will have to find some way to protect him from them.

Meanwhile, I will go and tell Bouncer's dad that Ob never said Man. U Red Devils were crap and then Ob will get back on the team. It will be most embarrassing for me, but I have to do it, so I will.

Probably tomorrow.

Later

I have done it. It was deeply, deeply embarrassing but I have done it.

I rang Melissa and told her I did not feel I should wait until tomorrow as we had arranged, because I might not have the courage to do it. Melissa at once said that she would come with me to back me up.

We spoke to Bouncer's dad.

He was very good about it, but I was *mortified*. It will be all right. Ob will be playing again for the team so now no one can say that I have been mean to my brother. We went there the back way and therefore did not see our *enemies* Batbugs and Arnold and Scats and their girlfriends, Awful and Sneaky.

I have also spoken to Mum, indicating that in my view it might be better if she laid off Ob on the matter of apologizing to Auntie Thelma Taylor and left *me* to persuade Ob gently into doing it, as I am nearer his age than she is.

For a supposedly Trained Professional Educational Psychologist, Mum showed little sympathy to this approach. She was still in orbit over the Thelma bust-up, with no sign of an imminent return to Earth.

"You can all crawl on your knees to me, and still nobody is getting any dinner!" was all she said. I have spoken to Dad on the matter. He and I will cook alternate days until she gets over it. Him first, which means baked beans. I suggested he might try to win Mum round on the grounds of Ob's general good behaviour and respect for the Institutions of Zog but Dad said, "What good behaviour? I hadn't noticed," so that was a non-starter.

I am hampered in negotiating a truce with Mum and Dad on Ob's behalf by the fact that I cannot under any circs. reveal the background detail. I do not want them thinking I am upset about being called names all over again and trying to beg favours off them. I will tell them the truth to save Ob if I have to, but for the moment we will wait and see. I have done as much as anyone could expect for Ob, and I don't want them knowing every *single* detail of my personal life, when it is private and hurtful stuff.

With regard to the problem with Mum, Ob can get himself off the Thelma hook if he wants to, just by going with Mum to Auntie Thelma's and apologizing. I will speak to him with that in mind.

I am working on how to get Ob out of the bother he will be in with Batbugs and his mates. That may not be as bad as Ob obviously believes it is, judging by the way he is acting. Melissa and I are agreed that

Batbugs wouldn't do him any real harm, not being a thug by nature, but Ob probably doesn't see it that way, and he is the one who is on the receiving end. We think Graham D. was simply scared out of his tiny mind at the thought of Tina (Mrs Hare) telling his mum what happened in the park, and that he will probably get over it and forget about Ob. *Maybe.* Trouble is that Ob is not convinced. Right now he is looking worried, and staying in his room.

Later, after dinner (so-called)

Dad's effort with the baked beans, sausages and chips was truly disgusting. It looks like I'll have to take over all cooking duties until things are squared with Mum, unless we are all to wind up with food poisoning.

Tuesday 25th August
Subject:

Survival Tactics 1 (Ob)

Melissa and I had a consultation with Ob in the Sky Cabin this morning. We told Ob that if he kept out of Batbugs' way for a few days Batbugs and his mates would forget all about him with the excitement of Sneaky's party coming up. Ob pointed out that that is easy for us to say when we are not being picked on.

"What's going to stop them getting me when we go back to school at the start of September?" Ob said, looking worried. "I can't hide in our house for ever, can I? I have got to go out again some time."

Ob thinks we might be able to get Hobsbawn on our side. Ob says Hobsbawn is bigger than they are.

"Hobsbawn is soft," I told him, scornfully. "Hobsbawn is a mummy's boy! Everybody knows that."

Ob didn't say anything for a moment. Then he said, "You're the one who started calling him that, Zoë. But you calling him it doesn't make it true, any more than people calling you Fat Elephant makes *you* one. Hobsbawn is big and he could be *quite* tough if he wanted to be, only he doesn't throw his weight about the way the others do, or mouth as much. Anyway, there is no one else who might take our side, is there?"

"There's Ivor Magella," Melissa said. "You know Ivor fancies you, Zoë. He asked after you when I was at the pictures. We could recruit him. If we had Hobsbawn and Ivor on our side looking after Ob, they wouldn't dare touch him."

"Ivor's no use," Ob said. "Ivor's a plonker."

Later
Subject:

Survival Tactics 2 (Domestic Matters)

There was no cooking this morning. We all had cornflakes. I do not intend to cook them anything in the middle of the day because they can get by on toast and I do not see why I should get lumbered with it just because I am a girl. On the other hand, I had agreed with Dad in a weak moment that I would do the dinner, so I will have to stick to that. Cauliflower Cheese is easiest I think, and no problem. Dad suggested it, as it soothes his burnt stomach. (He can get the cheese out of the pot afterwards, because I'm not doing that, I refuse.) The issue I have to confront is that of avoiding doing Cauliflower Cheese every day for ever until I grow up and leave Zog, and my approach to this is complicated by the Sky Cabin issue.

The Sky Cabin work is not yet signed up with the builder, so I am placed in an awkward tactical position, as I need to have both Mum and the Creative in a positive-thinking mode Sky Cabin-wise, but they are at loggerheads over Mum's downing domestic tools, which arose as a result of the Auntie Thelma row. Everybody going round grinning about Thelma was the straw that broke the camel's back. It has set Mum off into Outer Space Orbit on her campaign for domestic justice, with everybody doing their fair share around the house.

This gives me a problem. If I support Mum's stand that everybody should do their share of the housework so that she can get on with writing her book, I will eventually wind up doing *their* fair share, because they will all agree to help and then find excuses for not doing it. On the other hand, if I try to sweet-talk Mum back into making the dinners and doing the dishes as usual I will be deserting the cause of Women's Rights. Not taking her side would ditch my Sky Cabin chances for sure, in Mum's mind.

I have decided to work on it a bit at a time. If I can negotiate with Ob to apologize to Auntie Thelma, that should soften Mum up. Maybe if she got pleased about that she might relent on her no-further-domestic duties-till-this-is-sorted-out stand. She usually does relent, because things just don't get done when she doesn't do them. Till then, I must lie low, avoid being allocated extra domestic commitments, and say not a word on the Sky Cabin to-be or not-to-be question until Mum and Dad have re-established their normal relationship, domestic-wise, and Mum comes down from orbit.

Later
Subject:

S. Banjerdee's Rotten Party Again

Melissa came round this afternoon (having waited in vain for a second post, when everyone knows that there isn't one) in a terrible state about the fact that her invitation to Sneaky's rotten, stupid birthday party has not shown up.

We have to conclude that Melissa has *not* been invited, and is not *going* to be invited. Melissa was in a state because her mum hasn't noticed yet that there is no invitation but her mum will soon. Melissa doesn't want her mum to know that no one in the Tennis Club likes her.

"That's stupid, Melissa," I told her. "Everyone in the Tennis Club likes you – except Sneaky, and Sneaky doesn't like you because you are her rival for Arnold's heart."

"My mum won't know that," Melissa said. "I will be the only Junior Tennis Club Member not invited, and she will want to know why and I don't know what to tell her."

We talked this over in an urgent meeting in my Sky Cabin and as a result I have taken action to save our friendship, because being friends with Melissa is more important to me than any old Banjerdee party where I would be called rude names, possibly in front of Mrs Banjerdee.

I have returned my invitation, with a polite note written on it saying *Zoë regrets she will be unable to attend, as she has been in contact with an infectious disease*. This *diplomatic* excuse should get round any Mrs Banjerdee problem. Sneaky will no doubt get the message that there is no way I would go to her stinky party without Melissa.

Melissa and I will do something interesting and worthwhile instead.

It was only *after* I posted my invitation back that I realized that Mrs Banjerdee would see the *Fat Elephant* thing written on it, which is most embarrassing, as I did not want any more grown-ups to know. However, in the circumstances, what is mere pride beside my loyalty to my Best Friend Melissa?

"I still don't understand why *you* were invited and *I* wasn't!" Melissa said. "Sneaky doesn't like you either. And she doesn't like Ivor Magella and she invited *him and* his little sister Miriam, and Miriam isn't even in the Tennis Club and is ten."

"Mrs Banjerdee goes around with Mrs Magella," I explained to her.

"*You* were invited," Melissa pointed out. "And your mum is not particularly pally with Mrs Banjerdee, is she?"

I had previously told a white lie by letting Melissa *think* I was invited because my dad is famous, and Mrs Banjerdee likes famous people. I said this to soften the blow of what she sees as her social ostracization by fellow members of the Tennis Club who are supposed to be our *friends*, which will be all the worse because everyone will know she has not been invited when she doesn't show up.

"What is your dad famous for?" Melissa asked me. "I didn't know he was famous."

"My dad wrote a book," I told her. "And Mrs Banjerdee is artistic. She paints pictures. So probably she wouldn't let Sonja *not* invite me."

"You said his book was no good!" Melissa said grumpily.

"It was the *Sunday Times* that said it was no good," I told her. "And Mrs Banjerdee reads the *Sunday Times* because there is a lot of it and she has to do something all Sunday with Mr Banjerdee never coming home, so she will have seen it in there. And not many people round here have ever had their names in the *Sunday Times*."

Melissa thought for a bit. "Nobody reviews plumbers in the *Sunday Times*," she said.

"Right!" I said, relieved that she had got my message.

"But my dad is a very good plumber," she added.

"So?"

"People like to keep *in* with plumbers," she said. "There isn't another one round here. So she has to *like* my dad, hasn't she? It is more than just an ordinary business relationship. So I don't understand why she let Sonja *not* invite me, when everyone else is invited, even Miriam Magella."

Later
Subject:

News Sensation!

Mum had a builder in the roof space. The man had a notebook and a calculator and they were taking measurements so he could do a *detailed* costing on making my Sky Cabin proper!

Fantastic! Fantabulous! Mum is a big, big person. She is in orbit, having this awful feud with her family, and yet she still goes ahead with the Sky Cabin! My mum is a Great Mum.

I have spoken very severely with Ob about the need for him to go and tell Mum that he will apologize to Auntie Thelma, fully and in whatever terms Mum likes to dictate, with absolutely no reservations whatsoever.

"Why is it always me?" Ob said, unreasonably, because he was the one who insulted Thelma after all. The rest of us are only in trouble for aiding and abetting the offence.

"Because you are the one who put Mum's back up and now she is being *wonderful* in true Mum style and you have just got to put it right!" I told him firmly and he eventually went and apologized to Mum. They are going to visit Auntie Thelma Taylor as soon as it can be arranged, and Mum has let him off with a warning. Ob told me he can live with that, as we are getting *our* Sky Cabin. I did not dispute the *our*. Let him dream!!!

I made a point of going to Mum and thanking her personally and fulsomely for her helpfulness, and innocently enquiring about the time Cauliflower Cheese needs to cook to emphasize that Ob is not the only one who has been making concessions, and that I am cooking Dad's dinner.

"Don't worry about it, Zoë," she said. "I know you hate cooking. I will do it. I was only getting at your dad because he acts like a chauvinist little boy sometimes, and I thought he needed a lesson!"

Ob says they went out for a walk this morning while Melissa and I were holding discussions in the Sky Cabin (gloriously now to-be) and he supposes Dad bought her flowers or something like that. In my view the flower trick has long been discredited, but you never know. She is out of orbit, so whatever he did, it worked.

This is FAN-TAB-U-LOUS!

What caused this change and averted the complete rundown of Zog relationships? We will probably never know. That is the problem with being a young adult. Old adults pull stuff between them. One day they are fighting and everything is off, and the next day they are hugging and co-operating and everything is on, and you never know what has really happened. It just happens, and then you find your life is completely and utterly changed, but you *never* know what has happened to cause it.

Later still

As Melissa and I have vowed to stick around in sympathy with Ob, who is scared to go out in case Batbugs gets him, we spent the rest of the afternoon discussing possible decoration of my Sky Cabin when the builder has finished.

Unfortunately Mum tumbled to the fact that something was amiss.

"Why were you not out riding your bikes or something?" Mum asked me, when Melissa was just going. "You haven't many more days' holiday left, and it seems a shame to have you and Ob and Melissa all locked up in the house. Is something going on?"

Mum is not a Trained Professional Educational Psychologist for nothing.

"We prefer to stay in," I told her. "Don't we, Melissa?"

"Yes," Melissa said.

Then Melissa went home. The back way again, so that she wouldn't be seen by *them*, our *enemies*, who have not invited her to the party.

I rang Melissa to see if she had got home safely, as she had not rung me to confirm her arrival, as promised. Melissa's mum answered. She says Melissa isn't allowed to use the phone any more. There have been too many phone calls to our house. She wants to know what my dad will say when he sees our phone bill, with what she called "all these unnecessary calls".

I told her I was ringing Melissa on an urgent matter, and most, if not all, of our calls were strictly necessary. I went on to point out that our phone bill is tax-deductible because of Dad ringing and faxing

Newark, New Jersey, so my dad is more relaxed about phone bills than some people I could name. Well, words to that effect anyway.

"Well, I'm afraid life doesn't work that way for plumbers, Zoë!" Melissa's mum said. "So in future if there are any more calls that *must* be made I will tell Melissa to reverse the charges when she rings you!"

Wednesday 26th August
Subject:

Another Betrayal

Melissa did not ring me this morning, but I put it down to her mum's ban, so I rang her instead. Melissa was in a state of great excitement. It appears her party invitation went astray because it had the wrong post code, and has now belatedly been delivered to her house.

"Well, you still have two days to send it back saying you are not going," I told her. "The party is not till Saturday."

There was a long silence.

"I don't want Mum to know about *enemies*," she said. "How could I explain to Mum about not going when she knows I have been waiting and waiting and waiting for my invitation to come?"

"I refused *my* invitation because *you* were not invited," I told her, calmly but pointedly, although by this time I was boiling inside. "In my view, if you go you are going over to the enemy, and that is unforgivable. What is my mum going to say if she finds out I am not going and you are? First I told her I would go for her sake, despite not wanting to. Then I told her I simply couldn't go because you were not invited, and now you suddenly say you are going! So where does that leave me?"

By this time, of course, I was *quite* exasperated with my friend, so-called.

There was a pause while Melissa tried to think of some way to wriggle out of her moral obligation to me, and the betrayal of all our friendship has stood for. Of course she couldn't. She resorted to *weasel* words, instead.

"Your mum knows about you being called Fat Elephant. Your mum will understand perfectly well why you don't want to go," Melissa said. "You can get away with that as an excuse. I can't. You went round crying buckets and wailing in front of your mum about being fat, so your mum knows you don't really want to go. I didn't. I am not like that. I kept my chin up. Mum didn't know I was upset when I thought I wasn't being asked. So I've *got* to go to the party, Zoë, even though I don't want to. There is no way I can get out of it. And besides that, there is my relationship with Arnold to consider, and not letting S. Banjerdee have a free run."

I put down the phone without replying.

I have left instructions with Ob and Creep that if Melissa calls they are to say I am busy meditating in my Sky Cabin and am not to be disturbed, and that I do not wish to see Melissa or talk to her ever again.

There will be a problem if Mum sees her first, though. I have given Creep instructions to do guard duty for me, but he might forget.

Later

Melissa did not come. I feel very let down and betrayed.

It appears it is now me and Ob against the world, and we are surrounded by enemies, including almost everyone we know.

I never wanted to go to the rotten party anyway, but no doubt Melissa will enjoy herself palling around with her Arnold and will tell everyone what a relief it is for her to be free of the Fat Elephant at last.

Later still

Melissa still hasn't phoned me or called at the house. Our friendship is therefore at an end. I am very, very, *very* upset, and a further embarrassing thing has happened: I was out in the *back* garden (not the front, in case Melissa came. Creep was on watch at the front, to turn her away).

Mum Bluebottle saw me and called me over to the fence. "Is anything the matter, Zoë?" she said.

"No," I said.

"Are you sure, dear?" she said.

I didn't say anything. She has no business interfering in my personal life when everyone knows hers is such a mess. Her old husband is back and answering ads for jobs and all he does is potter round the house and I think she is making a fool of herself over him. I would not have taken him back, but then I have my pride.

"Zoë?" she said.

I looked up at her.

"Whatever's the matter, dear?" she said. "I've never seen you crying before. Something must be the matter. If you won't talk to me about it, you must talk to your mum."

"I am not crying," I told her.

"Zoë-Zog, look at me!" she said.

I don't know who told her that Baby

Name. Zoë-Zog is a stupid, rotten made-up name, Dad's pretend. Mum Bluebottle has no right to use it when she is talking to me and I nearly told her so, except that I could see she was trying to be kind, and she thought using my stupid, rotten baby name was the way to do it. Well, she was stupid, rotten wrong. It just annoys me that people think of me like that ... *Zoë-Zog*. My name is Zoë Thelma Curley, which is a proper grown-up name, even if I don't happen to like it very much, particularly the *Thelma*.

"Have those children you play with been calling you names again?" she asked. Evidently even Mum Bluebottle knows about the Fat Elephant thing. My mum must have talked to her. I wish people wouldn't talk about me like that, particularly to people like Mum Bluebottle, who is a *silly* love-sick woman who will put up with anything to hang on to Dad Bluebottle, though I can't see why.

"I really don't like to see you like this, Zoë," she went on when I made no reply. "Things can't be that bad. When you grow up you will probably look back on it and think how *small* a thing it was. It looks big to you now because now is when it is happening, but these things do blow over, Zoë. You've got to soldier on."

Then she went into her let-me-see-you-smile-your-lovely-smile-for-me stupid, rotten baby routine.

"Can't," I said.

"Come on, Zoë!" she said. "Why not?"

"Because my mouth is full of this ugly brace!" I said, and I clicked it at her with my tongue, and went back into the house before she could tell me that the brace would straighten my teeth and I would be lovely then. I will not be *cheered up* by stupid adults who don't know how it feels to be hurt. Next thing she will be round at the front door telling Mum about me. Not that that matters much.

Mum knows I am upset. She is too sensible to try to talk me out of it or to go on asking me questions. She knows I don't want to talk about it because I told her so when she started on again about me never going out of the house. She then changed tack and tried to be nice, talking about the Sky Cabin Plan and possible decorations.

"I don't think I care very much," I told her.

"Yesterday you were all excited about it," she said.

"That was yesterday," I told her.

"Zoë-Zog?" she said.

"Zog is just Dad's stupid, rotten childish *pretend*," I told her. "I would prefer it if from now on you call me Zoë, as though I was a proper grown-up person, which I am.

I'm fed up with this stupid, rotten Zog stuff. It is for kids."

"Whatever you say," she said. "Zoë."

This is awful. I hate the whole world. Particularly my False Friend Melissa. Ob is the only real friend I have, because Ob has taken a stand against my enemies. He told me later that Mum and the Creative have been quizzing him about what is the matter with me, but he is not saying anything, because he is loyal, even if no one else is. He says Mum asked him a lot of questions about me when they were driving over to Auntie Thelma's so he could *grovel* to Thelma and say how sorry he was for being rude, but he didn't let on. Dad asked me about him too, and why *he* was acting upset, but I haven't told him or Mum anything.

I suppose Mum and Dad think that just because they are going ahead with the stupid rotten Sky Cabin thing everything will be all right for their little children for ever, but that is not the way Life works. What goes on inside a person is much more important than stuff about whether they have Sky Cabins or not, and who is cooking dinner. It is in a person's heart that hurt lives, not in a person's head.

Mum and Dad are out of it... How can they still go on making kiddy Zog-world jokes and stuff? They are the ones who belong in their Zog-world. I don't. I have outgrown all that little girl pretend stuff. It gets on my nerves.

I am stopping writing this, fed up.
End of Zog, for ever!

Thursday 27th August
Subject:

Mum Drops Me in It

A truly, *truly* awkward thing has happened. Apparently Mum was out shopping when she met Mrs Banjerdee. They went for coffee and Mrs Banjerdee said something to her about how sorry she was that Zoë was unable to come to Sonja's party and she asked Mum who was sick at our house, and was it really infectious, because Sonja was *so* hoping Zoë would come, as she wanted all her friends from the Tennis Club to be there on her birthday.

Well, I for one *cannot imagine* Sneaky saying that, but of course Mum does not know what is going on, and she was caught out.

Mum glossed over it some way, but she ended up saying something about *of course*

Zoë would be coming, Zoë wouldn't miss it for worlds, without asking me first, which is practically unforgivable.

"But I don't want to go, Mum!" I said. "You had no right to say I would be going when I don't want to."

"Why?" Mum said. "Is this all because Sonja Banjerdee called you a silly name? Surely you are grown up enough not to let that bother you, Zoë? I thought we had talked through that little complication in your life, and we had agreed that you would go and show them that you are a big girl inside."

"Well, I just don't like her," I told Mum. "I don't see why I should go to her crummy party. I won't like *anybody* there, and they won't like me, so why should I go to be not liked and called names?"

"That just isn't true, Zoë, and you know it," Mum said. "Everyone likes you really, because you are a very likeable person. Melissa will be going for one, won't she? And Melissa is your friend."

Silence.

"Some problem with Melissa, too, is there?" Mum said.

"Melissa is not my friend any more," I said.

Longer silence.

"I haven't *any* friends left," I said.

It was very embarrassing.

"I know that isn't true, Zoë," Mum said, at last. "But I can see that you think it is, and that is important to you. So I can appreciate why you might not want to go to the party, and I am not going to ask you what the matter is, because you would have told me all about it if you wanted to."

"That's right," I said. "It is a very *personal* matter."

"Well, OK," Mum said. "I know you don't want to go, and that's enough for me. If you don't *want* to go, I am not going to make you. But I have kind of covered up for you with Mrs Banjerdee, and she is going to find out eventually that no one is sick at our house, and that will look as if I have been telling her lies ... which, in a way I have, because I had to back you up, hadn't I? I can't make you go, but I can ask you to consider getting me off the hook with Mrs Banjerdee by going to the party, even though you don't want to. *Please*, Zoë? Just for me? So I won't look silly?"

So I had to say I would go to Sneaky's awful party because I couldn't let Mum down, even though I really don't want to go and I don't know how I will face all those people, particularly Melissa, when I told her very specifically I was *not* going, and now I will turn up and look *stupid*.

I told Mum I would go and put in an

appearance for her sake, but I did not intend to stay any longer at the party than I had to, just to put her right with Mrs Banjerdee, because I really, really do not want to go. I am doing it for her, so Sneaky's rotten mum will not be able to go round the town saying Mum told her lies about someone being sick at our house.

"That's very *big* of you, Zoë, and really appreciated by me," Mum said.

So the result is I am going to the party, after all.

Later
Subject:

Melissa

Melissa came.

Mum let her in when I was upstairs and the first thing I knew about it was when Mum put her head through the trapdoor and said, "Zoë, Melissa is here to see you."

So I had to come down to speak to Melissa, even though she is not my friend any more and has no right to come to my house to see me without being invited.

"You have a nerve turning up here uninvited," I told her when Mum had diplomatically cleared off. I was really cross with her.

"I *had* to come," Melissa said. "It is really, *really* important and urgent. Only the one I need to speak to is Ob, not you. But I couldn't ask for Ob, could I? Ob is a boy! So I am going to tell you so that you can tell him."

"Tell me what?" I said.

"No more enemies! Well, except Sneaky and Awful, that is," Melissa said. "I have fixed it so Graham and Arnold and Scats won't clobber Ob the way Graham said they were going to, so there! That's Ob's problems taken care of. Sneaky and Awful are *our* enemies not his, so Ob doesn't have to bother about them. They are girls. So what I was going to say to Ob is that I have fixed it so he needn't stay in the house all day and he will be all right when school starts."

"How did you do that?" I asked her.

It appears that Melissa went to Graham D. off her own bat and she told Graham D. that she would *personally* speak to her friend Tina-next-door (Mrs Hare) and tell her who he was and where he lived. Then Tina would go to his house and tell Graham D.'s mum how rude he was whistling at her bum in the park.

"Or we could do a deal, if you don't want me to do that," she told him cunningly.

"What deal?" Graham D. asked her, and according to Melissa he was really, really worried, because he thought Tina would arrive and tell his mum everything and then he would be *sunk*, probably for ever, and have to go to Mrs Hare (Tina) and apologize and it would be awful.

"You promise to lay off the Curleys, and I won't tell on you!" Melissa told him.

"Who cares about the Curleys?" he came back.

"*I* do!" Melissa says she told him. And she told him laying off meant not bashing Ob or interfering with him in *any* way whatsoever, and that the deal also included telling his friends and his *girl*friends not to go calling *me* names either, or else she would get Tina (Mrs Hare) round to his house pronto.

And he said, "What *girlfriends*?"

And she said, "Awful Alison and Sneaky Sonja that you and Arnold are so crazy about!"

And he said, "No, we are not!" and got all hot and bothered and said if she went round saying things like that she was telling lies.

It seems that Sonja and Alison wrote "Blind-as-a-Batbugs" over his name on *his* invitation and he got wild about it and he wasn't going to go to Sneaky's party either but his mum said he had to, because she is friends with Mrs Banjerdee, and it would be embarrassing. His mum said that Sonja and Alison were only silly little girls and it was their stupid idea of a joke and they didn't realize how *sensitive* he was about having to wear his glasses all the time and not being able to play football properly in case they broke and went in his eyes. And he told Melissa he really likes football but so many people laughed at him missing the ball when he was goalie and couldn't see, and now he can't play again ever, because his eye will *never* come right.

"I think that just serves him right!" I told Melissa. "He deserves to have bad eyesight and stupid glasses."

"He doesn't deserve to be called names just because he can't see straight," Melissa said. "You wouldn't like it if it was you because you may be fattish, sort of, now, but it is fat that everyone *knows* will melt off when you grow a bit, and poor Graham will never be able to see straight, whatever happens. You should never have started that Blind-as-a-batbugs stuff going, Zoë."

"He could get contact lenses," I said.

"Some people can, but he can't. They hurt his eyes too much," she said. "And you of all people should never have called him a stupid name like that because you know how it feels, don't you?"

There was a lot more like that. I was really cross with Melissa for saying it at the time but I have been up on my Sky Cabin cushion thinking about it and I now think she is right. I am going to ring her and own up that I was wrong and say so, because I think it was really *big* of her to risk losing my friendship by saying that to me, but she did. Melissa did it for me. So I am going to show her that I can be as big and as rounded an individual and as grown-up a person as she can, any day. I am going to ring her and say so. Like *now*. Because she has fixed everything so it will be all right and she has proved herself a really big, warm-hearted friend, and I cannot allow the day to pass with this gulf between us.

Later

Did it. I have telephoned Melissa. We are friends again. I am going round to Melissa's house *now* to help her plan how we can make her Den really nice, so it will be as nice as my Sky Cabin will be (almost) when the men have finished working on it.

Dad says the builders should have my Sky Cabin all fixed and ready by the end of the first week after we start school and I have arranged with Melissa that we will take turns entertaining each other and doing our homework together every night, if we can get the mums and dads to agree to our doing it together and if we can get her dad to run an electricity line out to her Den so there will be light.

If we can't we will do our homework in her kitchen and/or my Sky Cabin (which will have electricity, Dad says) but weekend entertaining will be *exclusively* in her Den so that will even the entertaining up. And she is going to bring her CD player round on nights when we are doing our homework in my Sky Cabin so we will have music, if Mum lets us. We are going to pool the money she makes from Rupert-sitting for Tina-next-door with my next birthday money so we can build up a CD collection with all the good ones. My dad has only to fax and he can get ones from the States that no one else round here can, so we will be the envy of everyone.

It is also good because we will be seeing so much more of each other that we will not need to telephone so much as before, and that will free Melissa's telephone line for her dad's incoming plumbing calls, which will more than offset the cost of getting electricity in her Den. That is what we are going to tell Melissa's mum anyway.

We are trying her mum first because her mum is easier to persuade, according to Melissa, and if her mum says she *needs* electricity in the Den then she will get it. I said we might be able to get her mum to buy Cromwell a kennel for outside the Den, but

Melissa does not think this would work, and anyway her mum says Cromwell is old and may not live much longer, poor old thing.

Melissa is also trying to arrange that I should be in on the paid Rupert-minding as well, as a kind of back-up to her and her Mum.

It turns out that Mr Hare is using the street outside Melissa's house to sell the fancy sports cars he has parked there. He sells used cars through ads in the paper. Melissa's dad surmises that they may be stolen. Melissa's dad is considering ringing the Council about their bit of road being a used-car salesroom. Melissa is concerned that this will lead to trouble with the Hares. It could be that the Big Deal Rupert-Sitting will go out the window.

We think it is a pity because Tina Hare has been so good to us, buying us crisps and telling Batbugs he was a rude thing, but in this life you can't win them all.

We are agreed that what with Mum Bluebottle's troubles with Dad Bluebottle and Tina Hare having a possibly crooked car salesman to put up with it is possibly *unwise* for us to worry too much about boys, as it does not get you far and can adversely affect your career.

So we will go to the party, but we will take no notice of Arnold or Graham D. (though I had given him up anyway) and when school restarts we will concentrate on our education, with a view to making our own way in life, at least until we meet someone smashing.

I agreed it anyway. I am not so sure about Melissa. I think she is still gooey on Arnold, despite all the no-boys stuff she has been spouting.

Even later

I have telephoned Melissa to inform her that it will not be necessary for her to bring her CD player round to my new Sky Cabin, as I now have a CD player with twin speakers of my own. It is a pink one. Mum Bluebottle came across with it. It's a much better one than Melissa's.

"That's a thank-you for your unpaid babysitting!" Mum Bluebottle told me.

"Where's *my* pay off then?" Ob put in, after she had gone.

"Considering you spent most of the summer avoiding Cyril-sitting you can hardly expect anything, Colin," Mum said.

So there *is* justice in the world.

Friday 28th August a.m.
Subject:

Sneaky Busted

This has been a V.B. Day. (That means *Very Busy Day.*) I am very busy discussing with Melissa what we will wear to the Party and getting things ready, so I have not had much time to write, but there has been a *brilliant* bit *vis-à-vis* Sneaky Banjerdee.

Halfway through the morning, when Mum had sent coffee up through the trapdoor and Melissa and I were drinking it and discussing our Lives and Laughs, there was a ring at the door.

Mum answered, and she called me down.

It was Sneaky S. Banjerdee, looking very down in the mouth. Obviously she was mad cross at having to come and madder crosser when she realized Melissa was there and she would have to say it in front of my friend. *Obviously* Sneaky's mum had made her come.

Sneaky gabbled something about being very sorry if I have upset you, Zoë, by calling you silly names.

"That is quite all right, Sonja *dear*," I told her, with some dignity. "Of course I paid *no* attention to what you called me. I really don't mind in the least."

And Melissa laughed at her.
Sneaky went off looking *busted*.

Later
Subject:

Ob and the Sky Cabin Deal and a Mystery Solved

We had a big game of Monopoly to celebrate the Sky Cabin deal being on. We had it in the Sky Cabin to-be. Ob was the hat and I was the shoe and Melissa was the Rolls Royce and Creep (we allowed him up because it was a celebration) was the dog.

Mum made us little sausages on sticks. Creep got Mayfair and Park Lane right at the start and we kept landing on them so he got hotels and in the end he won. Mainly he did it by sitting on three five hundred pound notes so we thought he had no money and was going broke. The worst bit was that he kept getting doubles and I kept landing on Pall Mall.

Nobody goes broke because of landing on Pall Mall but I did, and so Melissa got all my money and then she landed three times on Mayfair and Park Lane so she was out, and that only left Ob with Fleet Street and the Utilities, so he got stuffed, but it took ages and ages and ages, the way Monopoly does.

Monopoly is not a game of skill *really*,

otherwise there is no way Creep could have beaten us.

He kept explaining how he did it, so in the end we sent him downstairs.

Ob and I had a serious conversation today, cementing our new alliance.

Neither of us really, really, *really* wants to share the Sky Cabin with the other one, but by negotiation and discussion most of this morning we came up with a *brilliant* solution to the problem. We then co-operated in a joint approach to the Creative, outlining the solution we had arrived at. I acted as spokesperson, with Ob backing me in our new spirit of co-operation.

"A partition either side of the place the new stair comes up?" Dad said. "What for?"

"So I will be private and he will be private. There will be a door to my space and a door to his," I said.

"Two Sky Cabins," Ob said. "One each. Instead of one big space we would be fighting over all the time."

"The space in-between where the ladder comes up would be neutral territory," I went on to explain. "Ob and I could store things there, but only by mutual agreement. And there would be room for your fishing stuff too, so that Mum can't complain about it cluttering the house."

Part of my original deal with Dad was that I would store his fishing stuff in return for his support on the Sky Cabin issue, and by putting it outside what will be my space and into neutral space between my space and Ob's, I have cleverly extricated myself from the difficult position of being seen to favour his fish killing, while keeping him on my side.

Ob then showed him the sketch we had drawn, which was a ground plan of the new Dual Sky-Cabin Deal, as agreed between us.

"Explain it!" he said.

"That's my space with the Z in it and Ob's is the other one with the C. The two thick lines are the partitions and there are two doors, one for each of us, facing each other, with the stair space in between," I told him.

"Two skylights?" he said, looking at our plan. "That's going to cost extra!"

Ob and I had anticipated this objection.

"We will both need natural light for when we are studying up there at weekends," I told him. "You will save on the electricity bill. It will be ideal. The principal use of these spaces will be for us to do homework and school projects so that Mum's kitchen will be clear and we won't have Creep bothering us all the time."

"Taylor," he said. "Not Creep. You must stop calling him Creep, Zoë. You wouldn't like it. And I am not sure your mum will be happy about homework unsupervised."

"What our little brother is called isn't the problem," Ob put in, evading the unsupervised homework issue, because we knew it was our weakness. "It is what he does that is. We cannot do our school stuff properly with him hanging about."

"*Two* skylights where there was *one* before, *two* partitions where there was *none* before, and *two* doors," the Creative went on. "I am not made of money, you know. It is a big concession having the roof space opened out at all. If I had not just put through my Big Deal in the States I wouldn't even think of it... But I suppose with your mum getting the research grant for her book..."

"What research grant?" I asked, because we hadn't heard about that.

"Your mum is getting some money for her research, that is all," he said, suddenly gone very offhand, so we knew it was sensitive stuff. "We heard about it the other day. Didn't she say?" And he went on to say how proud of Mum he was. Then he spoilt it by launching into a speech about how disturbing it was that money was available for non-creative projects like Research in Educational Psychology in the New Britain, but none was available for playwrights and poets and Creative persons like him –

jealous, as usual!

So one Mystery is solved. That is what cheered her up and got her cooking again.

It is nice to know. She might have told us. Probably she didn't because it would have sounded too much like boasting, and Mum is very *quiet* about her work, not like some people I could mention.

We are clubbing together for a box of Congratulation Liqueur Chocolates *For Our Clever Mum from the Minions of Zog.* (I like the Pernod ones and Mum knows that so probably she will save them for me, if the Creative doesn't wolf the lot in his work room as he usually does.)

Anyway after we decided on the chocolates, Ob and I turned him back on to discussing our scheme and I think we have won.

Ob and I are agreed that this is a supreme example of what can be done by two otherwise opposed parties (us) working together for the common good and being prepared to set aside vital elements (his pool table and my exclusivity) in order to reach a workable compromise.

That's what I've convinced Ob of, anyway. I am just hoping he doesn't notice that I have managed to get my *exclusivity* back by having a partition with a door to keep me private, while his pool table is definitely and finally for ever *kaput* because if it wouldn't go in the whole space, then there is no way he can ever get it in the half-space.

This is a deal worthy of the absent Citizen Turtle. He would be delighted with it. If and when Ob realizes that he has been really, *really* diddled by me in the course of our prolonged negotiations, I don't want to be around.

I am stopping now, as I have written lots and lots and lots more stuff than I meant to and I am really, really tired and I need my Beauty Sleep before the Party.

Saturday 29th August

Panicsville.

Mum started doing our clothes for school, and found lots of bits missing, so we had to drop everything and head townwards. Of course, our school being an illogical school, you can only get the rotten stuff they *permit* you to wear in the one place, and that one place isn't here.

I had to ring Melissa and put off yet another bike ride because we had to go late back-to-school shopping, but as it turned out it didn't matter.

"I am going for a spin in my dad's new sports car," Melissa informed me loftily, but

I noted that I was not invited to come with her. Probably because it will be only a two seater and therefore impractical for family driving, as I told her.

"It will whizz by your old thing!" Melissa said, and she went on and on about the soft top that pulls down so you can be like a film star with your long hair blowing in the wind. (She has short hair, but I suppose now she will grow it long.)

I think the amazing thing is that Mr Hare next door has talked Melissa's dad into purchasing one of the flashy cars he was selling. The last thing I had heard, Melissa's dad was going to report him to the Council for carrying on a used-car sales operation in the road outside their house, and now he has gone and bought one, so presumably he is back on good terms with Mr Hare again and the police won't be getting any anonymous tip-offs about might-be-stolen cars. Which is good from the point of view that our babysitting prospects with Tina will not be blighted by a feud between neighbours.

Melissa kept on about how wonderful their new flashy car was so in the end I said, "Is it one of the ones your dad said was probably stolen?"

Melissa was not very pleased.

"Don't tell your mum!" Dad warned me. "If she hears about it she'll want one too."

I told him Mum *deserved* a sports car to brighten up her middle-aged life. He doesn't drive because he is too Creative for mundane stuff like that, he says, and can't stand all the machismo that goes with it and anyway machines don't work for him, witness his PC.

I bet Mum would like one, though. She could drive me to school in it, and she could race against Melissa's dad if we met them on the way. If Melissa's dad ever lets her in it...

"I doubt if going *varoom, varoom* will make Melissa's dad any better as a plumber," the Creative told me, resentfully.

I steered off the subject, bearing in mind the Sky Cabin position, but I plan to return to it later. If Melissa's dad the plumber can have a natty new sports car I don't see why my mum the Educational Psychologist and Author to-be cannot have one.

Later

Our car broke down, which makes my *sports car* point. In my view a new sports car for Mum should be a priority, and I told Mum that I intend to tell Dad so. She was kicking our car at the time, and did not reply.

We had to come all the way from town in the bus with our bags and Ob was objectionable and got Mum mad so it was a difficult journey and we did not get back here till half past six and now I am in a rush to get ready for the Party.

I am hoping it will be *brill*, now I am going, because if it isn't brill I will have wasted precious minutes at the end of my holidays.

Signing off now. Got to get ready for S. Banjerdee's party.

Much, much, much later

Party was *brill, absolutely*, but *not* the way we thought it was going to be!

Too tired to write it now. Am busted, am going to bed.

Sunday 30th August
Subject:

The Party

Now we know who has stacks of boyfriends and who has not (ha-ha)!

Sneaky and Awful got their comeuppance, which was well deserved, in my view. It was supposed to be a set up for *them*, the Birthday Girl and the Birthday Girl's Best Friend taking the Best Boys, but it all backfired, and Melissa and I have walked off the winners.

Melissa and I agreed that this was the case when reviewing matters in my Sky Cabin this morning, as Best Friends do.

"That will teach S. Banjerdee to go having show-off parties nobody else can afford!" I told Melissa.

"It is funny, though," Melissa said. "The real bother was the adults mucking our stuff up, the way they always do."

We have both agreed that Mrs Banjerdee's behaviour was most unsophisticated. For a start, she should not have invited her revolting wrinkly friends to her daughter's disco, and if they were going to show up they should have come sober.

One of the Wrinklies made rude and uncalled-for remarks to the Disc Jockey. The Disc Jockey shouted back at the rude Wrinkly. They started punching each other. Then they were wrestling and rolling about on the floor. It was dead good.

The hotel staff had to rescue the Disc Jockey from assorted Wrinklies, and after that it got even better. The Hotel Manager came roaring down to sort things out and Mrs Banjerdee chucked her fruit trifle over him because she said he had spoilt her Little Girl's Birthday Party. Then Mr Banjerdee got mad with Mrs Banjerdee, but not as mad as the Hotel Manager was. He sent for the police. The result was the whole party was chucked out in the middle of the night and the Banjerdees are banned *for ever* from the Manor House Hotel.

"Mr Banjerdee threw the Manager into the swimming pool and we are hoping we will get a day off school to go to court and be witnesses when he is sent to prison!" Melissa told Mum, who had popped her head up through the trapdoor when she heard us laughing.

"Oh dear!" Mum said. "Poor little Sonja."

"We were very nice to Sneaky," we told her. "It isn't our fault that her mum and her dad got arrested, and she had to sleep the night at Awful Alison's house while they were calling their lawyers to get them out of the clink."

That was truly *all* we said. We just called her *Sneaky* and we called Alison *Awful*, which is what nearly *everyone* we know calls them, and neither Melissa nor I can understand why Mum got on her high horse about it. She read us a lecure about *our* unsympathetic attitudes. She went on and on and on about it the way mums do, positively *rabbiting* about how terrible it must have been for poor Sonja and how would we have liked it if it had been us?

I pointed out to Mum that this is not the only time this summer that the strange behaviour of adults has mucked up our lives and that if adults could learn to behave properly and not totally *inexplicably* their children would have happier lives. Faced with this point, Mum was most unsympathetic and refused to discuss it.

We didn't tell Mum the best bit though, because we held it to be highly personal and not a grown-up's business.

Melissa *was kissed by Arnold*... Well, almost. It was sort of on the back of her ear when we were bombing our plastic supper plates in the ornamental duck pond after we were turned out of the hotel. We had to hang about because no one had expected the party to end as early as it did and the cars to take us home hadn't come, so everybody was running round the flower-beds in the dark and Miriam Magella fell in the water and got soaked.

I *dared* Arnold to kiss Melissa and he did, even if it was on the ear and kind of soppy and not very nice, according to Melissa.
So that means Melissa now counts as having a boyfriend, and has been kissed, though she states that as far as she is concerned Sonja can have him now, because the kiss was very ordinary, and not the kind of super-romantic

kiss one might hope for, first time round, even though the hotel garden was moonlit.

I have not been kissed yet because Melissa was so embarrassed when Arnold kissed her that she forgot to dare anybody to kiss me (which was the deal we had come up with before going to the party, in case the chance arose). I had taken out my brace just in case, but it didn't happen. However, on reflection I would not wish Graham D. to kiss me, as I consider a kiss between two people who do *not share* a great deal in common not to be the way I want to start my kissing career. However, *Vince* Hobsbawn got a lift home with us in Melissa's dad's car and because it is a small car and most unsuitable for a plumber, I sat on Vince's knee because our house is nearest and I was getting out first. Melissa and I are agreed that sitting on Vince's knee counts as having a boyfriend, so now we have both got one, though we do not intend to marry them.

Melissa is reconsidering her Love List, having found Arnold unsatisfactory as a kisser. I am not putting Vince on mine because although we have agreed to call him Vince now because he says that is his name I cannot forget that his nickname is *Hubie* and I cannot give my young heart to someone whose pram-name was *Hubie* and who is probably still called *Hubie* at home by his mum.

"Do not be so hasty, Zoë," Melissa told me. "Perhaps you will grow to love him. And Vince is a very nice name and he is a *very* kind boy and he did not go round calling you names when the others did."

Melissa is no doubt disturbed by the turbulent emotions of having been *kissed* at such a young age, before almost anyone else has got round to it, but I am not so easily thrown into the arms of an immature boy like Vince Hobsbawn. My opinion now is that Melissa has lower standards than I have, and may already have formed a secret attachment to Hobsbawn now his name is Vince, but is afraid to let her Love be known as she considers I have prior claim to her beloved.

I intend to talk this over with her later, when she has stopped going round boasting about having been kissed and having paid employment as a babysitter and having a dad with a sports car (probably stolen by the man next door, who sold it to him).

Monday 31st August
Subject:

Ceremonial Closing of This Notebook

By special arrangement with the Mistress of Zog (under pressure from the Creative, because he was indebted to me for yet again hunting down his pipe) I am spending this, the last night of my holidays, in a sleeping bag in my Sky Cabin to-be, so it is therefore officially in being and declared open, by Edict of Zog.

Ob is doing the same in his half (not to be confused with my Sky Cabin, and of course pool-table-less) and we have a blanket strung up where the partition will be, so I have my *exclusivity* while I write these last words propped up on my cushion before going to sleep.

I feel I have kept my word.

I promised I would write something each day in this book for one whole month and I did... Well, there's something *about* every day, anyway.

Apart from one casual-seeming request from the Creative (refused), no one has asked to see it and I do not intend that anyone ever shall until I am a Famous Writer, at which point I may decide to take these notes as a beginning for the book I will *then* write, when I have time and don't have to give up living and everything and go back to rotten stinky school.

When I have finished writing this I will put my book in a special box which will be kept locked at all times and I will keep the key on my person so that small brothers can't get at it.

Well, that is it then. Finito. The End. For Now.

Goodbye, Notebook.

Zoë T. Curley

Minion of Zog,
The Sky Cabin,
Zog

TANGO'S BAY
Martin Waddell

Brian Tangello – Tango – is not one of life's romantic heroes. Even his few friends are amazed to hear of his love affair with young Crystal O'Leary, the girl he fancies and who seemed to have no interest in him. Next thing they know, she's pregnant – and that's when the real story of Tango's baby begins. By turns tragic and farcical, it's a story in which many claim a part, but few are able to help Tango as he strives desperately to keep his new family together.

"Stylishly written, sensitive, funny and moving… A book with a depth that can only reward all who read it." *The Times*

"Waddell is as ever an excellent storyteller." *The Independent*

MAD ABOUT THE BOY
Mary Hooper

"Ooh, I'm so mad! Fancy having a boy like that living here."

For years since her mother died, it's been just Joanna and her dad – and that's the way Joanna likes it. Then Tatia moves in... Worse still, there's the *boy*: Tatia's son, Mark, "the boffin", who's silent to the point of rudeness. Yet Joanna's expected to welcome him into her home with open arms. Anyone would be resentful – and, boy, is she mad!

You'll laugh out loud at this entertaining and perceptive account of a girl's determination *not* to adapt to a new family situation.

THE BOYFRIEND TRAP
Mary Hooper

"I didn't know much about Sarah's love life. Mum thought she hadn't got one... Could Mum be right? If she was, then I was going to play Cupid..."

Arriving at her older sister's London flat, with a bag full of romantic magazines and a head full of True Love, Terri is dismayed to discover thet Sarah doesn't appear to have a single boyfriend! Something must be done, decides Terri – and quickly.

"A brilliant read." *My Guy*

TALL, THIN AND BLONDE
Dyan Sheldon

"Maybe Amy was right. Maybe if I lost a few pounds, and did something with my hair, and had myself stretched, I could look perfect too. I turned around again. Or maybe not."

Jenny Kaliski and Amy Ford have been best friends for years. They share the same interests and sense of humour – and the same contempt for girls whose only talk is of boys and fashion. Now, almost overnight, Amy has turned into one – while Jenny finds herself attached to a group of unfashionable oddballs, nicknamed the Martians. Torn between the weird and the glamorous, Jenny's soul-searchings are brimful of humour and heartache.

JOHNNY CASANOVA
Jamie Rix

Johnny Worms is hot to trot, the unstoppable sex machine, Johnny Casanova... Well, so he believes. So when love's thunderbolt strikes in the form of Alison Mallinson or a beautiful vision in purple what can Johnny do? And is it his fault that Cyborg Girl, Deborah Smeeton, finds him irresistible?

Follow the far-from-smooth course of Johnny's love adventures in this hilarious romp by the author of *Grizzly Tales for Gruesome Kids*, a Smarties Book Prize Children's Choice.